D1523687

FYI

An Unintended Consequence

Patricia E. Gitt

ISBN: 1545230986
ISBN 13: 9781545230985
Library of Congress Control Number: 2017906991
CreateSpace Independent Publishing Platform
North Charleston, South Carolina

This is a work of fiction. Names, characters, places, and incidents either are the product of the author's imagination or are used factiously, and any resemblance to actual persons, businesses, companies, events or locals is entirely coincidental.

Also by Patricia E. Gitt
CEO
ASAP A settling of scores
TBD A game changer

DEDICATION

In memory of Michael A. Gitt, my father, who taught me to believe in myself, and that with passion, persistence and hard work my dreams would come true.

Great fury, like great whiskey, requires long fermentation.
Truman Capote

CHAPTER 1

Jolted awake, Taryn felt a chill brush over her. It was as if she were pinned to the mattress. As she grasped for consciousness, the feel of her husband's arm stretched across her stomach made her smile. Once again Jesse had moved the covers exposing her upper body to the cool room. He often reached out for her in sleep.

Without moving so much as a finger, she began to look around their bedroom for the cause of her anxiety. Her eyes roamed first to the open bedroom door, then slowly over the triple dresser opposite the foot of the bed, and next to the small sofa Jesse loved to burrow into when reading one of his mysteries. The curtains fluttered in front of the partially open window scattering light reflected from the city below. Her eyes next fell on Jesse's pants tossed over a chair before going to bed. While she was neat to the point of compulsiveness, Jesse inhabited their apartment with bits and pieces of clothing, books, and socks left scattered and forgotten. Before they met, her home had a pristine orderly appearance—everything in its place and a place for every little thing. It hadn't taken long before she had accepted Jesse's habit of dotting their apartment with his things because Jesse had turned her apartment into their home.

"Honey?" Jesse murmured.

"Go back to sleep. I'm just going to get a glass of water. My mind doesn't want to settle."

"Mm. What time is it?"

"Three o'clock. It's too early even for you. Go back to sleep."

"All right. Wake me if you want to talk." As he fell back into a deep sleep, Taryn listened to his even breathing, jealous of the ease with which he could close his eyes and drop off. Lately her mind had a hard time slowing down, and instead of sleeping, she had been spending her nights tossing and turning. Was this another sign of trouble?

Careful not to jolt the bed, she eased her legs onto the floor, slipping her feet into fluffy slippers, and reached for her thick terry robe draped over a nearby chair. During the night, her ponytail had loosened from its elastic band. Absently pushing the sun-streaked hair behind her ears, her mind continued to search for clues to her unease.

As she entered the kitchen, Taryn was aware of the nighttime sounds of a city just outside the window. New York hummed with light traffic, the occasional siren of an ambulance, along with the background rhythms of a city that vibrated twenty-four hours each day. Tonight she counted herself among its nocturnal residents.

Aware of an enormous thirst, she filled a glass with cold water and quickly gulped it down. "I shouldn't have eaten that spicy pasta, especially so late in the evening. Maybe this nervousness is simply due to my poor food choices."

Still standing at the kitchen sink, her mind tried to grasp a glimpse of something, more like a wisp of smoke than an actual thought. As the image of Gibraltar Bank's logo crystallized, she froze. It was something she hadn't thought of in more than a decade. *Just my nerves.* Taking another deep drink of water, she continued to allow her mind to wander. Was this sleep-generated impression a warning? Was her firm, 4G Investments, going to have problems from a dissatisfied client? "Oh shit! It's that damn interview in *Economic World*!"

"Honey? What's bothering you?"

She turned as the familiar figure in pajama bottoms and robe swinging open moved close. Her eyes drew in all six feet of a body kept in shape with regular workouts at the gym. The sight made her fingers itch in anticipation of touching each ridge and ripple of exposed skin.

As she felt Jesse's arms pull her close, Taryn dropped her head on his shoulder. "I don't know. I woke with a premonition of trouble. I just came up with one possible answer. That magazine article on 4G Investments. It comes out soon."

"Come on. Talk to me," Jesse coaxed, leaning back to get a better look at his troubled wife. "I doubt anything you said to that reporter would cause problems."

Taryn looked into his eyes and loved him anew. How had she lived forty years without this all-encompassing partner in her life? "OK, put on a pot of coffee, it looks like neither of us is going to get any more sleep."

As Jesse prepared the coffee, she paced. "If not that profile, then is a client about to close their account? If it's sizable enough, it could compromise one of our funds."

"But you have already lived through that scenario. I remember you telling me that you changed procedures for vetting new investors. That you began an interview process akin to a psychological profile. You told me you wanted an insight into the person's investing patterns. You do realize it's highly unusual for a firm to do more than a cursory financial-background check. Usually it's the prospective investor who researches a hedge fund for credibility and reliable results." As he pulled her back into his arms, he gave her a full body hug, chuckling as he pushed a stray strand of hair behind her ear. "My life is so much simpler. I don't have clients. I don't have a boss. I just have an agent demanding I deliver my work on time."

"I wasn't going to get caught again with another nervous Ned. That was our first year in business. He was a necessary lesson that no amount of investment was worth the hand-holding and aggravation that weird man demanded every time there was a blip in the market. And they say women are difficult to deal with. Ha."

"Here. A freshly brewed kick. I've already added the sugar." Jesse handed Taryn her favorite ceramic mug with *Money: one way of keeping score* printed on it. "Sip and relax. It's early. We have lots of time to get you back on track."

Pacing the kitchen, holding the hot mug to her chest, Taryn reviewed her weekly list of appointments. "Is my upcoming meeting with that college investment officer going to demand weeks of time-wasting trips, or will the initial meeting be attended by all interested parties? If they can be handled via conference calls and e-mails, that would keep me in New York. I won't be happy flying off to South Dakota during a raging winter storm." Momentarily sidetracked, she gave her husband a mischievous grin. "Although a visit during summer would be fun. You could join me. Sort of a mini getaway."

She was delighted with the responding twinkle in Jesse's eyes. "Before I pack for that getaway, why not open your laptop and see if your schedule triggers anything? Later, I can go over your quarterly reports. Maybe I'll spot something."

Ever since she was a kid, Taryn had kept check lists. Some people accused her of being obsessive, but they kept her on track, prepared for unexpected events. She had separate lists for work including meetings, clients needing attention, investment opportunities to followup on, and then one for Jesse, wanting to be available for his every need. In truth, Jesse was a dream, entirely self-sufficient, not demanding. He even loved to cook.

Jesse was known for writing articles geared to people uncomfortable with financial jargon but interested in understanding the complexities of financial planning, investing, and a variety of financial products. Because he wrote his columns using everyday language, his audience, to the delight of his agent, kept growing.

"Aren't you on deadline? Do you have time to review the latest 4G financials? I brought a draft home. I'll get it."

As Taryn turned to get her briefcase from the hall table, Jesse reached for her hand and pulled her back into his arms. "Yes, I have the time. Nothing is more important than my wife…and don't run and get the draft. Let's have breakfast and see if anything else comes to mind."

"Thanks, sweetheart. Maybe I can narrow this fear down to the interview. That reporter was sharp. I hope she sticks to what I said and not what she's conjectured. I don't know why I let Melissa talk me into doing it."

While Taryn continued pacing and thinking aloud, Jesse opened the refrigerator and pulled out the fixings for their breakfast. As he began whipping up scrambled eggs and frying bacon, he said, "Oh, you might check into Joseph Baldino's latest communications."

Taryn stopped pacing and smiled. She knew Jesse was just trying to deflect her fears. At one time, Baldino had been a sore point with him. Now it was an inside joke. When Taryn first told Jesse about Mr. Baldino, she tried to reassure him that he had been carefully vetted. But on meeting the aging thick-set balding man for the first time, Jesse told her he felt he was in the presence of a thug. That was five years ago, and she continued to reassure Jesse that the man was one of her favorite clients, always pleasant, easy to deal with, and had increased his investments with 4G on a regular basis. Maybe it was a male thing. Regardless of what she said, Jesse still thought the man was smarmy.

The salty aroma of bacon filled the kitchen as Jesse turned off the burner and dished up their breakfast. After placing the plates filled to almost overflowing on the table, he reached for the coffee pot and refilled his mug. "You must be rattled. You've hardly touched your coffee," said Jesse as he reached over and gently settled Taryn in her chair.

"This looks wonderful. Thanks." Not wanting to disappoint him, she began to nibble at the edge of her food.

"Honey, are you all right? By now you would have wolfed down the entire plate."

She saw concern and tried to let him know she was fine. "I'm a bit off. Probably lack of sleep. Why not go back to bed? I'll sit a bit and clean up when I've finished."

Jesse nodded and took his plate to the sink. "Come and get me if anything comes to mind." As she watched him leave, Taryn wished she could join him. Her body needed him. But her mind had already refocused on work. If there was a problem brewing, she wanted to be prepared.

CHAPTER 2

Sleep no longer a possibility, Taryn pushed her breakfast to the side and slid her laptop in its place. Out of habit, she clicked on the 4G Investments website hoping to refocus her thoughts away from the shadows lurking at the edges of her mind. She loved the strength projected by the opening page with its dramatic color photograph of the lower Manhattan skyline. The buildings sparkled with light reflected from the setting sun and the firm's name sat securely off to the side very much part of the drama of the scene. 4G Investments was her dream, and seeing the opening page reminded her of the gamble she and her friends took in building the firm into a respected member of the financial community.

Next she clicked on the page featuring 4G's management team and smiled at the familiar faces of women who had been friends since third grade. How did we go from eight-year-olds to women running a hedge fund? The answer stared back with sophisticated photos of Linda Foster, Ellie Thompson, Kathy Ryan, and herself. As a group they were tailored, crisp, and attractive women, each captioned with a brief profile describing their responsibilities as partners in the firm.

Linda with a cap of straight light-brown hair that curved at her jawline looked as neat as the financial systems under her command.

Kathy's smile hid an exceptional facility with financial strategies that guided 4G's investment programs.

Ellie with a short cap of curls exuded a friendly open personality so aptly suited to her role as head of client relations.

As if she were seeing her photo for the first time, Taryn was stunned by the seriousness of expression. As managing partner of the firm, she now wondered if her responsibilities had somehow erased the fun-loving girl she remembered from grade school.

Memories flooded her mind of those early years. A reminder sat on a nearby bookcase shelf. It was a treasured photo taken thirty-six years before showing four girls dressed in sneakers, jeans, and hair ribbons, triggering thoughts of the day when she had started it all. The day she decided she needed to earn lots and lots of money.

Taryn rose and took the picture off the shelf and touching each happy face with her finger, smiled. At eight years old, that meant $5,000. It wasn't as if her family denied her anything or that she felt poor. It was something she had read in a book…that having money bought you freedom. She loved her family, but at the time all she wanted to do was get away from Dunkirk, New York.

"I call the first meeting of 4 Girls Babysitting Service to order. Treasurer, Kathy, please read your report." Before Taryn could continue, the girls broke out in giggles. "This isn't funny," Taryn said and waited for her best friends to settle down. The four were sitting around her family's dining room table, the site of homework, afternoon snacks, and today's meeting.

"You sound like your dad," Ellie said. At that the three girls broke out in a new round of giggles.

Taryn sat back and waited for them to calm down. "Sorry. It's just this is serious."

As Kathy handed around her colorfully printed pages, each clean-scrubbed face focused on the charts. "Our new organization has earned twelve hundred dollars since June when school let out for vacation. All funds have been placed in my savings account until we decide what to do with them."

The cheers were accompanied by laughter drawing Taryn's mother into the room. "What's this? Is someone celebrating a birthday?"

Looking over to her mom, Taryn wanted to share their exciting news but felt she had to get her friends' permission first. "No, Mom, I'll tell you later." Just how much she would share with a grown-up she hadn't figured out. Taryn had never told her mom about her dream of a life beyond little Dunkirk, a place where nothing ever happened.

"Mrs. Cooper," Linda piped up, "we've formed a babysitting service and are trying to see where we go next."

"That's very commendable, girls. I knew you each had after-school jobs babysitting. Is this a new idea?"

All four voices answered yes at once. "Well, I'm proud of you." With that she returned to the kitchen to finish dinner preparations.

"You didn't tell your mom?" Linda asked. "My mom knows everything I do."

"I didn't know how to tell her," Taryn replied. "We hadn't really figured things out."

At that, Linda pounded the table. "Well, when do we get our money? My jobs are the worst of the group...all boys, the little brats." All but Taryn clapped their hands.

Taryn needed a break before she told her friends her newest idea. So, she got up and went into the kitchen where her mother handed her a plate of cookies. She knew they all wanted to go to college anywhere but in their hometown or nearby Buffalo, New York. Of course, they were only in third grade and had nine more years to earn grades that could qualify for college scholarships. She didn't know why she had decided at age eight that money would help her get the future she dreamed about—an Ivy League school, big-city career, and most of all travel. Safaris in Africa, the Forbidden City in China, Blue Footed Boobies of the Galapagos. Anywhere away from boring Dunkirk.

With the cookies on the table, Taryn looked at each of her happy friends. "I don't think we should split up our earnings. I think we should add to them. Invest everything we make for the future."

"Invest? How? We need our parents' signature to open a savings account," Kathy shrieked.

"How do you invest twelve hundred dollars?" Linda asked. "I was hoping to have enough to buy a new bike."

"Why not get my dad to take our money and put it in stocks and stuff?" Taryn answered.

The room now deathly quiet drew Mrs. Cooper back. As she set the tray with lemonade and glasses in front of the girls, she asked, "Why so quiet? A minute ago the neighbors could hear your laughter."

Without looking up, Taryn said, "Mom. This is private."

"I see. I'm just in the kitchen if you need me."

After her mother had left, Taryn handed around the glasses of freshly made lemonade. "Look, if we want to get out of Dunkirk, we have to have money. Real money. Remember Charley, my cousin's friend? Well, I heard that it cost his parents over sixty thousand dollars to send him to Dartmouth. That's each year."

"That's a lot of babysitting," Kathy said slumping down in her chair.

"My parents keep after me about my grades. 'Don't you want to get into a good college?'" Ellie said mimicking her dad's gruff voice. "And we're not even in high school," she screeched.

"What do you tell them?" Linda wanted to know.

Ellie moaned. "I keep telling them I'll do better. To give me a break."

Looking at her friends Taryn knew she was lucky. Her dad was the president of the town's only bank. Kathy's dad owned a local auto-parts manufacturing company. Neither had ever heard the words "we can't afford that" from their parents. But, loving numbers, Taryn had kept a diary of each dollar earned, received as a gift, or saved since she was six. Maybe it was the pretty piggy bank she'd received for Christmas that made her determined to save every cent she could for the future. Ever since, after slipping her small change through the pink slot, she'd pick it up and jiggle it, dreaming of the day it would become too full to make a sound.

"Taryn, I'm sure we could convince your dad to help us. He owns the local bank and must know about these things," Kathy said breaking the silence.

"You know, once we set up an account we will have to get papers, keep records, and file taxes," Taryn added.

"Geez! Now you do sound like my dad," Ellie groaned. "Every few months I see him huddled over folders and cussing that Uncle Sam's stealing all his profits. That if it kept up, he'd have to take in a partner at the store."

"I've always thought money was a grown up's thing. I never thought I'd have any. My parents are teachers. They keep telling me they don't earn very much," Linda said resting her head on her arm. With a frown, she grumbled, "I guess I could ask Santa for a new bike."

"What would we invest in?" Ellie asked. "I put my birthday money in a bank's savings account."

"Well? Are you in?" Taryn watched as her friends reluctantly nodded their approval.

"I guess we could use more money for…whatever," Ellie said.

"Well, at least you're interested. So here are the things we need to find out. Let's divide up this list and meet next Saturday. We can compare notes and begin to plan our company." Taryn wondered how she was going to approach her dad. *Maybe it's better to wait until after dinner when he's relaxed.*

"Mom," Taryn yelled. "Can I have Ellie, Linda, and Kathy over for lunch next Saturday?"

Emerging once again from the kitchen, Mrs. Cooper looked at the previously fun-loving girls all wearing serious faces. "Of course you may, dear. I'll be happy to invite them for lunch. Are you doing anything special?"

"Nope, just getting together, like today. Thanks, Mom." As her mother left, Taryn thought of more problems they'd face. "You know, making money is serious stuff. We can't just give it to my dad. We have to think ahead. Develop some plan. We work too hard to lose everything because we're stupid."

"Yeah," was the chorus echoing around the room.

"Well I can't think about it now. I'll take the first two questions, and you divide up the rest. Maybe next week we can write up something to show my dad.

CHAPTER 3

The market had been open for an hour when Bobbie Klein announced the arrival of the rest of the 4G founding partners. Linda handled systems management and maintained her office down the hall from Taryn. Ellie also had an office but was often found traveling to meet with 4G clients. Kathy, the mother of three boys all under the age of twelve, usually worked from home. Her computer was her lifeline to 4G's world.

"Show them into the conference room, Bobbie."

"Sure thing, Ms. Cooper. I'll see what they want with their caffeine."

"You know how they love their pastry."

Laughing, Bobbie quipped, "I should after all this time. If I didn't know any better, I'd think you were having a sorority reunion."

Taryn gathered her notes and again wondered how four girls who had been friends since grade school grew up to start a hedge fund. The journey had been one step at a time, and here they were, captains of finance. Princesses of finance would be more appropriate.

"Hi, gals. Thanks for changing our monthly meeting. My schedule just got away from me," Taryn said as she took a seat at the round conference table and took a sip of coffee to settle her thoughts.

"No problem for me," Kathy said. "My boys are in school, so I'm pretty much free from eight to four." Laughing, she added, "In case you need me in the office on a more regular basis? I could use the mental stimulation."

"Right," Linda piped up. "Like you want a real job. Raising your three hellions isn't enough trouble?"

"Actually, I'm jealous of Kathy and her family. Living alone all I have is time. True, it's filled to overflowing, but I could use some disruption in my life." A former high-school English teacher, Ellie always said she wasn't the motherly type. Taryn knew her students would disagree. They had all adored her. But that was years ago, before Taryn, as managing partner, launched the friends into the world of high finance. Since then they were a well-oiled team with each building on her prior professional experience to handle varied facets of the firm.

Taryn thought about Ellie's comment. She deserved to have someone special to share her life with. When asked why she never married one of her many suitors, Ellie had said she hadn't been able to commit. Maybe it was time. They were all in their mid-forties. Linda, who had divorced her husband and swore never to marry again, had been saying that finding interesting and available men to just date had become a challenge. She swore that her divorce turned her off marriage. Now all she wanted was a playmate to go to dinner and the theater with. Kathy had married her college sweetheart. As for herself, Taryn had given up on ever finding a husband when Jesse literally swept her off her feet.

As her thoughts returned to the business at hand, she sat straighter in her chair and waited until she had the group's attention. "The memo in front of you outlines an idea that has been brewing for some time. With the market fluctuations increasing impacted by electronic trading programs, and our commitment to focus on companies and financial products in this country, it has been a challenge to keep our rate of return goals. What do you think of transiting away from hedge funds and creating a new business with longer term targets?"

"The very nature of hedge funds is trading on the volatility of assets," Kathy said. "When we launched 4G, it was to maximize our technical expertise in managing financial opportunities."

"True. And for ten years we have kept to our plan of delivering an average fourteen to seventeen percent annual return. If our investors wanted something in the forty-seven percentage range, they would have invested with one of the larger, more aggressive funds," Taryn replied.

"And we know how well that goes in a down market," Kathy piped up.

"Well, three of our funds will be closing by year's end." Taryn turned to Ellie. "You're in touch with our clients. Do you feel they would be open to new investment opportunities with 4G? Especially those in funds that will be closing?"

"Absolutely. In fact, remember that little man who looks like he'd come straight off a boat at Ellis Island? You know who I mean. He's one of your original favorites?"

Smiling and remembering her earlier conversation with Jesse, Taryn asked, "Ellie, do you mean Joseph Baldino?"

"Yes. Anyway, we had been having a conversation about what he would do when we closed our funds…you remember most of his investment is in those early funds."

"And?"

"He's looking for us to present something fresh and new. When I asked what he meant, he said he wanted to see something grow before he got too old. That it was fine to make money. But he's already done that."

"Ellie brings up an interesting point," Taryn said. "Mr. Baldino must be in his mid-eighties. He made his first of many fortunes buying up small buildings on the lower eastside of Manhattan. Then he branched out to the Bronx and upstate New York. When we were introduced, he had begun divesting some of his property."

"How did you two meet? Kathy asked.

"Arthur had worked with him briefly when he was still at my dad's bank. They had become friends. As Arthur put it, he learned more about real estate from Mr. Baldino than he could have read in a book. And when we began 4G, Arthur had us meet over dinner. The man intrigued me. He was textbook for an immigrant building a fortune quietly, one brick at a time. When he learned that we were going to set up a hedge fund, I saw a twinkle in his eye. I remember him saying, "I love a good gamble, but don't play those Vegas games. Don't understand the odds."

"So? What's on your mind?" Linda asked.

"Let me explain my idea before we discuss specifics. I will need your help in researching the missing pieces before we make any decision. If this takes off, we could expand our firm's objectives." Seeing that she had their full attention, Taryn leaned forward, elbows on the table, and in an earnest voice began to explain the most important business idea she'd had to date.

"My plan is to move out of hedge funds entirely and become a venture-capital firm. We'd start slowly, beginning with a small fund managing no more than four companies. Of course, we'd continue managing our remaining hedge funds for another two years, at which time they are also scheduled to close. Look, instead of short-term trading, we would be taking a longer view. It's an entirely different pace and would get us more involved in the management side of these firms." Taryn's enthusiasm had her racing on. "I want us to focus on the health sciences. Our challenge will be in identifying early scientific start-ups before they seek financial assistance. Discovering promising gems, while still in the hands of the scientists and engineers, enabling us to avoid competing with the deep pockets of the big pharma and large health-science companies. Then…"

"And if a company proves successful, help find a buyer," Kathy said. Finishing Taryn's thoughts had become a natural part of the dialogue. Both had the financial education and experience required to make these leaps in logic, unlike Ellie who specialized in education and Linda who had focused on management systems.

"How did this come about? Why health sciences?" Linda asked.

After taking a sip of her coffee, which somehow didn't taste quite right, she continued. "Remember Kathy, you wanted to take your boys home to spend time with their grandparents and asked me if I wanted to join you. Linda, it was while you were married and weren't available to take quick weekend trips." About to comment further, Taryn decided not to rub salt into Linda's wounds. Her ex had monopolized all of her free time, preventing her from joining her friends for quick trips and social dinners.

"Ellie," she added, "that particular weekend, you were on one of your spa getaways. Anyway, on a whim Kathy and I stopped by our old high school, and Mrs. Allen asked me to address the class."

"Oh, and you began chatting with that gangly boy, thinner than the frames of his horn-rimmed glasses, Kathy said. "I didn't hear what you two were going on and on about. Later you simply said he was curiously fascinating."

"Dad said he called to get my phone number. In speaking with him last week, he mentioned that he would be graduating from John's Hopkins in June and wanted to continue his work on inflammation and how it impacted the body. That he was ready for more sophisticated testing and wanted to see if we would back his research."

"Who is he working for? Where has he found all the lab equipment he would need for a project of this nature?" Linda asked.

"Bingo," Taryn said. "That's where we come in. He sent me a report documenting his research, how far he has come, and how much he will need to complete the next phase of his study. He says he has promising results proving his thesis that inflammation is at the core of most disease.

"Listen, I've been reading about companies researching this very thing. Why is this kid's research different? Can he meet with us and explain his work in laymen's terms?" Ellie asked.

"Yes, Ellie. To your point, check the science publications to see what they have on inflammation. You might also look at the non-traditional outlets including Mayo Clinic's website and those quasi-medical programs advertising dietary approaches to controlling inflammation. I want to see if his theory has original components or has been widely reported by other scientists.

"Linda, here is Reggie Farmer's overview of his work including a timetable for each subsequent phase. Will you see if you can devise a working plan that would enable us to assist him with staged infusions of cash? Think long term."

"Kathy, check our Bloomberg Terminal for relevant research being done by other companies. Don't forget the subsidiaries as well as their foreign affiliates."

"Taryn, it can take a big pharmaceutical company fifteen years and one-billion dollars to bring a new drug to market. Just how much and how long were you planning on keeping our investment in house?" Kathy asked.

"Just long enough to patent his research. Then attract either a sale or investment by a major firm…one we can work with to go the distance. Of course his work may not be successful. Then we'd face a loss. But we can reevaluate our investment at the completion of each phase. That will keep us involved in the management end of things, enabling us to determine if we want to continue going it alone or bring in a partner. He maybe be a scientific genius, but we don't know anything about his management capabilities, or his fiscal skills."

Watching as the three women made notes on their tablets and laptops, Taryn decided they needed to hear more about Reggie's research in terms of theory and its practical applications in medicine. Taryn thought the kid was more than this one intriguing bit of science, he embodied the next generation's curiosity. Raised on computers, they were able to make leaps in thought not possible in previous decades. With computers, research and calculations were available at their fingertips. Now in his final graduate year in biomedical studies at Johns Hopkins, Reggie Farmer was ahead of current science even by today's standards.

"As to why health sciences," Taryn continued, "well we need a cohesive focus. Not only to crystallize our new business model for prospective investors but to narrow the field of promising firms for consideration. Over the years Ellie and I have shared information about the medical miracles scientists are working on. The field encompasses multiple aspects of medical research, development of new medicines, surgical procedures, and medical devices. I keep thinking of Buck Rogers and the death ray…now the laser is used in a variety of surgical procedures, treatments, and diagnosis. Kathy, you have always been fond of saying that health sciences were the next frontier of humanity. That we should be focusing on preventing or curing early stage diseases before people became bedridden. This way we can work toward that goal."

"Right." Kathy's brow wrinkled with the seriousness of the topic before them. "Taryn and I had been discussing my mother's fight with heart disease. I had felt so helpless. Outside reading everything I could on the latest treatment for her particular condition, there was nothing I could find to help her. At sixty-four she was in the last stages of her condition. Imagine if there had been an effective treatment when she had first been diagnosed at the age of fifty."

The room became suddenly silent. They all remembered Kathy's sorrow when her mother finally passed away. While her passing had been peaceful, the years leading up to it had been filled with suffering.

"OK. Who's in?" All, with coffee cups raised, signaled their agreement. "Good. Let's reconvene next Monday. We can go over the missing bits and pieces you've come up with. I'll call Reggie and invite him to New York to join us."

"We may need more time," Linda said. "Especially when the work is by someone still in grad school. I've glanced at Reggie's overview, but I want to understand how close he is to producing a drug for phase-one trials. Or if he is only working on proving a theory. Then we will need to know how he plans to pursue his research. Without that information I can't set up a schedule for each infusion of cash. My job will be to limit the downside while waiting for some profitable breakthrough," Linda added.

"There is also the matter of Johns Hopkins and the conditions under which they have supported Reggie's research. We may be forced to partner with them and eventually share in any profits," Kathy added.

"Again, something down the road. We can ask Reggie about his relationship with the university when he meets with us," Taryn replied.

"You don't establish a venture capital fund with one company. What else is on your mind? I know you have been going to those dog-and-pony shows and studying possible investment opportunities. Has another firm peaked your interest?" Kathy asked.

"You're right. A couple of those companies show promise. In fact, we already have a prospect. Remember, we currently have a financial stake in Solo Pharma. I am pretty sure Timothy would be

interested in our becoming more than minor investors. As partners we would not only provide additional funding but also take
over his management responsibilities. He's always complaining
that he studied science and not business."

Taryn sat back in her chair, watching each of her partners as
they considered her proposition. "What do you all think?" she
asked. "I think it will add spice and a new purpose to the firm."

"Agree," Kathy said.

"Me as well," Ellie added. As Taryn looked over to Linda for her
approval, she noticed a somewhat puzzled expression.

"Is there something else on your mind?" Linda asked. "While this
is an exciting prospect for the firm, when you walked in this morning, you looked unusually serious and tired. As if you hadn't slept."

Taryn realized her friends knew her too well. Linda was especially sensitive to her moods. They would expect her to share her
unsettling dream of the night before. They didn't keep secrets.
"Actually I didn't sleep all that much. I woke with one of my pre-
monitions of trouble."

"And Jesse? What did he say?" Ellie asked.

"Ah, Jesse. Well he calmed me down by listening to me vent.
Then I sent him back to bed. I guess it's your turn to hear me out."
As Taryn tried to find the words to explain her midnight fears, she
knew she wouldn't mention the Gibraltar Bank logo. That was one
secret she'd kept locked away, buried in her past. Not even Jesse
knew that she had worked for the bank.

"Have any of you run into a possible problem with one of our
clients? Ellie, that's your area. You're good at ferreting out dissatisfied investors."

"Nothing at my end. In fact, everyone seems happy. When I
called earlier this year and asked for feedback, there had been
no surprises. Those who wanted more of a return still did but in
today's marketplace were satisfied we had been paying attention to
business."

"Linda, anything in systems? Something about to breakdown? Any hints we may have attracted the attention of a hacker?"

"No. I run a tight ship. Our consultant visits weekly, and we discuss the latest trends, criminal activity, and of course our dear government's interference into our record-keeping. I could write a crime novel with all he's been telling me."

"Taryn, what's going on?" Kathy asked. "Has something come up?"

"Probably nothing. But last night I awoke in fear that all was about to come crashing down on us. Probably just one of my superstitious dreams. So don't worry, but keep alert to anything new that could throw a monkey wrench into the business. OK?"

"Maybe you and Jesse need to get away for a weekend of R and R?"

Looking at Ellie, Taryn smiled. "That's a great idea. This new business venture is probably putting my checklists on overload." Laughing, Taryn rose and gathered her papers. "Sorry I can't join you for lunch. Next week. Promise." The three friends gathered their things, and Taryn wondered if she was capable of slowing down and enjoying her success. It probably was stress causing her stomach problems. Yes, more time with Jesse and definitely more time with the girls. They were closer than family. Her father once said that to the four of them that nothing was impossible. Over the years they kept proving it.

CHAPTER 4

Kathy couldn't wait for Linda and Ellie to gather their things. "Come on, ladies, I've made reservations for a back booth at Pete's Tavern. They fill up quickly."

"We aren't exactly dressed for pub dining," Linda complained. "I bought this suit at Bergdorf's to show off at this morning's meeting. You know, dressed as a financial mastermind."

"Just because we are lunching at a pub doesn't mean we have to be slobs," Ellie snapped. "Anyway, you should wear a skirt more often. It looks good on you."

Kathy led the group through the already crowded bar area, heading for the reservations desk. "Hi John, is our table ready?"

"Sure thing, Mrs. Ryan. Just as always, a corner booth in the back room. Follow me, ladies."

Settled at their booth, Linda looked at the daily specials featured on a blackboard at the end of the room. "Don't you wish we could order beef on weck? Like the sandwiches we had after school at Joe's coffee shop back home?"

"Sure do. That thinly sliced beef was great, but the Kimmelweck roll topped with kosher salt and caraway seeds was my favorite. I'd lick all the salt off first and then bite into the sandwich," Ellie said, moistening her lips at the thought.

Linda and Kathy laughed. They all ate the sandwich that way.

"So?" Kathy asked. "Venture Capital? I for one love the idea. With three boys who will at one point all be in college at the same time, this seems a more secure business model than our incremental hedging of fiscal bets. Not living second by second will be a vacation all by itself."

"The financial markets are always a gamble. Investing in specific companies would be a more satisfying way to earn a living. While I provide Arthur with background for his trades, I never feel I've accomplished anything. He and Taryn are the ones who control the firm's exposure," Linda said.

"Good old Arthur." Kathy smiled. "Over the years he's been like an uncle to all of us. But he and Taryn are more like stepfather and daughter. I guess it's because he worked for her dad before helping us found 4G."

Linda saw the waiter approach and quickly ordered. "A gimlet and a glass of ice on the side."

"Chablis, for me," Ellie added.

"Just coffee," Kathy said and saw two pairs of eyes looking at her. "I'm trying to lose weight. You do know alcohol is sugar!" They nodded in agreement but didn't change their orders.

"Do you want to order now or after I bring your drinks?" the waiter asked with his pad open and pen poised.

"Now. We'll have medium burgers all around. Sweet potato fries and horseradish on the side," Kathy said, looking at her friends to see if she had left anything out. "Oh and a side order of raw onion," she added.

"Thanks, Kathy. I don't have a husband to worry about," Ellie quipped. "I don't know how you can eat a burger without onions. You don't know what you're missing."

Once again alone, Linda returned to business. "Well, it's no secret I could use more income. That rat bastard of a husband cost me almost everything I'd made since I was fourteen. While 4G has helped me regain fiscal freedom, the volatility has increased my liquor bill."

"I'm working to fund my two nephews' and niece's college educations. So I guess Taryn's idea won't impact me as much. However, I do like the idea of supporting the next medical miracle. Instead of in-and-out trades to maximize fractional increases in our investments, we will be financing new marvels in the health sciences."

After the waiter set down their drinks, Linda raised her glass. "A toast then, ladies. To 4G Ventures."

Kathy sat quietly, not wanting to interrupt the cheerful mood. When they had taken their first sips, she said, "Don't you think Taryn is looking a bit frayed at the edges? I'm worried about her. Maybe her intuition or hunch of pending trouble is the cause, but I'd be happier if she checked herself out with her doctor."

"My sister looked a bit like that early in her second pregnancy. You don't think she and Jesse are starting a family?" Linda asked.

"I would only wish them that happiness. They'd make terrific parents. Wouldn't you love to play doting aunts? Having gone through pregnancy three times, I'd be happy to be her coach."

"You really think Jesse would let you take his place? That man hangs on her every breath. A child would only intensify his attention, if that was possible," said Linda, adding another ice cube to her drink.

"If not pregnant, she could be coming down with something. Before she married Jesse, we used to discuss the latest medical and health news. Come to think of it, that's probably where Taryn got interested in the health sciences," Ellie commented.

"That interest goes back to high school when she began to volunteer in the kids' ward at our local hospital. In addition to our babysitting business. I never could keep up," Kathy added. "With my working from home and Ellie on the road, Linda, you see her more than we do, so keep us informed. OK?"

"Sure. I'll find some excuse to drop by her office at least once a day. While we work down the hall from one another, I rarely get to see her."

"I guess we've become so specialized in our responsibilities, we rarely spend time together. Not like we did in the beginning. I miss that," Ellie said.

As lunch progressed, sharing news of family and New York life, Ellie announced, "Well, I have something I overheard that's going to one up all your news."

"Give. Don't keep us in suspense. Especially if it's gossip," Linda replied.

"Well, a friend of mine was walking down lower Broadway when she overheard a conversation between two men and a woman all in their late twenties or early thirties. Apparently they worked for a design firm and were discussing a fellow employee who made the stupid move of posting his recent conquest of a particular female executive on the company's intranet. It seems that this young man had been trying to sleep his way to the top, having affairs with first his direct report and then moving his roving eye to more senior women in the firm."

Laughing hard enough to almost spill her drink, Linda couldn't contain her glee. "Well, at last. Equality in the workplace. I'll drink to that."

"Me too," Ellie responded. "Finally there were enough women in upper management to be targeted. More importantly, these co-workers apparently saw through his scheme."

"Where do you get these stories, Ellie?" Kathy chuckled as she raised her glass. "Here's to men evolving from abusers to schemers. I wonder if the women felt harassed or amused. They had to see through him."

As dessert of one cheesecake and three forks was served, the conversation returned to Monday's meeting. "OK," Linda said. "I have my work cut out for me."

Kathy and Ellie nodded in agreement. "Enough business for now. I have another idea. Let's take Taryn out for a fabulously expensive dinner. As old friends, not business partners," Ellie suggested.

The applause was heart-felt. "What a great idea. Just like we use to…before we worked together."

Amid laughter, Kathy said, "Yes, Linda, and we always had to make reservations at seven o'clock to make sure you left your office. Now, Taryn's the last one to leave the office due to an overloaded schedule. Nothing changes."

CHAPTER 5

As she brushed her shoulder length auburn hair, Taryn Cooper Walsh thought of her husband. "I can only give you love to last forever," she sang, looking forward to spending the night in her husband's arms. How lucky she was to have found her soul mate—a man who not only understood and supported her business but made her feel younger than her forty-four years. When Jesse took her in his arms, she forgot everything else.

"Honey," Jesse said as he entered the bedroom and kissed the top of her head. "I am so proud of you." He held up a copy of *Economic World* magazine so that it reflected in her dressing-table mirror. Taryn saw her likeness on the cover. It was of a smartly tailored executive smiling for the camera. She recognized the pose she had perfected upon entering banking two decades earlier. It was the same expression she wore on the 4G website. The photo that had her wondering why she looked so stiff. Taryn nodded and resumed brushing her hair.

"I just read Pamela Green's article. She not only featured 4G's success, she proclaimed you the financial woman of the future.

Listen to this…" As Jesse continued to read the two-page profile, Taryn's thoughts turned inward. She had only granted Ms. Green the interview at the insistence of Melissa. When the plucky reporter had first approached her, she had declined. Not one to deny her capabilities or the success of her firm, she wasn't someone who sought the spotlight. Learning that Pamela had contacted her at Melissa's suggestion, Taryn called her friend to ask her advice.

"Pamela Green? You should do the interview. Remember that biography the company wanted written when I became CEO of United Chemicals? Well, Pamela followed me for a full week, and when I read the completed manuscript, I found she hadn't betrayed one confidence. In fact she still hasn't."

"If I remember, the book sold well, and there wasn't a hint of negative publicity."

"Right. She kept to our ground rules, the condition to granting her access to me, and a week of meetings with my staff."

Taryn remembered asking, "What if I'm misquoted or, worse, positioned as a money-hungry Wall Street scoundrel?" But her friend had prevailed, insisting that she could trust Pamela to write a fair piece. Having read the article earlier, Taryn was relieved that Ms. Green had done an excellent job of fairly portraying the firm and its goals. As she continued to brush her hair, she thought, *Well, I can cross that fear-generating possibility off my list.*

"Finally someone recognizes your brilliance." Jesse's voice interrupting her thoughts.

Looking up at the man who had brought love and passion to her life, Taryn took the magazine and tossed it onto a nearby chair. "This doesn't change anything. I still have to wear high heels every day and dress like Hollywood's version of a female overachiever. You work at home wearing sweats. Anyway, it's not as if I started 4G to have it fail."

"Did you happen to also notice that the article included a quote from Arthur? He mentioned that working in your company was heads and shoulders above the trading desks at male-dominated firms. That everyone at 4G speaks without resorting to profanity."

"My, my, don't you realize that men on those desks speak a code learned playing sports? Women learn manners. In my case if I used profanity as liberally as men, my friends would have thought I was bordering on stupid with a severely limited vocabulary."

"Darling, I work with women all the time. My editor and agent are women. Believe me—you are special. I've seen you with your back up and had to look up some of the words you spewed. They certainly had more than four letters but were equal to anything my male friends would use." Pulling her up by the shoulders and holding her close, Jesse pressed her body into his and gave her a deep kiss.

As she sank into his arms, Taryn thought of the article's opening phrase, "Against the Odds." To her it meant that at forty, she had fallen in love for the first time with a man perfectly suited to her hectic life. He didn't complain when business took her away for a week at a time or that she brought work home. He placed her first in his life, while maintaining a successful career as a financial columnist. All with his ego intact.

CHAPTER 6

The day was getting away from him. Here it was 11:00 a.m. and all Jesse had accomplished was reading the morning financial news and sorting through his mail. Getting up for his third cup of coffee, he spotted the note Taryn had posted on the refrigerator. She always anticipated his needs. Not like his first wife, the bitch. Married right out of college, it lasted less than one year. After the proverbial divorce from hell, Jesse gave up on marriage, or so he had thought. Then, five years ago fate, God, or the spirits sent him Taryn. His wife was a treasure, beautiful in spirit, pure of heart, and with curves that made him crazy.

> Darling, I should be home by seven and thought we'd have a light dinner of omelets and ice cream. You might want to fix something more substantial for lunch. My day includes a business lunch at the new Danny Meyer restaurant.
> Love you.

Jesse couldn't delay any longer. His agent said the publisher wanted him to write a market update on investing in gold for the upcoming issue of *Investment Business Report* newsletter. *Yeah, and both are hoping to turn investing in commodities into a regular column. Bless their hearts.* Returning to his desk, he began working on the final edit planning to e-mail the column by late afternoon. Or at the latest in the morning. This time his concentration was interrupted by the phone.

"Jesse," he answered, his mind focused on his computer screen.

"Good morning, grump," said Maureen. "I thought you would like to get out of your comfy sweats and come downtown for a business lunch. On me, of course."

"It must be big, or you wouldn't be picking up the check. I'll know just how big by the restaurant," Jesse answered, now all smiles. Maureen had been his agent for more than a decade and knew he didn't like dressing for business meetings. He'd told her it made him feel he was in a straight-jacket.

"How is Buddakan?"

The famous Robert De Niro restaurant was a way over-the-top showplace and the perfect venue to impress a potential business prospect.

"A surprise. Do you have room on your credit card to pick up the check?"

"You know I have a house account at the best places. So are you in? It's one p.m. today."

"I don't know. I was hoping to get the column in by late afternoon."

"Isn't tomorrow your deadline?"

"Do you know everything I do in my life?"

"Just those things that make me money. Jesse, I wouldn't interrupt, but this could be a great opportunity for you."

"I'm persuaded. I even have a new suit. And before you give me grief, Taryn picked it out. This must be the deal to buy that Fifth Avenue apartment you've been dreaming about. The one facing the Metropolitan Museum with great views of Central Park."

"It just may be. You won't do so badly yourself, pal. I'll only get fifteen percent. Just remember that. Oh, and wear that new tie Taryn bought you in Paris. The Hermes. I don't want them to think we're too anxious."

"Wait, before I get into my executive uniform, tell me just what this deal is about. You're acting more bossy than usual."

"How about a book, video, and educational program for middle schools across America? No more now. See you at lunch."

The column forgotten, Jesse sipped the dregs of his coffee while trying to figure out just what Maureen had said. Schools? When did he ever get involved with kids? His audience were people who thought they were savvy investors unlike his wife's hedge-fund clients who had already accumulated their fortunes and wanted more.

CHAPTER 7

"I'm so glad you chose Brasserie 8½." Taryn's greeting elicited a cheerful smile from her luncheon companion and valued friend, Melissa Lynn Horn. As she edged into her seat at a booth off to the side of the large open dining room, one of their regular waiters approached.

"Hello, Walter. We'll need a few minutes." Across the crisp white tablecloth sparkling with crystal and flatware, Melissa nodded in agreement.

"Very good, Ms. Cooper."

"I know what I want, and first it's to catch up with you."

"We don't get together often enough," Melissa replied. "We seem to meet only at corporate board meetings where your sharp fiscal analyses often cause grown men to blanch."

"Well, why did they invite me to join their boards? So they would have a second token female to assuage their shareholders?" Seeing Melissa's smirk, she quickly added, "No offense. I don't mean you were a token appointment. But you are the first woman to sit on these boards."

"As for being the first, they probably thought I'd be grateful to be joining their elite group. You do understand that you were their second try at appointing a compliant woman. That was until the first time you wrecked their plans with cold profit-and-loss analytics. They were stunned to find you had a brain."

"Very funny. I do the best I can with what I've got. I am who I am."

"I must say though, the first time I met you I saw an image of myself. Armani suits, silk blouses, all in back or navy. Look at us all these years later. You've softened your look, let your hair grow, and I've moved on from black and navy to a brighter color palette of reds, greens, and blues."

Looking at the stunning CEO sitting across the table, Taryn was embarrassed. How could someone almost six feet tall with the body of a model compliment her on her fashion sense? "You were always a standout, Melissa. Your designer suits may have been basic black or navy but so elegantly detailed how could you think you were dressing in a uniform? Anyway, now I dress for Jesse. He likes me in soft knits, not the structured menswear styles I used to wear. I always thought of clothes as a kind of uniform. In this case to make me look like I belonged on Wall Street."

"Ah, Jesse. That isn't all he's changed. Those knits reveal a well-toned body. And you told me you hated to work out. Is that the blushing bride I see?"

"I can't help it. After four years of marriage, I'm still smitten. So what's a bit of weight training and jogging? Just you wait. You are going to be bitten by the love bug, and then your attitude will change."

"You've know me long enough to realize that I intimidate men. Being CEO of an international corporation seems to take the starch out of their libido."

"You just haven't met the right man. I'm going to make it a personal challenge to find suitable prospects and invite them to dinner. You'll be safe. Jesse adores you and will run interference." Picking up the menu, she added more to herself, "I wonder why I haven't thought of that before?" Something made her look up, and she caught Melissa's smirk. "Ellie is in the same predicament. Finding a charming man. I know, I'll invite her as well." With that settled, Taryn returned to studying the menu

"Now that Pamela Green's profile on you is in the current issue of *Economic World*, you will be the talk of the financial world. What did you think of it?"

"Interesting that you brought that up now."

"Why? You're not worried?"

"To be honest I awoke the other day in dread. Worried that something was going to happen. And in reviewing the possibilities, I thought of Pamela Green's interview and all the trouble it could cause."

Melissa reached across the table and held Taryn's hand. "She's a pro. I thought she did a marvelous job of showcasing 4G Investments, and she certainly wrote it in such a way to emphasize a different style of management…that of a smart woman in charge. Give yourself a break. I've asked EF about it, and he's in your corner. Told me to tell you to take a bow."

"How is EF? You haven't mentioned him in a while. Less since you moved out to Sands Point. Jesse would love the four of us getting together again." Taryn noticed a slight change in Melissa's expression from cheerful to thoughtful. Wanting to be sure her friend hadn't read anything into her comments, she rushed to add, "I knew you were never romantically involved, but I always thought of you two as a family."

"My move out of the city has been an adjustment for both of us. But the change was needed. I had to find a life, and he had to return to his. When we lived in the same brownstone, we tended to shut the rest of the world out."

On seeing her friend quieten in thought, Taryn settled into her business mode. "You're right about the interview. The visibility will help attract new investors. After all, you sell products, I sell myself."

"My life is spent managing people. It's my job to oversee my team making sure they accomplish our corporate goals. I direct, they act. By comparison, Taryn, your life seems serene."

"Are you kidding? Just because I spend my day on computers researching investment opportunities or attending think tank presentations on the latest drug trial doesn't mean it's quiet. Hell, Melissa, the stress screams at me. Of course it is my stress. Still when I make decisions on how to spend other people's money, the level of tension increases with each hundred thousand dollars involved."

"And that fear? Another premonition? I remember you calling me hinting that there was a possible enemy at UCC. It's only because of your warning that I quietly looked into possible malcontents, and once I had identified that creep, I prevented him from doing any serious damage." Melissa's smile held gratitude. "So listen to your gut. If it's nothing, then at least you checked things out. If it actually develops into something, you'll deal with it in your swift take-no-prisoners style."

Laughing at the typical back and forth of whose job was more stressful was normal. It was the language of career women sharing business-related concerns.

Taryn paused to sip some water. "I miss our little luncheons. Another thing I seem to have little time for lately."

"We will just have to add personal time to our schedules. Enough, I'm starved," Melissa said. "I need food."

The restaurant was off the beaten path and was a favorite of the two women, both secure in their own egos and preferring privacy to trendy dining spots frequented by their male counterparts. As Walter approached, Melissa closed her menu. "I'll have the grilled snapper with steamed greens and a glass of chardonnay."

"Sounds good. I'll have the same, but a virgin mary for me, Walter."

As the waiter walked away, Taryn noted her friend's questioning look. "I'm not drinking much lately. My stomach seems a bit off. I'm sure it's nothing. But I have a full afternoon and don't want to spend it in the ladies' room."

"Is it anything you should see a doctor about? Anything you want to talk over?"

Taryn shook her head. "It could be stress. I seem to process that internally. Not like you. Didn't you tell me that while the outside world sees a polished, composed executive focused entirely on her job, your Achilles's heel was migraines?"

"Sad but true. And here we are accused of being perfect." Melissa's reply caused the two women to break out in laughter.

"Yes, and when I learned there was no perfect, life got a whole lot easier," Taryn added.

Over drinks and enjoying their luncheon choices, Taryn and Melissa discussed the latest challenges inherent to their growing empires. Taryn mentioned that 4G might be changing focus but didn't elaborate. It was too soon. Melissa mentioned her upcoming quarterly investors call and the news that the corporation was investing more heavily in their biomedical research.

"Holy shit! I have a steering committee meeting in twenty minutes," Melissa announced as she signaled for the check. Taryn added her credit card to Melissa's, and handed the folio to Walter who left to process the payment.

"Melissa, I'll check with Jesse tonight and get back to you about that dinner. I think you might like one or two of his writer friends. They'll see the stunning, sexy woman, not the CEO leader of men. Trust me."

"Thanks…I think."

As Melissa's car pulled away from the curb, she wondered how Taryn was able to appear fresh and affable while masking her ferocious attention to her business. She remembered meeting the slightly younger woman the year she opened her investment firm. It was at a cocktail reception. Not one to be fooled easily, she had at first taken Taryn as a bright young woman with a dream, not someone with the capabilities of a mathematical savant. Later as they became friends, Melissa learned that Taryn took her facility with numbers for granted. They represented order—each problem had its distinctive pattern from which she derived her decisions as to what and how much to invest on behalf of her clients.

Normally content with her life, Melissa envied her friend's marriage. In all of her forty-eight years, she had yet to find the one man who inspired passion, trust, and wanted to share her life. She thought she'd found him once, only to realize he had placed her on a pedestal. He never saw the whole of her life…an ambitious, flesh and blood woman. *Oh well, maybe Taryn is right. I should try harder.*

CHAPTER 8

"Reggie, let me introduce you to the 4G team." As Taryn introduced each of the women, she watched the kid for any hint of disdain. Was he of the new generation where men and women were equal, preferred dealing with men, or was he wrapped up in his own universe? What she saw was a beanpole of a young man, who looked as if he would rather be in his laboratory than facing this polished group holding the keys to his dreams.

"Reggie, Kathy and I have reviewed your brief. Would you give Linda and Ellie an overview of your work on inflammation? Once they understand what's involved, they will be in a better position to ask their questions."

Nodding and then clearing his throat, Reggie Farmer pushed his glasses in place on the bridge of his nose. Taryn watched him wipe his palms on his pants and realized his discomfort was probably increased by having to make a speech explaining his work to an audience of strangers. Then again, his generation rarely held face-to-face conversations.

"When I was in grade school, I was diagnosed with the beginning of rheumatoid arthritis. It started in my shoulder, and at first I thought it was only sore from playing baseball on the school team. The coach would ice it after each game until one day when he asked me if I had ever told my mom that my shoulder constantly hurt. When he found out I hadn't, he sat me down and called her. To my embarrassment she rushed to school and took me straight to the family doctor. Well, after seeing a specialist and having an MRI, I learned that I would eventually be faced with increasing limitations as the arthritis grew worse. Apparently it was not only the wear and tear on my shoulder causing me to ache after each game, but my body was still growing, and with each inch I was adding new stress on my joints. So sports, normal growth, and the beginning of the inflammatory arthritis were combining to destroy my body."

"Were you severely limited?" Ellie asked. "Or is this something that grew slowly and you just adjusted to it?"

"I'm not severely limited, at least not yet."

"How old were you?" Linda wanted to know. She had a niece who played soccer on her high school team. The wear and tear on her young body worried her family.

"Ten. But I swore I wasn't going to be a cripple. So I began to read everything I could find, mainly online. There were foods that were supposed to be inflammatory. Then there are the nutritional herbs that are supposed to control inflammation. And, of course I drove my mom crazy as each new substance, folk medicine recipe, or drug was touted to either cure or limit its impact on my body."

"All when you were ten?" Ellie asked, eyes wide in disbelief.

Looking a bit embarrassed, Reggie shook his head. "No. It was an interest that grew a little at a time until high-school chemistry. When I mentioned my interest in arthritis to my teacher, Mr. Simon assigned inflammation as my term project. He said to gather all the information I had collected and suggest future avenues of study. And that was the real beginning of my focus on science and the search for a better understanding of just why inflammation can be the body's repair tool or why it can jump into overdrive and cause damage."

"Reggie, I am particularly interested in your research because if you solve this puzzle, we could be on the threshold of an entirely new way of looking at another one of the body's mysteries," Taryn said. "And that could lead to cures of…how many diseases and conditions did you estimate in your brief? Hundreds?"

"We just don't know. We don't know if inflammation is due to mechanical wear and tear such as in my shoulder or if it is bio-chemical in nature. If you look at tomatoes and spinach as con-tributing to inflammation, then you might say it was biochemical. But when you suffer from an overused joint like my shoulder and it becomes inflamed as part of the healing process, then it might be considered mechanical. And there are others suggesting it might be a bioelectric process."

"And where are you in your research? What do you need to con-tinue to prove a thesis? What are your expectations for, let us say, the next five years?" Kathy asked.

Taryn watched the intense young man, now clearly in his ele-ment, as he quickly answered each question. Somewhere between the beginning of his presentation and now, he had relaxed into his role of a scientist enthralled with his work.

"Sorry. It's simply too early to give specifics of either a time-frame or end point to my research."

Taryn recognized Reggie's ambition and drive. Both good signs if 4G was going to become an investor, build a company around his work, and make sure he had the support of a solid management team.

Reggie took off his glasses and wiped them on a crumpled handkerchief. With a calm not previously shown, he looked at

Taryn. "I want to find out how inflammation begins to attack the body's defenses. I'm close to establishing that process, and when that is achieved, I will begin to test for specific conditions, including something as common as cholesterol production."

"Why cholesterol?" Kathy asked. "Mine is considered safe because of the healthy ratio between LDL and HDL, but the total is over two hundred sixty and considered high. I was advised to try to lose ten pounds and begin taking a statin to help reduce the numbers."

"Statins are widely prescribed, but they have side effects. If I can establish that point at which cholesterol stays within the safe range, we will be in a better position to develop safer drugs. Think of it this way: if there is a breakdown in a body part, it causes inflammation, and then the body produces cholesterol and rushes it to the damaged section…like putty to fix a leak. Inflammation is the signal…it's just too early in my work to identify the key to controlling that mechanism."

"Reggie, the health gurus advise staying away from eating the night shade plants you mentioned, limiting caffeine and alcohol, among other recommendations. Are you working with any of these theories?"

"The simple answer is yes. But as my backgrounder states, it is more complicated than that and the reason I want to continue my research. I am ready to provide you with access to my work… anything to convince your firm to provide necessary funds. I am so close to finding the key. I can't stop just because Johns Hopkins shuts off my funding."

Taryn was pleased with the two-hour meeting and noticed that in addition to Kathy's concerns about inflammation, each one in the room had a brush with it in one form or another. Like Kathy, her cholesterol numbers were approaching dangerous levels. While she could control the math of finance, her body wasn't paying attention to her attempts at keeping fit.

After Reggie had left, the room grew quiet. "OK then, what did you think?" Taryn asked, breaking the silence.

"I'm in," Kathy said first.

"Me too," Ellie added. "This kid is serious and seems willing to work with us. I might have been concerned if I thought he was someone who wouldn't take business advice."

"Linda, I told Reggie I'd call in the morning and discuss our thoughts. I would like you to pay him a visit sometime this week and see just what his setup requires. You might also quietly look into the connection with Johns Hopkins. Until we have Reggie in house, I don't want to alert anyone of our intentions."

"Ms. Cooper," greeted Taryn's valued assistant as she entered the large sunny office. "I wasn't sure if you wanted me to open this. It just came by special delivery."

As she looked at the ordinary number ten envelope, Taryn replied, "Let's see what we have, shall we? You never know who is looking for money." It was common for her to receive requests for funding. She welcomed these requests, always on the lookout for the next investment opportunity.

As Taryn carefully slit the envelope open with a brass letter opener given to her by a favorite aunt, she withdrew the photocopy of a news clipping. FYI was scrawled on the upper-left corner of the page in heavy black marker. There was no other notation. It was part of a business roundup from her hometown paper in Dunkirk, New York. After giving it a once over, Taryn sat back in her chair and then refocused on the offensive item and read every word to her assistant.

"4G Investments is reported to have been cheating its clients with overstated fees. Information was obtained from an anonymous source. Rumor or fact, we will be following up with the firm for comment."

"What the hell?" Taryn said as she picked up the envelope and looked for a return address. Not finding one, she looked at her assistant, stunned.

"Ms. Cooper?" Bobbie said. "Are you all right?"

"Bobbie, this is probably some crackpot. I don't want you to say anything about this. Promise?"

"Of course, Ms. Cooper. I promise not to say anything."

"Here." Taryn handed over the offensive paper. "I want you to check online for this particular issue of the *Dunkirk Clarion* and see if this…this article actually ran in the newspaper. If you can't find it on this date, check each day for two weeks before and one week after. I also want the name and contact information of the columnist. That's if it is an actual article and not some prank."

Bobbie quickly glanced at the article, folded it, and replaced it in its envelope. "On it."

What she needed was Arthur Mallory's advice and keyed in his extension. After years in banking and helping to found 4G Investments, he was her most valuable counsel. "Arthur. Can you come in? I need to show you something."

"Sure. On my way."

"Bobbie," Taryn called out to her assistant sitting by the open office door. "Show our little surprise to Arthur when he gets here."

As she swiveled her chair to face the window, Taryn tried to think of who might want to spread a rumor casting doubt about the way she managed her firm. A competitor? Had someone read the interview and wanted to cause trouble? Regardless, she had to prevent this from being leaked. Even a hint of something of this kind would make her investors nervous. Was this the premonition of trouble she'd experienced two nights before?

She and Arthur went way back to when she was a kid and he worked for her father at the bank. Now a silent partner in 4G, he was family. This time she was counting on his experience to avert a potential crisis.

As the mature man in conservative dress settled in a chair opposite, she leaned forward, clasping both hands in front of her. "Arthur, have you read our little surprise? Bobbie is checking to see if this item actually ran in the paper. So far she hasn't confirmed its authenticity."

"She had better extend her search to the internet including Facebook and Twitter."

"Facebook and Twitter? Social networking isn't in my skills set. I don't trust the accuracy of the information."

"Even if this is a faked news article, someone went to a lot of trouble to create this little falsehood. The newspaper exists, and the rumor is targeted."

"Arthur, are you telling me that someone is trying to damage 4G's reputation?"

"Welcome to the new world. And you thought the SEC was a challenge."

"I have to give this some thought. I was going to pass it off as a prank. You're telling me I have to take this infuriating bit of nonsense seriously."

"Taryn, you run 4G as one of the most highly respected firms in the business. Put your thinking cap on, and I will do the same. There must be an incident prompting this behavior. Between the two of us, maybe we can come up with one or two candidates."

CHAPTER 9

Arthur returned to his office two doors down from Taryn's, wondering who wanted to cause her trouble. In all the years he had worked alongside her at 4G, he had never heard a negative word from investors or business associates. He knew better than most how committed she was to running an ethical firm. It was something she learned from her father. As president of the local bank, he drilled his only child on the importance of truth and honor in life and in business.

He had known Taryn since she was in grade school. Back then, a newly minted CPA, he had gone to work for her father, Bennett Cooper, president of the Dunkirk Savings and Loan. "Where did time go? That was more than three decades ago."

As he reminisced, Arthur thought how proud his mom would be of the man he had grown up to be. She had lived to see him become vice president at the bank but not his current role as silent partner and mentor to 4G's founding partners.

The son of a man who died in combat while serving in the army in Vietnam, Arthur considered his mother as his symbol of family.

She had worked on the army base as a nurse trying to keep him in school. His strongest memories were of her pulling him out of one scrape after another. But it was her stories about his dad and the dreams he had for his son that had stayed with him. He could still hear her voice as she told him how she had pictured them going to ball games, fishing on the lake, and playing basketball in the back yard. Arthur grew up loving to hear those stories of what might have been. Thinking of his mom, he couldn't remember if he told her that he loved her enough. When she died, he wished she had known how grateful he was for not giving up on him.

Twenty years her senior, Arthur knew how independent Taryn was. Back when she was in grade school, and her eight-year-old friends began trusting him to invest their babysitting money, he treated her as a business client—albeit a favored one.

He thought back over thirty years and that first meeting with Taryn, Kathy, Linda, and Ellie. Since then, nothing Taryn did had surprised him. From that first consultation, he tried to impress upon each of the girls the seriousness of money and the importance of investing their earnings. Then, one day as they discussed the group's finances, he had to tell them it was time to become an official organization complete with records of their transactions, just like any adult client of the bank. Up to that point, the few dollars they had earned babysitting had been placed first in each girl's interest-bearing savings account, and when it had grown sufficiently, into the bank's CD offerings, and later into T-bills.

Thinking of how far he'd come brought Arthur a warm feeling of contentment. Nearing his mid-sixties, he had the life he dreamed of all those years ago. He'd married the love of his life, Lorraine, and together they raised their twin daughters Chloe and Cynthia, who today were bright, lovely young women. He lived in a home with all the comforts and had surpassed his personal financial goals. But it was his relationship with Taryn that was pivotal to his feelings of success. Outside of his family, she was the only other person he had devoted his time and efforts toward helping realize her dreams. Today she was a financial leader, astute, capable and had built a successful hedge fund in a highly competitive field. With retirement from the bank a decade away, Mr. Cooper, his longtime boss and friend, suggested Arthur leave the bank and become part of 4G Investment's founding team. Arthur smiled at the memory of that pivotal conversation. What Cooper wanted was for Arthur to be onsite and continue protecting his daughter.

Pulling out the 4G Investment's phone list of business associates, Arthur began looking for someone who might want to cause the firm harm. When that didn't trigger anything, he opened his daily diary looking for a clue to someone who might be targeting 4G and Taryn for ruin. When these cursory checks failed to uncover any possibilities, Arthur made a list of files he'd review next. They held specifics of client investments and might turn up a name of someone who had lost money with the firm or had become disgruntled. It would take time because while the files were all computerized, Arthur placed personal notes in the paper copies kept locked away in his office.

CHAPTER 10

In the midst of studying a research report, Taryn was distracted by the sudden appearance of Fergus Donavon, her office manager, who along with Arthur, was the bedrock of her organization. "Yes, Fergus? What's wrong?"

"That company you made a small investment in…the one in upstate New York? Well, you need to call the insurance company. The building just burned to the ground."

"What? Solo Pharma? It's in a fireproof building."

"Timothy just called to say there was a gas main leak, and someone in the adjoining space must have lit a cigarette. The entire concrete building blew."

Reaching for her phone, Taryn punched in Timothy's cell. "Tim? I just heard. Is everyone all right? Anything salvaged?"

"It's all gone. The lab, equipment, our files. Everything."

"But is anyone hurt?"

"What? Ah no. Not physically anyway."

"Tim, you sent me copies of your latest research. Isn't that all you need to start up again?"

"Yeah, and one hundred thousand dollars."

"OK. I'll overnight a package to your home with everything we have here at 4G. Look it over and get back to me after you've figured out if anything is missing. Then figure out how much you'd need to rebuild. I'm here if you want to talk. We'll get through this. Promise."

Taryn couldn't help picture the intense young man who lived for his research. His family had a history of Huntington's disease, and still in his twenties, Timothy was living with the threat that he had inherited the defect. Taryn believed he would eventually develop some drug to, if not cure the disease, at least lessen its impact, giving patients an improved quality of life. Timothy had told her of watching as his dad deteriorated from the disease that attacked nerves in his brain. At first he couldn't control his balance; then his thinking became muddled, and finally increasing dysfunction included psychic episodes. Taryn was deeply affected watching the young man relive the terrors that had befallen his father and had committed herself and the firm to aiding his research.

"Fergus, please make copies of all Timothy's research and overnight them to his home."

"Sure thing, Ms. Cooper."

Punching in the Solo Pharma account, Taryn discovered that 4G would collect a healthy $15 million on the insurance the firm had taken out when they had structured the initial loan. "Bobbie, please set up a conference call with Ellie, Kathy, and Linda.

"Hey gals, the venture capital fund has to begin sooner than we thought." After telling them about Timothy's lab, she made a decision that would change her view of business going forward. "Listen, we'll recover enough on the insurance to rebuild. We'll reorganize Solo Pharma into our first venture capital investment. I'm suggesting we use the insurance and investor capital to rebuild Timothy's facilities. If I'm right, not only will he succeed…especially with Linda sitting on him, prodding him with her timetables, but

I am sure he is close to running a phase one trial." Taryn listened to Kathy provide her thoughts on redesigning Timothy's physical space and began making quick notes on a pad. She'd flesh out these points in a memo to each and begin structuring the new company around Solo Pharma's needs.

"And, gals, once Tim has the eye of the FDA, we can turn around and look for outside investors. Then Solo Pharma and 4G will begin to realize profits. Do I have your approval?"

Smiling as she hung up, Taryn guessed she would get approval for her actions. Unlike some hedge funds, her partners didn't want to just make money at the expense of a firm. They believed in building something worthwhile and that with quality management and investment policies, they would generate healthy profits. She'd have Arthur contact their lawyer to start developing a new prospectus for the first 4G venture capital fund. While Solo Pharma and Reggie were the only two scheduled for the new venture, her prior research in health science start-ups showed some promising additions for consideration.

As she continued making notes of the steps necessary to include Tim's company as part of 4G's new venture, Taryn stopped short, tapped her pen on the pad, and smiled. "Shit! Timothy needs a calm assistant to help restore his confidence along with his company. And I know just who to send. Reggie. With his expertise in genetics, he can help catalogue the cellular studies Timothy has been working with. Once order is restored, Reggie can resume his own work on inflammation in an adjacent laboratory. Right! One building with two separate research entities. Cost effective and easier for 4G to manage its investment dollars.

Taryn felt eyes on her back, as though someone was looking over her shoulder studying her computer monitor. Was she was being irrational? She was sitting with her back to a wall of windows thirty stories above Sixth Avenue. No one was looking at her trading targets. Squaring her shoulders, she shook off fatigue. What she needed was a hot bath and a cozy dinner at home with Jesse.

The last item of the day was contacting Arthur to discuss his call to the firm's broker. It was a daily end-of-day routine before she left for home. Arthur was the one who actually communicated all 4G Investments trades to their broker, Stephen Harrington, at the bank's trading desk. Arthur was more than capable of handling the firm's trades, but as with most details of 4G's activities, Taryn felt that as managing partner the ultimate responsibility fell on her shoulders.

"OK, Arthur, I just sent you my suggestions for the day. They're in line with yours. Unless you have any changes, you can contact Stephen at the bank. I'll look at your report first thing in the morning."

"Right. I see you agree with that trade I highlighted in my memo. If we gain even one point, we can add that to the profits for the month. Good night, Taryn. Say hello to Jesse for me."

Hanging up the phone, Taryn felt a chill. *Someone's walking over my grave.* Laughing off her fear, she gathered her files placing them into her drawer. A stray envelope sat at the bottom of the pile. With a shaking hand, she ripped it open and pulled out a sheet of paper. Impatient to see what it contained, her eyes blurred as she saw FYI scrawled in heavy black marker bordered the top of a photocopy of another news clipping.

The luscious husband of 4G Investment's Managing Partner was seen at lunch clinking glasses with an extremely attractive woman. Is the paragon of investments' husband cheating?

"Bobbie, are you still here?" she all but yelled. Seeing her trustworthy assistant rush through the door, she restored a modicum of control. "Please look at this, and try to tell me how it got on my desk."

"Ms. Cooper, I've never seen this."

Taryn heard the concern in Bobbie's voice. She guarded Taryn and everything around her. The girls often joked that Bobbie had trained at the Secret Service and would take a bullet for her boss.

Slumping into her chair, Taryn handed over the second missive and waited for her assistant's reaction.

"Ms. Cooper, this is serious. We have to call someone in to find out who is trying to scare you."

"Not yet." Taking deep breath, Taryn, who with the first FYI clip was somewhat concerned, was now thinking this hazing was only the beginning of trouble. A trouble that was yet to be identified. "Look, Bobbie, we don't have anything to go on. Promise not to say anything about this. I'll show this to Arthur in the morning."

"But this needs attention."

"Yes. But I can't afford for any of this to leak. It could spook our investors. So let me think on this, and we'll take it up first thing in the morning. And you might do another online search to see if this actually ran in the *Clarion*, like you did for the other one." Seeing Bobbie hesitate, she looked at her and smiled, "Just lock this up with the other one. Go home. Enough drama for today. OK?"

"Yes. But I'm not happy about it."

After Bobbie left, Taryn looked around her office and saw everything in order. Knowing her computer was protected and her office was secure, she tried to relax. Why then did she have the strongest feeling of being watched? It was something she sensed, smelled, like the energy before a lightning strike. Her office was a smoke-free zone. But the scent was more electrical than of burning tobacco.

Always thinking better with pen and paper than on her computer, Taryn began one of her lists. On top of the page she made two columns: *Pros* and *Cons*. Then under *Pros* listed everyone connected to 4G. When she got to the *Cons* column, she thought hard about those competitors who would love to see her fail. That column hadn't taken long. Still not satisfied she closed her eyes trying to visualize her world. When nothing important seemed to come to mind, she felt a sense of loss. Am I so focused on work I've become oblivious to everything else?

CHAPTER 11

"I'm home," Taryn called as she dropped her keys on the entry table of their New York apartment. Weary beyond words, she was looking forward to kicking off her heels and snuggling down on the sofa next to Jesse...wishing he could help her figure out how to handle those horrendous clippings. Thinking the first was a prank, she hadn't wanted to tell him about it until she knew if it was a serious threat. So far Bobbie hadn't found anything either online or in the newspapers. As for telling Jesse about today's surprise, well, she'd see how the evening went.

Rushing out to greet his wife, Jesse blurted out, "Honey, come with me." Jesse reached for her hand and lead Taryn into the library where he poured her a glass of champagne.

"Are we celebrating something?" Her husband was always so measured, calm, never getting too excited or deeply saddened by events in his life. Even at their wedding, he just grinned and hugged her until she melted into his arms. Seeing this unexpected show of delight animating her husband's handsome face, she pushed her own troubles to the back of her mind. It was unthinkable to bring up this latest clip and cloud his excitement.

"Yes. Your husband has just been given the assignment of a lifetime. One I know you will want to be part of…officially or unofficially, of course."

Raising his glass, he all but sang, "Here's to actually helping people. Kids in fact. Creating something worthwhile that will outlast us."

As Taryn drank to her husband's toast, her mind couldn't even begin to understand what he was talking about. "Kids. Worthwhile, outlast us? Jesse, could you start at the beginning? It's been a tough day. I am afraid you have me totally confused."

Where was this leading? It was a subject she hadn't thought about since Jesse asked her to marry him. Back then they had discussed planning a family, but with both busy building their careers, it was something they had put off planning. Was he reopening that discussion now?

Taryn took a moment to consider her reply. "Jesse, are you asking me if I want to raise a child? Sweetheart, I'm forty-four; my days to conceive may be over."

"No, no, Taryn. Not children of our own. That's a conversation for another time. I mean do you ever think about doing something to help them? Like develop a financial education program for schools?"

"Now you have my attention. Is this something Maureen cooked up? And, if so, please tell me everything and why you are so excited."

"I had lunch with Maureen today at Buddakan. She picked up the check for three."

"What? Your fiscally conservative agent who could make a buffalo jump on a nickel paid for a four-star lunch?" *And that squelches that rumor.* Taryn's smile brightened, even more eager to hear Jesse's news.

Laughing, Jesse sipped his champagne and nodded. "You know that I became focused on writing financial columns and books to help people learn how to manage their money. It's been a crusade of mine so they won't bankrupt themselves out of ignorance."

"Like your father did?" she asked softly. Taryn remembered hearing the story that after a successful life as a physician, Jesse's dad had made several bad investments that reduced their family to living on his retirement account and social security. After a life of hard work, he couldn't provide his wife the retirement they had dreamed of, traveling the world to see all the things they had only read about and had no time to enjoy. Both lives cut short by early deaths. Jessup's from a heart attack and Diane's a decade before from cancer.

"Yes. Well, the Staller Foundation wants me to create a financial responsibility program beginning with a book, lesson plans, and video lectures for the middle schools across the country."

"Didn't Muriel Siebert do something similar in the late 1990s? I seem to remember she had to practically fight City Hall before the Board of Education adopted her original program for high schools."

"Yes. And she was developing one for middle schools when she passed away. Anyway, apparently, the wife of the CEO had been part of an outreach by American Express's Office of Responsibility in 1994. They partnered with Home Extension Agents across the country and developed one of the first video seminars focused on providing teaching tools to create programs on finance in schools."

"You know, Jesse, nothing has really changed. Kids don't understand anything about those credit cards they use until they owe so much money they have to declare bankruptcy."

"One of the reasons your husband could afford to buy you that country house you dreamed of is because their parents aren't much more informed."

Taryn was so proud of her husband. Here he was knee deep in work and ready to take on a massive new project because he wanted to help kids. "I love you," she whispered as she moved toward her husband, wrapped her arms around his neck, and gave him a sweet soft kiss. "You are one in a million."

Taryn listened as Jesse talked about his luncheon and the plans to begin locally with a middle-school program. Test it in several of the city's poorer neighborhoods and then build an entire coordinated program from lesson plans to video productions featuring television and film personalities. "You know your mom and dad would be so proud of you. Didn't they always hope you would help people understand the importance of learning how to manage their money?"

"I wish they were here," he said, hugging her close. "They'd love you." Taryn wilted in his arms. "Honey?" he asked. "Is everything all right? Normally you would be full of rapid-fire questions. Is this something you aren't really interested in?"

"Oh no, Jesse. It's not that. I guess I'm more tired than I thought. It's probably just my stomach. It's acting up. Can we go over this tomorrow in the country? Your middle-school age group is rather special to me. You know I had a business at that age." Smiling, her love for her husband had once again lifted her spirits. Her newest problem could wait. Now was Jesse's time.

CHAPTER 12

"Taryn, dinner is cooking, the wine is chilling, and you've set the table beautifully. Even used your aunt's silver. It's just a casual gathering of friends. Relax, it isn't as if you were entertaining business associates."

"Jesse, I've never done anything like this before. Melissa and Ellie are friends. Yes, we have talked about men…" Looking up and seeing Jesse smile, Taryn quickly added, "You know they adore you. But I've never played matchmaker. I want them to be as happy as you make me."

"Look, Jack and Marty are from my world. True, Jack writes thrillers, and Marty is a sports reporter, but they're good guys. Don't you think both gals could use a little social relief? Enjoy the company of a man not all buttoned up in a business suit? What is that old saying? 'All work makes for a dull boy,' or in this case, gal?" He chuckled at the worried look on her face. "What's the worst that can happen? Everyone has an enjoyable evening and our single friends don't make a romantic connection? Don't worry.

The evening will be fun, I promise." Reaching out to his wife, Jesse gave her a deep kiss. "There, all settled?"

"Not at all. You just started a different set of nerves humming."

Jesse had greeted each of the guests with laughter, and knowing the individual preferences of each, had their drinks ready and waiting on the bar. Taryn had opened bottles of chardonnay for Melissa and white zinfandel for Ellie. Jesse poured scotch, adding two ice cubes for Jack, and a tall rye and ginger ale for Marty.

"Welcome, all," Taryn greeted emerging from the kitchen with a tray of cheeses and crackers. "Jack, I haven't read your latest book, but the reviews give it high praise. What part of the world did you visit to write it?"

"Ah, Taryn, you have to take Jesse to the Galapagos. It's a world away from this crazy town. When I returned, I sat in my apartment and went over my photos of the seals barking for a mate, the blue-footed boobies dancing to attract their female companions. Just raw nature pairing up. Sex is universal."

"I have always wanted to visit the Galapagos," Melissa said. "Unfortunately, my recent schedule hasn't permitted the two weeks I'd need to do it right."

As he looked at the attractive redhead, Jack couldn't imagine a prettier companion. "Well, I wouldn't mind visiting again. I had to cut this trip short to meet a deadline. There wasn't time to visit the giant tortoises or some of the other islands."

Taryn watched her friend break out in a charming smile and wondered if the male population was blind. Melissa was smart, lovely, rich, and available. So what if she's a CEO?

Settled at the dinner table, Taryn picked up her napkin and announced, "I am happy to report that I had nothing to do with dinner. Jesse is serving one of his favorite dishes, paella…complete with lobster. I, for one, can't wait to dig in."

The hum of dinner conversation moved back and forth with each guest giving a brief description of their jobs. Melissa said that she worked at UCC, leaving out her title of CEO. Ellie mentioned that she was one of the principle partners of 4G investments and listened attentively to Marty discuss the world of professional sports. Everyone loved Jack's thrillers, so he told an entertaining tale of a reader's reaction to his latest book at a personal appearance and book signing. Apparently one young man found the murder not grisly enough. "What in the world have we come to when readers become inured to a bloody murder?" he asked.

"How old was this critic?" Ellie asked.

"I'd guess in his mid-twenties."

"Well then, he's been desensitized by the visual violence seen on television dramas, film, and video games."

"I'll have to think about that before I begin a new manuscript," Jack replied.

"Melissa," Marty said, "you might like to attend a Yankee game with me this Sunday. I'll be sitting in the press box."

Jesse broke out in a belly laugh. "Marty, your invitation would be better issued to Ellie. She's a fan."

A surprised Marty looked at Melissa. "You don't like baseball? Isn't that un-American?"

"Apparently I missed that genetic gift. Personally, I find watching baseball as exciting as watching paint dry."

The room broke out in good natured laughter with Marty simply unable to accept her reply and turned to Ellie. "Do you understand her?"

Ellie smiled at the befuddled man, the picture of a collegiate athlete gone a bit soft around the middle. As she reached over to pat him on his hand, she said, "Don't try to understand Melissa. She has other interests. As Jesse said, I'm a fan. I used to go to all the home games with my dad and never got over the excitement of a ninth-inning no-hitter."

"Then I happily extend my invitation to join me at Sunday's game. I'll pick you up. Just give me your phone number and address when this feast takes a break."

"I'd be delighted and honored to sit in the press box. That would be a first in a lifelong love affair with the game," Ellie replied.

"Jack, how do you come up with ideas for your thrillers?" Melissa asked over dessert of cherry pie.

"Mostly I read the daily newspapers for some recent scandal or a destination I've wanted to visit. Today's politicians provide a wealth of dastardly deeds to use in developing plot twists and turns. Then there are the characters themselves. They often become bossy telling me how to wrap up a story."

"Have you ever used social media in one of your books?" Taryn asked.

"Not yet. But I have been thinking about it. Socially, the Internet is like the wild west of yore. A place where all kinds of schemes can be perpetrated. Theft of identities, money, trade secrets, even creating rumors to ruin a company. In fact some of what you read as news is no more than the invention of some blogger."

Jack's comment about internet rumors ruining a company had Taryn wringing her hands carefully hidden in her lap.

"My company has a full-time team to ensure that our computers and phones are kept scrubbed. I get their reports and am surprised by the range of activities they've thwarted," Melissa said.

Taryn knew Jack would understand what she was facing. As an author of thrillers, his mind sought out the how's and why's of a crime. Could she ask for his help? Her pie and coffee forgotten, Taryn decided to wait until she and Arthur had completed their preliminary research and filed Jack away on a mental list of people she could call upon for help.

Taryn's attention refocused on the dinner conversation, and she was pleased to see that even if Melissa and Ellie didn't find a romantic partner, they would all become friends. She had to make time for more evenings like this, especially as the weather turned warmer. The Connecticut house had room for overnight guests. She was sure that a weekend out of the city would be fun for all and just maybe give her a chance to settle her nerves. Mindful of her recent health issues, Taryn had only sipped at her one glass of wine, but her enjoyment of Jesse's paella had still been marred by a queasy stomach.

CHAPTER 13

"Done. Hit send, and I'm free for the rest of the week. Next week's article can wait until Monday."

Jesse wanted to concentrate on 4G's quarterly statements. Maybe he could spot some anomaly Taryn had missed. He had never known his wife to worry about something when there hadn't been a good reason.

Digging the file out from under a pile of his own work, Jesse headed to the cushy love seat across the room. Just as he settled in, the ringing phone interrupted his thoughts. Resigned, he picked up the receiver. "Jesse Wash."

"Well, hello, hubby," was the saccharine response.

"What do you want, Sharon?" It was the voice he hoped never to hear again.

"Now is that any way to treat your first wife? The one who turned you from a nerd into a dashing Wall Street trader?"

"Why are you calling me? Call your third husband. Let him take care of you."

"Don't be like that. And we're getting divorced." Her tone had gone from flinty flirt to a soft kitten's purr.

Why wasn't he surprised? His ex was the epitome of manipulative bitch. "We haven't been in touch for twenty years."

"Don't go into a fit of nastiness. Actually, I read about your new wife being one of the outstanding women in finance. You certainly married the golden princess. So, I thought you'd help me out of a little financial jam. It isn't as if my needs are all that great."

Well, her claws are out. She probably sharpened them just before she called. "When we divorced I gave you a large cash settlement. You signed the agreement, which among other items said you wouldn't seek anything further from me."

"Sweetie. Don't be like that."

Her sugary tone could still get him riled. "What do you need?" he all but shouted before he remembered that showing anger only escalated Sharon's temper. He'd just have to hear her out.

"I am a bit over charged on my credit cards."

"How many cards and how much?" It was getting harder not to lose his patience.

"Only two cards and a total of thirty-five thousand dollars, which is nothing to you."

"How in the hell did you get into that mess? I know your favorite past time is shopping, but you always knew your limit."

"Well, I had a bit of a nip and tuck. It isn't easy for someone my age to reenter the social scene. It was just a little tightening and lifting here and there."

Her pause was ringing in his ears.

"And of course a wardrobe update. How am I to meet a successful man looking like bargain-basement Bessy?" The edge had returned to her voice. Jesse was sure that shrill wasn't far behind.

"Listen carefully, I advise people about handling their finances. So I am going to give you some free advice. Make an appointment with a credit-counseling service. They will review your finances, combine your outstanding credit-card debt, and maybe even be able to negotiate a reduction. And, I might add, you should do it immediately."

"Now listen, you bastard. Your pitiful one-hundred-thousand-dollar divorce settlement was chicken feed. The ink wasn't even dry on the papers when I read you signed a huge book deal. I want some of that money. Half is rightfully mine."

Closing his eyes seeking an inner calm, he tried again. "Look, Sharon, I had to borrow that one hundred thousand dollars to pay you. You know we didn't have anything when we split."

"Jesse, Jesse, Jesse, you don't get it. If I don't get thirty-five thousand dollars in two days, I'll go to that rich wife of yours. When I tell her what a mean spirited, controlling bastard she married, she'll be only too happy to give me the money."

In a cold, low voice he hadn't used since he last spoke to Sharon, Jesse said, "Don't you dare go near, Taryn. And don't threaten me. We're done." He had almost cut the call when he heard her shrill retort. "Not only will I see her, I'll show her a copy of the check for the two-hundred-thousand-dollar advance you got the day our divorce was final. I'll threaten her with a public disclosure during a live television interview on the Today Show…complete with a copy of that book. Now won't your readers love knowing their vaunted paragon of an author is a thief? A man who would steal from innocent little me?"

The sound of Sharon's slamming down her phone reverberated throughout his spine. Jesse hadn't told Taryn much about his first wife. She got the message that his marriage had been hell. Bless his innocent wife, she had no idea people like Sharon existed.

"What I need is a shower…long and hot to steam out the poison."

⇒⟡⟡⇐

Rage enflamed her normally pale face. *How dare he dismiss me…the bastard. I'm the reason he's a success.*

"Let's see, where is that article?" As Sharon sorted through a pile of magazines, the only one not a gossip or fashion publication fell to the floor. Opening at the page she'd turned down when first reading the profile on 4G, she studied the accompanying photo. The neat young woman certainly wasn't the glamorous wife Jesse divorced.

Sharon, feeling a bit better, studied the new Mrs. Walsh's hair with its no style cut. Her clothes, tailored, and to Sharon's fashion-conscious mind, were quality but had no flare. Nothing sexy—all just plain boring.

"Ah, here we are." Sharon saw the words *wealthy, financial whiz, one of few women to make it on* Wall Street, all underlined in red ink.

There must be a bit of dirt online. I need something to get wifey to give me $35,000. She smiled at the thought that her ex would be furious on hearing that his princess had given Sharon the money he refused her minutes ago. Well, he deserves it for that puny divorce settlement.

CHAPTER 14

"Ms. Cooper, you look a bit tired," Bobbie commented as she handed Taryn the daily mail.

"It was a late night. I must be getting old if I'm tired after a night at home with friends." Looking at the concerned face of her assistant, she added more warmth to her usual smile.

"I have to finish updating your schedule. The invitations to investor conferences you left last evening are piled up. Do you realize that you will be out of the office midday all next week?"

With a sigh she handed her assistant yet another invitation from the morning's mail. "If this doesn't conflict with anything else, please add this to your scheduling puzzle."

Left to sort through her mail, Taryn placed marketing materials to one side and stacked industry journals in another pile. Spying a plain white envelope without postage, her skin began to crawl. "Bobbie," she said her breathing taking a hitch.

A surprised Bobbie rushed into the office and saw her boss staring at her desk blotter. "Ms. Cooper, is that what I think it is?"

"Bobbie, do you happen to have any gloves in that junk drawer of yours?"

"Let me see." Rushing out of the room, Bobbie remembered she had just purchased plastic gloves she needed for coloring her hair. Handing the unopened package to her boss, she said, "I just bought these at the drug store. Will they be of any use?"

"Do you remember seeing this in the stack of this morning's mail?"

"No. I'd certainly remember that particular envelope."

"Was anyone in the office when you arrived?"

"No. Oh, I did see one of the building handyman leaving. Freddie. You know him. He is the one we call when something goes wrong with the air-conditioning system."

As she pulled a pair of thin gloves from its package, Taryn's mind was already thinking of having Arthur check it for finger prints. Careful to not tear the envelope, Taryn pulled out another copy of a newspaper clipping with its familiar FYI scrawled in the upper left-hand corner. Her breath stuck as she quietly read the clipping.

"This reporter is hot on the trail of possible insider trading by someone at 4G Investments. Will print proof as soon as it's available."

"Here, Bobbie, put on another pair of your gloves and then take this…this latest to Arthur. You might read it first. Then after he's read it, ask him to stop in."

Bobbie pulled on the plastic gloves and picked up the note, carefully replacing it in its envelope.

Before her assistant left, Taryn cautioned, "You had better re-mind him not to touch either the paper or envelope. If you have extra gloves, give him a pair. If you don't, run down to the store and get a box. This is the third such surprise. I have a feeling we're going to need them."

"Then what should I do with it?"

"Put it with the previous ones."

Left to consider the third clip delivered as mysteriously as the previous ones, Taryn knew she'd receive another one on Monday. *This isn't a onetime thing; it's the beginning of a campaign.*

"Did Bobbie show you our latest mail?"

Arthur waved the packaged clip in his hand. "Taryn, we have to take this seriously. Three clippings in less than two weeks? I suspect it is the work of one woman."

"Why a woman?"

"Only a guess. But women use words; men use guns."

"Do you know anyone who can check this one for fingerprints?"

"I do. But I don't think we'll find any in the police database."

"Maybe not. Aren't finger prints held in other places? Don't you need to be printed for the military or a government job? Could we check the paper? Or is that only in the detective novels?"

"This feels like ordinary copier paper. It could come from any place. Let me check into a couple of other options. My concern is how many hands have already obliterated the original prints. If you receive another one, you don't touch it with bare hands."

"Bobbie and I are already using plastic gloves. Now you're confirming my fears that there will be more." That thought caused the blood to leave Taryn's face. "Arthur, will you excuse me for a minute? I'll be right back."

"Taryn? Are you all right?"

"No. Yes. I just have to go to the bathroom. This latest irritant isn't helping."

Arthur got up and took Taryn's hand, feeling her pulse. "Taryn, nothing is as important as your health. This stress has your pulse racing."

"Don't worry. It's temporary, Arthur. I'm as healthy as a horse."

"Please, if only for Jesse, get a checkup."

"OK. Promise."

⇒⊹⇐

Arthur was sipping an after-dinner cognac, lost in thought. "Dear?" Lorraine said. "Is there anything you would like to talk about?"

Looking across the table at the soft gaze of the woman he had loved for thirty years, he read her concern. She had been his joy, his confessor, and his cheerleader the whole of their marriage.

"Is it something about Taryn?"

"For a wife to ask her husband about another woman in his life usually means he's in deep trouble."

"Maybe another wife and another man." Rising from the table, Lorraine walked over, leaned down, and gave him a kiss on his head. Arthur relaxed as he always did when Lorraine responded to his need of comforting.

Arthur slowly rose from the table and reached for her hand. He felt Lorraine squeeze his as he led her to the living room, settling her on the sofa. Then joining her, he took a breath. "Maybe you can help me deal with this." It took him a moment before he continued. "Yes, it's Taryn. I know you are fond of her. It's just that when she has a problem, I take it on myself to help resolve it."

"Arthur, look at me," Lorraine said as he was about to turn away. "I couldn't have been loved by a better man. Your daughters love and respect you. Our friends think the world of you."

"One of the things that convinced me that I had to ask you to marry me was your total understanding of my special relationship with Taryn Cooper. In all these years, even after I took the gamble to leave the bank and become part of 4G, you stood by me."

"I've always known Taryn is special. It's just that she and I are friends, but you two are family. I'm not jealous of the time and attention you give her. It wouldn't be like you not to worry about her."

As he lifted her chin and looked into her eyes, he kissed her with all the love he felt…then, sitting back he began to highlight the FYI threats, knowing that Lorraine was someone who'd listen.

CHAPTER 15

The keyboard was clicking away as each new Facebook profile was created. One new profile for each e-mail address.

Now to create my little group. Future postings would come from one of these people and shared with a wider online community of friends.

The first profile was Betty Jenkins—owner of Fashion House and member of Dunkirk business community. Her information included a degree in fashion merchandising from the University of Buffalo. Divorced. No children. Career highlights featured an executive training position with a New York City department store, where in two short years she rose to position of buyer. She opened Fashion House a decade later. The fact that Betty Jenkins and Fashion House didn't exist wasn't important. There had been a *Fashion Shop* twenty or so years ago. It had closed when the owner passed away. Sticking close to the truth was always a good idea.

Settling into the task of creating the desired number of fictitious people, each new profile became easier. All that was needed were details including date married, names of children, hobbies, and information hinting at a career or personal lifestyle.

Let me see, I have three women. I also need a couple of male profiles to broaden my outreach. At the least, men who might be aware of the object of my poison-pen postings.

It didn't take as long to create profiles for an ad executive and an economics professor. Good. The men should provide a potential group of friends in finance.

With each key stroke, the five profiles went live. The next challenge was to search Facebook listings for people who were active in acquiring a diverse and wide group of friends. After selecting forty-four potential women who spent the majority of their online time gossiping and twenty followers of men in advertising and higher education, invitations were sent, thereby launching the beginning of a fictitious Facebook circle of friends.

It would take a bit for acceptances to arrive and once a goodly number were received, the next phase in the campaign would be the issuing of false postings. No one on this list would ever meet, so privacy was assured. All activity was restricted to one laptop and an e-mail address created for this particular purpose.

It had been a long day beginning at 6:00 a.m. shutting down the computer, the schemer headed for the liquor cabinet and a bottle of Russian vodka, a gift from an old friend. With a satisfied smile, the glass quickly filled with a healthy double shot and addition of two small ice cubes…the reward for a successful day's work.

CHAPTER 16

"Ms. Cooper, your executive team has arrived for your Monday morning meeting. I've shown them into the conference room. Is there anything else?"

"Not at present, Bobbie. A quick pit stop, and then I'm on my way."

"Taryn, are you all right?" Ellie asked as she entered the room.

Startled, she quickly checked to see if her blouse had escaped the waist band of her skirt. Reassured that it hadn't and every blouse button was fastened, she looked up. "Nope, everything's in order."

"You're pale, you have circles under your eyes, and it looks as if you may have lost at minimum five pounds," was Ellie's soft reply. "Still not sleeping the night through?"

"Ellie, my stomach has been a bit off. One reason I couldn't join you all for lunch last week. I'm sure it isn't anything serious. But if I look that poorly, maybe I shouldn't wear beige," she quipped. Taryn sat at the table, all business, and opened her folder. "OK, now what have you found?"

"I've looked over the possible competitors now under contract to one of the big pharmaceutical companies and any financial news on this particular field of research," Kathy reported. "Most of what I read relates to Lupus, with a mention of other possible health concerns impacted by inflammation. So Reggie Farmer may be on to something. Anyway, sometimes it's just a matter of who gets to market first. And probably most of the time, it's a matter of how solid the preliminary work is."

"I agree," added Ellie. "However, the nontraditional health publications by Dr. Weil, Dr. Oz, and others primarily discuss inflammation in connection with cholesterol. The bad kind. If I am reading their reports correctly, they believe that cholesterol, when out of control, causes the buildup of plaque, which will either clog arteries or break off causing stroke. That alone would make Reggie's work interesting. You know I've been on statins, and wish I could stop them. I live in fear of the cure-causing complications that are more worrisome than my cholesterol levels."

"Linda, will you draft a sensible timetable for our projected investment in Reggie's work?"

"Taryn, didn't you say that Solo Pharma has to be rebuilt? Could Reggie move from his Johns Hopkins laboratory and work with Timothy?" Linda asked.

"My thinking exactly. It all depends upon how wedded Reggie is to his Alma Mater and how far along he is in proving his work."

"As you all know, I took a quick trip last week to see Reggie's setup. We discussed those very things. I was impressed with his cautious approach to expenditures and his detailed schedule. It's my conclusion that Johns Hopkins won't interfere with his work once he graduates. I didn't go into any financial claims they may make in future. We can cross that bridge later. I also believe we can provide for his laboratory and office needs rather inexpensively. And initially those would be sufficient for about six months, unless he has an earlier breakthrough," Linda reported.

"That's just the information I needed. Thanks." As Taryn passed around copies of her tentative plans to combine Solo Pharma's rebuild with Reggie's needs, she thought once again how well the team worked on solving any problem at hand. They seemed to fit. Each with strengths that made 4G a cohesive entity.

"Linda, why not visit with Timothy and get some kind of estimate on rebuilding his laboratory. You could also check with a local building-management firm. It might be practical to build a larger facility and defray costs by renting out the extra space. Then, when we invest in other startups, we could consider moving them to that location."

Linda began taking notes on her tablet as the rest began reading her plans for 4G's first venture capital investments. Taryn sat back with a feeling she was back in control. This was her world. The potentially damaging notes were another matter. Something she was tackling with Arthur. He had always been her steadying hand, and now more than ever, she was relying on his support.

"Can you join us for lunch, Taryn? I've found a healthy alternative to last week's burgers. A new restaurant guaranteeing non-fried, sugarless, and all natural ingredients," Kathy said.

"And it's got four stars?" was Ellie's humorous reply.

"What do you want everything? It's got a four-star chef. Come on, Taryn. Take an hour off. Like the old days before we became responsible adults," Kathy coaxed.

"Just what Doctor Ellie ordered. Let's finish up, and I'll meet you at the elevator." It was too soon to share her fears about the news clips with anyone but Arthur. Even with Jesse. What she needed was an enjoyable break with her friends.

"Bobbie, I'm going to lunch with the girls. I'll be back in an hour. Is there anything I need to see before I leave?"

With a plastic-gloved hand, Bobbie showed Taryn a plain white envelope. "I swear, Ms. Cooper, this just arrived as mysteriously as the others."

"At least it wasn't found sitting on my desk." Signaling her assistant to follow her into her office, Taryn wondered what this newest missive would say. "Close the door, Bobbie. Let's see what we have now." As Taryn sat at her desk, she felt her stomach churn.

Bobbie handed her a pair of plastic gloves. As she opened the envelope, her eyes fell on the FYI scrawled at the corner of the page. Showing Bobbie the photocopy of a news clip, Taryn said, "Just like the last three. This clip has the same newspaper masthead." With her anger restrained, Taryn read the clip aloud.

"This reporter is hot on the trail of a possible connection between 4G Investments and illegal parties running a money-laundering scheme. Will print proof as soon as it's available."

As she handed the clip to Bobbie, Taryn, in a barely controlled whisper, instructed, "Like the others, please don't say anything. When I get back I'll call Arthur, and you can show it to him when he arrives. After he sees it, place this…this little item in our file, and lock it away in my safe."

"Yes, Ms. Cooper. Are you still leaving for lunch?"

"No. My stomach is in knots."

As Bobbie turned to leave, Taryn said, "On second thought, yes. I need to clear my brain. I am not going to let some malcontent interfere with my life."

CHAPTER 17

"Sweetheart, can we sit a bit? I have something I need to share with you." Taryn had made her decision to finally tell Jesse about her scary situation. Arthur hadn't been able to get any leads. Maybe Jesse's connections could help.

Nodding, Jesse sat on the living room sofa. "I'm all ears."

As Taryn removed a folder from her briefcase, she gave its contents a quick scan. It wasn't as if she hadn't imprinted the information on her brain. "I'm not sure where to begin."

"At the beginning. And, don't leave anything out. I know you. You'll want to give me the highlights so I won't be worried."

He did know her. That wasn't going to make this any easier. One of the things she respected about him was, in the almost five years of their marriage, he had never pried into her business affairs. Yet, every time she had asked Jesse for help, he had dropped his own work to assist her.

Taryn began to pace the room, trying to keep panic from her voice. As she stopped in front of him, she stood a little straighter.

"OK. For the past couple of weeks, I've been receiving mysterious mail. Each one hinting that 4G wasn't on the up and up."

"What?" Jesse jumped up grabbing the folder from her hands. After he read the four photocopied pages, he held the folder in front of her. "This is outrageous."

"It could ruin me," Taryn said, collapsing on the sofa, tears silently leaking down her cheeks. What the FYI mail hadn't done was to reduce her to tears…confessing her problem to Jesse had.

"Knowing you, these have been checked. Right?"

"Yes."

"Are they in circulation?"

"We can't find any evidence that they are anything but mock-ups."

"Who else knows about this?"

"Bobbie and Arthur. Now you."

"Why in hell have you waited two weeks to tell me about this? Do you think I'd blame you? Assume you have been doing something that was less than honorable?" With each question Jesse's voice rose slightly in volume.

Startled, Taryn stared at her agitated husband as her tears continued to flow. Where was the calm partner she relied on?

Now it was Jesse pacing the room as he continued his vigorous reproach. "You always want to solve the world's problems by yourself. Well, you can't. Remember when the investment you were looking into turned out to be fraudulent? Did you forget that I checked it out in time to prevent 4G from being drawn into what turned out to be a world-class financial scam? And that is only one of the more serious things you didn't feel you had to share with me. Why do you keep secrets? You are beginning to remind me of my ex who lied with every word."

Taryn didn't know much about Jesse's previous marriage other than he still bore the scars. Over the years he'd let things slip including her secret spending of their limited income, cheating on him with another man, and lying. "I haven't lied, Jesse. I just wanted it to go away." Before Jesse could continue his outburst, she rushed to add, "But that last clip arrived today. It hinted we were laundering money. That sent me over the edge. It's way out of my universe."

Taryn watched as her husband's eyes glared at her, while his hands pounded the back of the sofa, each blow sending tremors down her spine.

"You should be scared shitless! Whoever is doing this is out to ruin you personally and is doing it through 4G. Money laundering isn't something you read about in the *Wall Street Journal*. This is a shadowy world, one I'm only too familiar with."

Taryn bristled at Jesse's last remark. He was saying she was stupid. Not mincing words, she snapped, "Money laundering is in the newspapers. Especially since the US government began warning citizens that they would be prosecuted if they try to hide assets abroad."

Jesse just stared at his wife, his pointed figure punctuating each word in reply. "Money laundering as in drug money! As in crime! Your little message insinuates that you are one of a group of financial evil doers. That, my dear, puts you in Madoff's league."

Of course she knew in detail of Madoff's criminal behavior. He had built a Ponzi scheme defrauding his investors out of billions. Money was her world. Still, her bruised feelings were turning to anger. "I don't deal in drugs or in hiding money. I don't cheat my investors." Jumping up and wringing her hands, she pleaded, "Jesse, I need to find out who is doing this to me. Who did I cross? Is it a competitor? You know everyone I know," she yelled.

"Not everyone. Just those you've been involved with since we've met. Taryn, your life didn't begin at forty. You've probably held jobs you never mentioned."

"Jesse, you never asked about my life before I met you. My life began with you. There wasn't a plan or a strategy I developed that

I hadn't shared with you. For Christ's sake, you watched me building 4G."

As suddenly as his rage erupted, Jesse began to calm down. With a wave of his hand, he walked to the bar. Taryn was surprised. It wasn't like him to turn to drink out of emotion; he was purely a social drinker. As he poured a glass of wine and took a sip, Jesse stood silently, lost in thought. She had to restore her own sense of calm before she could continue. Nothing between them was worth uncontrolled anger.

Without moving from the bar, and in a soft voice, Jesse's love echoed in his next words. "Honey, neither did mine. But you are now facing a crisis. I need to know everything about your life before we met if I can help you out of this mess."

With those few words, Taryn was reassured that they were once again the partners in the life she so valued. "Sorry, Jesse, you know me well enough to know I don't dwell in the past. That's just me." Contrite, she settled back down, thinking of how she could make him understand her actions. "I've tried to get to the source of these lies. Yes, I should have said something to you when the first note arrived. Yes, I thought I could handle this on my own. Even though the information is false, it is about my world…all except the last one."

"You married me for better or worse. Do you think so little of me that you have to keep this to yourself? Or anything else in your life?"

Couldn't Jesse see how devastated she was? Shit. I have to go to the bathroom. As she got up from the sofa, Jesse turned. "What? You are simply dropping this bombshell and leaving the room? We haven't settled anything."

Taryn stood, numb, not knowing what to say. The last time they had a fight was when Jesse insisted they purchase their house in Connecticut. Life in the suburbs was the last thing in her life plan. It was a reminder of growing up in Dunkirk and how badly she wanted to get away from small-town living, where everyone knew your business. But they had compromised and now she enjoyed Connecticut as their weekend home away from the hectic pace and ever-present noise of Manhattan.

Jesse saw his wife retreat into herself. Not in thought but in escape. He couldn't let their emotions turn this crisis into something personal, that they would later regret. "Look. I don't want to fight with you. This is important. If we can't have a constructive discussion about your business problems…and, lady, this is a big one, then you should have married an empty suit. All looks and no brains."

With hands fisted, Taryn had all she could do not to scream. "You think you know me? How I run 4G? Are you crazy? I'm not dealing with your readers who play at investing. I'm handling real money. Billions," she cried. Of course this was serious. She needed his support, not a demeaning reminder that she couldn't solve this on her own.

Grabbing her hands and holding her at arm's length, Jesse had to stop himself from shaking her. "Just stop it. Listen to me. Don't interrupt."

Taryn had never felt so betrayed. To think that her own husband would treat her like an empty-headed female triggered her deepest fears. That she might not be as smart as she needed to be. Fear drove her to study harder and work longer hours, and only by keeping the problems to herself, had she been able to keep fear at bay.

Jesse waited for his distraught wife to begin to regain a semblance of balance. "Honey. Stop and think. I'm sorry my temper got the better of me. Now that I know what you've been facing, we'll tackle it together. Let's begin by trying to analyze the contents of these clips and then figure out a way to stop this creature who ever he or she is."

"You think it could be a woman?"

"Could be."

"That's what Arthur thought."

When she felt Jesse's arm around her shoulders, Taryn knew there was nothing he wouldn't do to keep her safe. Closing her eyes, she took a deep breath, letting her mind step down from its frazzled state. She was no longer alone. Dropping her chin so he couldn't see her tear-ravaged face, she whispered, "I'm so sorry. I feel so…"

"So vulnerable, exposed, alone?" Jesse drew her close. "Well, you have me."

CHAPTER 18

"Here are the changes to 4G's annual report. I'd like to see the revised draft later today. And Bobbie, hold things together. I am going to need some time. I'll call you if I need you."

"Fine, Ms. Cooper."

Clasping her arms to still a chill, Taryn was glad she had shared this growing crisis with Jesse. He reminded her they were a team, husband and wife for the good times and bad. It had been a rough couple of hours, but after the fiery language calmed, they had come through it strengthened—partners in the true sense, as well as lovers.

As her assistant left the office, Taryn sat back trying to figure out how to stop these harassing messages. It had been two weeks since the first had arrived, and since then she received three more. "Well, it looks like this hateful person, whoever she or he is, sticks to a schedule." Opening her folder containing photocopies of the clips, Taryn found her assistant's hand-written notes...one attached to each page. So far none could be found to have run in the newspaper identified by their mastheads or any newspaper in neighboring communities.

Grabbing her handbag and tote into which she stuffed the offensive file, Taryn headed out of the office. "Bobbie, I'm going out for a while. Hold down the fort. If you need me, send a text; please don't call."

⇥ ⇤

"Ms. Cooper, Ms. Horn will see you now. Go right on in."

"Thank you, Mrs. Hammond." Melissa had inherited her trusted executive assistant from her predecessor. She often told Taryn that Mrs. Hammond knew not only where all the bodies were buried, but when!

When visiting her friend in her sky-clearing office, Taryn was always surprised at the power projected by this impressive corporate officer. Today the strikingly tall, pencil-slim redhead was dressed in a textured green suit trimmed in black braid. "Very Spanish of you," Taryn quipped, hugging Melissa who had met her at the door.

"If I'd known this morning that we'd be meeting I'd wear something more feminine." Both women laughed. They believed clothes were costumes to be selected for the situation.

"Today black would be more appropriate." Looking around the office, Taryn decided it wasn't where she wanted to share her dilemma with Melissa the CEO. What she needed was the advice of her friend. "I am sorry to just drop in on you. But I hoped you'd have time to step out for a cup of coffee? We could even grab an early lunch?" She hoped she wasn't looking or sounding as desperate as she felt.

"Sure. I have an open afternoon." Moving over to her desk, Melissa opened a draw and withdrew a small pouch of a bag. "Let's go. Anyplace special?"

86

Looking at the miniscule purse, Taryn knew her friend had read her need. This wasn't going to be a business luncheon. Melissa had once told her she used this purse for personal meetings. It contained a basic lipstick, two credit cards, and one-hundred dollars in small bills.

As she followed Melissa from her building, Taryn saw they were headed to a small coffee shop on a side street, off the beaten path. "This is a place I go when I need to get away from the phones and think."

Once they had settled in a back booth of a still empty coffee shop, Melissa ordered a cup of coffee. "I'll have the same," Taryn said, taking a menu from the young woman.

"I'm in trouble. I thought if I told you about it, it would trigger a solution."

"Are you all right? Is it Jesse?"

Taryn set her coffee down and looked into the worried eyes of her friend. "No, thank God. It has nothing to do with Jesse. In fact, it's got to do with 4G. I told Jesse about it last evening. And he blew up at not having been told from the beginning." Melissa was her friend, so she confided, "It was truly awful."

Taryn, seeing that Melissa understood the depth of her concern, relaxed.

"I'm here. Now tell me what's going on. You look unnerved."

"Unnerved doesn't begin to cover it. I needed to see you because this is something you might have some insight on." Taryn paused, not quite knowing where to begin. "I am going to tell you all I know, and it isn't very much. What I'm hoping is that you will agree to help me find a way out of this mess."

"You know I will if I can. But what exactly is this mess you're in?"

Afraid her voice would carry, Taryn leaned toward Melissa, placing both elbows on the table for support. "Almost three weeks ago, I began receiving copies of newspaper clippings hinting that 4G wasn't on the up and up. No, that's not accurate. That I was cheating 4G investors and that 4G was involved in insider trading. That sort of thing."

"Those are the most outrageous lies I've ever heard! If anything you bend over backward to ensure that not only are your trading activities solid, but you also even communicate the bad news to your investors. I should know; I am one."

Breathing a sigh of relief, Taryn was reminded just how good and loyal a friend Melissa was. "You know we only invest in reputable situations, those connected to organizations, municipalities, and companies with proven track records." Turning her coffee mug around in her hands, she took a quick sip and noticed that her friend was sitting quietly, waiting for her to continue. *No wonder she's such a good negotiator. She waits for the other party to show their hand.*

"That's not all. The one I just received hinted that we were washing drug money."

"Have you tracked these clippings? Do you know if they have actually run?"

Taryn slumped back in her seat. "While the mastheads are of an actual newspaper, nothing has been found. I've even had Bobbie check newspapers in neighboring communities for similar information. She came up blank."

"And the Internet?"

"That was one of the first things Arthur said. That we needed to check out Facebook, Twitter, and Google, and he gave Bobbie a list of other sites. Melissa, I don't trust the online world. Never have and limit myself to secured sites. I'm scared. None of this can get out. It's all lies. If even a hint gets leaked, I'd be ruined. My focus must be on identifying this lowlife and stopping them."

"I deal with corporate rumors all the time. Maybe I'll spot a pattern."

"I brought the entire file including Bobbie's lack of findings. I told her to do her online searches on a new laptop she was to purchase with cash and set up with an independent email, nothing that can be traced back to us."

While Melissa looked over the slim file with damning information, Taryn's mind drew a complete blank. How did she proceed? What could Melissa do that she couldn't?

"Isn't Arthur a lawyer? Wouldn't he be in a better position to begin a search? You know a clandestine look at similar business situations? You can't be the first to fall into someone's clutches. From the wording, I'd say that so far this person was trying to cause fear without actually crossing the line by publishing false information. That would leave them open to criminal charges."

"Arthur has begun to research cases of harassment involving the spreading of rumors. At least those that have been prosecuted. However, he's afraid this is something more."

"He's right. This looks to be a personal vendetta. Carefully launched and maybe destined for public distribution. But Taryn, I don't know how I can help you. I certainly can't do anything at UCC. Even if I wanted to help, I've only known you for the past few years…ever since we began serving on corporate boards together. You and I have had entire lives we've never discussed."

Taryn began to squirm in her seat. "Right. Well, there isn't much to tell. You know that Linda, Kathy, Ellie, and I have been friends since first grade."

"Ladies, would you like to place an order?" the waitress asked, reminding Taryn where they were.

Taryn gave the menu a quick glance and then looked over to the counter for a clue as to what was the least she could safely order and saw a customer munching on a hamburger. "I'd like a hamburger, cooked medium. And more coffee."

"With fries?"

"No just the hamburger. Thank you."

"I'll have the same," Melissa added.

Alone again, Taryn thought of a way to describe her life before 4G. "Why not come over for dinner? Tomorrow if possible. Then I can fill you in on my life and Jesse can add what he knows since we've been together."

"Jesse is prejudiced. He thinks the sun rises and sets on you."

"Don't laugh at me. He can be very analytical where business is concerned. Especially when I get into one of my hermit moods where all my conversations are in my head. You should have seen him last night. It was someone I've never met."

"Fine. Tomorrow at your home around six-thirty?"

"I'll check with Jesse when I get back to the office." Reaching out to clasp her friend's hand, Taryn felt better. "I knew you'd help. And I could use your moral support with Jesse. He may look calm and contained, but last evening I saw a stranger gearing up for a fight. Like he does in the boxing ring with his gym buddies."

Melissa laughed. "Personally, it might be fun to watch a work-out. All that hard, sweaty muscle has to be sexy."

"Sexy Jesse is right. He claims boxing keeps him in shape. Unlike me he lives on a pretty physical plane. I say I am going to join a gym but never seem to do it. Jesse is out every morning by seven and home an hour later four days a week."

Melissa's mood changed from easy going to serious. "Taryn, I can't promise anything. I have our annual meeting coming up. My time isn't mine, and even if I have the time, I'm not a detective. You need a pro. Not an amateur. I could mess things up royally."

"What I need is a problem solver. Someone who thinks outside the box. And you, dear friend, are the best."

"A problem solver maybe. But this isn't a business. You need a profiler. Some expert to explain the kind of person who works from the shadows. You don't even know if this will end up as blackmail."

"Blackmail? Another scenario. Pay them, or they release these articles to the media," was a depressed Taryn's response to yet another aspect of this brewing crisis.

"Let me think about this," Melissa said. "Maybe by tomorrow I'll have an idea or two."

"Yes, tomorrow. Maybe Arthur will have turned up something by then. Or Jesse. Now that he's aware of this crisis, maybe he has found another way to track this creep down." Taryn's eyes misted.

"Stop that, or you'll have me in tears. I'll think this though and see you for dinner. I hope Jesse is cooking. If not, I'll order up."

CHAPTER 19

I t had been a long day during which the manuscript of the new
novel had been completed and e-mailed to the agent's assistant.
Weary of conjuring up words to describe happily ever after, the
author switched out of the document and clicked on the book-
marked site of a favored news channel.

Pouring a shot of tequila from a bottle sitting in a silver ice
bucket, attention focused on the day's Wall Street news. Being a
top-selling author of romantic fiction funded a portfolio of more
than five million dollars. This daily scanning of business news fed
an insatiable need for amassing even greater wealth. No matter
how much the portfolio increased, it was never enough.

Spotting an item about hedge funds on the program's lineup of
stories quickly cleared a fog-clouded brain. Another sip of the chilled
liquor, repositioning a pillow on the back of the chair, and with eyes
and ears focused, the writer waited for the upcoming report.

"4G Investments announces better than expected earnings
in a challenging market, citing increased interest from investors.
While actual breakdown of investments with this midsized firm

aren't available, it is speculated that Taryn Cooper, 4G's managing partner, has been able to provide consistent returns in spite of highly competitive market conditions."

A deep-seated need for revenge blotted out everything that followed. As the writer began entering a note on the ever-present smart phone, the letters quickly spelled out, "Need you first thing in the morning. Prepare for a long day."

A need for more alcohol followed with the swallowing of a larger than normal mouthful, causing a spate of coughing. The tequila was quickly spit back into the glass, with angry thoughts tumbling over one another. *Getting even was fine, but anger fueled mistakes.* It was an adage that had become a personal code when the need to create a double life first began. One little slip and the identity of a popular author whose celebrity was centered on mystery would compromise a carefully built existence that hid a troubled past.

How does she keep getting richer? More famous? She's a nothing! The oriental carpet was worn around its perimeter due to the periodic pacing of the overly agitated person. The purpose for this elaborate scheme was to first frighten and then ultimately destroy the object of a deep-seated hatred. With four of the mocked-up news clips already delivered, and the rest sitting in a folder kept in a personal file, it was time to consider the next steps in destroying the one person who had ruined a promising life.

It seems I haven't made even a dent in her firm's success. Like the Energizer Bunny, she keeps on going. It's time to redirect my efforts and target the company! Phase two, posting the clips online, is almost ready for beta testing.

Focused on ferreting out weaknesses in the financial firm, next steps included shadowing the managing partner of the firm. Finding a chink in the organization. Getting news of upcoming deals and investors by prodding someone to obtain insider information on 4G's next moves.

CHAPTER 20

"Look, Kathy, something is definitely wrong with Taryn. Have you seen her pallor? Her unaccustomed nervousness? And she's always running to the bathroom." Ellie's observations grabbed the attention of her two lunchtime companions.

With schedules independent of traditional office hours, the three women got together several times a month. Having been friends all their lives, as Ellie once said, they got withdrawal symptoms when separated for too long.

Of course Taryn couldn't join them at noon, a time their friend predictably attended dog-and-pony shows held by health-science researchers seeking funding. Noon seemed to be the usual scheduling of these presentations, with the rest of Taryn's day influenced by activities of the financial markets.

"Of course we've noticed. But why? Business is great. I just cashed my bonus check and deposited it into my children's college funds," Kathy replied.

"Ellie's right," Linda said. "We have to convince her to go to her doctor. In fact, we have the same physician. I could call and ask if she would like me to make adjacent appointments. Usually we follow up with a drink and dinner at a nearby restaurant."

"Doctor's don't schedule appointments at another patient's request. How do you plan to accomplish that feat of magic?" Kathy asked.

"Surprise, the doctor is my cousin, Ellie said. "You remember the kid we use to label mouse because she was always so quiet? Well, surprise, she grew into a respected physician."

"Do it. Here, use my cell," Kathy said as she handed Linda the small device. You suggest it to Taryn, and then Ellie can contact her cousin," Kathy prompted.

Punching in Taryn's office number, Linda prepared her lie. Not actually a lie, just a bit of devious scheming one friend would do to help another. "Hi, Taryn. Look I have to make my annual visit to our favorite doctor and wondered if we could coordinate appointments. We could have dinner after…just the two of us."

"I hadn't planned on visiting Serena, but now that you mention it, I haven't been on top of my game. Maybe she can find a physical cause for my upset stomachs. Let me check with Jesse to see if he has anything planned. I'll get right back."

"I'm thinking tomorrow would work best for me. Let me check and see if she can fit us both in on such short notice."

"I don't know. She's always booked."

"Not to worry. I'm aiming for three p.m. Can you be available? I'll go first so you won't have to be there until a little before four. If Jesse doesn't have plans, we could skip dinner, or maybe he could join us."

"I can do that. I would really like to stop this stomach thing, whatever its cause."

"OK, talk to you in a bit." Linda gave Ellie and Kathy a thumbs-up. "Now to convince Serena she has to see Taryn." As she handed the phone to Ellie, Linda held up crossed fingers. "Good luck, Ellie. I'd rather tell Taryn I'd booked the appointment so she can't back out."

Ellie nodded her agreement while keying in Serena's office number. "Hi, Cara. This is Ellie, Serena's cousin. I have a favor to ask. Will the doctor see Linda Foster and Taryn Cooper Walsh tomorrow afternoon? I'm calling for them, both are currently in meetings. Linda's appointment isn't critical but we believe strongly that she should check Mrs. Walsh. She's been experiencing stomach problems." All three were silent, waiting for the nurse to get back to Ellie. "Yes, and four o'clock would be perfect. Oh, and she can spare fifteen minutes for Linda as well?" Ellie said. "Please thank the doctor for me. Tell her that we will see her tomorrow." As she handed Kathy her phone, Linda's phone began ringing with Taryn's name appearing on the screen. Again, crossing her fingers, she answered the call.

"Jesse's on deadline so I'm free. Do you think Ellie and Kathy could join us? That's if you can get us an appointment?"

"Done and yes, your appointment is scheduled for four p.m. We'll meet you at Serena's office and afterward go to that little French restaurant we like."

With the phone call over, Linda sat back in her chair smiling as she shared Taryn's invitation that they join them for dinner.

"Wonderful," Ellie said.

"I thought that's what transpired," Kathy said. "Now I've got to run and be home in time for the boys. For me it's homework, dinner, and later story time. Tomorrow's dinner will be a mini vacation. Imagine, a dinner where food goes directly from the plate to the mouth."

CHAPTER 21

The French restaurant was one of their favorite neighborhood places and conveniently located right around the corner from the doctor's office. "What a great idea to enjoy ourselves while waiting for the lab to process the doctor's numerous tests," Taryn said.

"Just how many tests did she take," Linda asked.

"I told her about my queasy stomach and having to go to the bathroom almost hourly, and she just asked if there were any other symptoms she should know about."

"Well, I seem to be tired a lot," Taryn said as she took a sip of her red wine.

"She's pretty quick so I would guess she'll get back to you before end of the evening," Ellie said. "I trust my cousin to solve any of my medical mysteries. You are in good hands."

Their orders were being set before them when Taryn's cell rang. "Yes? Oh yes, Serena. You have the results already? I'm already nervous, so please just cut to the chase. I told you I was worried that it might be cancer."

Ellie, Linda, and Kathy knew of their friend's fear of the dreaded C ever since her aunt had died a horribly painful death.

As she clicked off, Taryn sat as if in a trance. "Are you going to share the doctor's report, or are we going to have to have a mystic read your mind?" Linda asked.

"Oh," Taryn said as if she were returning from some other place. As she looked at each of her dearest friends, she broke out into a broad grin. "I'm pregnant." The words were hardly spoken when all at the table raised their voices in congratulatory cheers.

"Taryn, were you and Jesse planning on a family and didn't tell us? How could you withhold something as important as that?" Kathy asked.

"No. Not even on our radar. And with all that has been happening at the office, I thought my physical problems were simply due to stress."

"Well, enjoy the moment. When your child arrives, stress will have a new meaning. Just ask me," Kathy said.

"Would you mind if I left? I want to rush home and tell Jesse."

"Of course not" was the unanimous reply.

Kathy signaled their waiter over. "Harry, would you please wrap Mrs. Walsh's dinner to go."

"Certainly." As Harry rushed off to the kitchen, Taryn clasped each of her friends' hands. "Thank you so much for making me see the doctor. I would have put it off and missed the excitement of being pregnant. I know Jesse would too."

⊰⊱

Taryn had taken the first taxi she could find and was rehearsing her little speech to Jesse. Then, as an errant thought, wondered if he would welcome the news.

"I'm home," Taryn called as she dumped her things on a hall chair. As she entered the living room, Jesse looked up in surprise. "I thought you were having dinner with the girls."

As she handed him the plastic bag with her dinner, she dropped into his lap. "Something unexpected came up, and I rushed home to share the news."

With the recent problems at work, Taryn saw Jesse's look of concern and not wanting to alarm him, gushed, "We're going to have a baby."

"But...what...how?" Jesse stammered.

"How? Well, I guess we've been practicing and finally got it right," she quipped.

As he hugged his wife close, Taryn felt tears on her cheek. She knew Jesse was a softie, but rarely had he teared up at good news. Then again, this wasn't just good news; it was their future as parents.

CHAPTER 22

It had been another hectic day at work when Taryn walked into the lobby of her apartment building. Tired as she was, Taryn perked up and smiled at the greeting from the doorman. Tonight it was one of her favorites, William.

"Ms. Walsh, I have an envelope for you. It was delivered earlier."

"Really? I'm not expecting anything. Thank you, William."

As she walked toward the elevators, she looked at the plain white envelope and recognizing it, felt the skin on her arms prickle. It looked like the previous mysterious notes, each had been typed on an old daisy-wheel typewriter, not the crisp imprint of a computer-generated address. Slipping it into her handbag, Taryn was determined not to focus on its contents. What she needed was to spend the evening enjoying her husband.

A smile lit her previously somber face as Taryn was greeted with Jesse's encompassing hug. The warmth of his body had enveloped her with feelings of safety. "Let me get rid of my things and freshen up. I'll meet you in the den. I could use one of your special predinner drinks, but now it had better be hot tea."

Wearing one of her favorite at-home silk shirt and pants outfits, Taryn walked into what she felt to be the coziest room in their apartment. "So how was your day?" she asked sipping the hot beverage.

"I missed you. That's how." As Jesse pulled her close, Taryn felt so very much loved. Cozying up on the sofa, they sat quietly for a moment savoring their closeness.

"I had a long chat with Maureen discussing ideas for the school campaign. I want to develop a financial program in three stages. It will give me the flexibility needed to design an entirely new approach to teaching personal finance to middle-school kids, not merely a rehash of book-based programs already out there."

"How long do you have before you present your ideas to the client?"

"He's being very patient. It seems he wants this program launched nationally. That's going to require more than my creativity. He is going to have to get the endorsement of school boards and teachers across the country. There's no way you can't implement a program without their support at the local level."

"Have you thought of enlisting someone known in the educational field to accompany you on these exploratory meetings?"

"No, but I could mix it up so that we could enlist several known experts on finance." Turning, he gave his wife a deep kiss. Taryn returned it and cuddled closer. "Not only is my wife lovely, sexy, and sweet, she's smart. I'm a lucky man."

Taryn promised herself that she'd try not to think of the white envelope, and since she hadn't read its contents, she was certainly not going to bother Jesse about it tonight. For the present, Arthur and now Melissa were looking into the FYI mailings. She wasn't aware if Jesse had taken any action of his own, but tonight she just wanted to forget the whole mess. He'd learn about this latest surprise tomorrow when Melissa arrived and the three began working together to search for the perpetrator.

It was their habit that when Jesse prepared dinner, she'd clean up. Now, as Taryn left the kitchen clean and tidy, she passed her handbag on the way to the bedroom. *Hell with discipline. I can't wait.* As expected, when she slit it open, Taryn found another FYI news clip. In a whisper, she began reading it aloud.

"Is the financial woman of the future desperate? Or seriously ill? The mere shadow of her former self has Wall Street insiders talking."

With cold resolve, Taryn replaced the clip back in its envelope and returned it to her handbag. Her clammy skin was the only sign of the terror that had invaded her mind. How did they find my address? How do they know I've lost a few pounds? Wasn't the hate campaign designed to destroy 4G? With arms crossed and clutching her elbows to keep from shaking, Taryn knew she had to get a grip. She had to appear normal so as not to alert Jesse about this home-delivered threat. Her home was sacrosanct. If Jesse found out that this villain had sent a message to the apartment, he'd hire bodyguards to stay with her whenever she went out. She had seen him angry and knew her sweet, loving husband would destroy anyone who threatened her.

Taryn decided that a day or two wouldn't make any difference. That would be soon enough to share this latest threatening note with Jesse and the others.

A sudden taste of undigested food had her rushing to the bathroom. Not wanting to alarm Jesse, Taryn turned on the sink taps, and with head over the toilet, emptied her stomach. Tears followed, and reaching for a tissue, she hid her face and wept.

CHAPTER 23

Her fear had escalated with each attack on her integrity. Now having one of the FYI clips delivered to her home, Taryn was facing her mortality. Was this campaign designed to destroy 4G or her life? Am I going to be physically harmed? Or simply have my reputation and firm ruined? What she knew she had to do before she could share the latest FYI clip along with her escalating fears with Jesse later this evening was update all legal documents, not the least of which was her last will and testament.

"Arthur, thank you for staying late."

"Taryn, after more than thirty years together, you know I'm here for you."

A little sigh escaped as she tried to gather her thoughts, her eyes focused on all former versions of her legal life spread out on her desk. "Look, I need a drink. Would you care to join me?"

"Of course, the sun set over the yardarm several hours ago. Let me get it." As Arthur went to the cabinet on the far side of her office, he opened it revealing a neatly arranged bar with a full range of hard-liquor choices, assorted mixers, crystal glasses, and a small ice maker. "Scotch and two cubes?"

"You do know me. Yes. That's fine. On the other hand, I'd better have club soda."

"Taryn, are you ill?" Arthur asked.

"Yes and no. I saw the doctor and it was decided to keep my diet simple for the next few months. That means no drinking." She had yet to share her news with Arthur. "You go ahead. Please."

When Arthur gave her the glass, Taryn raised it in toast. "To a new addition to the Walsh family."

Arthur slammed his glass down on the bar and rushed to enfold Taryn in a hug. "Congratulations. I couldn't be happier for you and Jesse."

By the time her glass was half empty, she had steeled herself to the task at hand. "To surviving. If not, to being prepared."

Arthur had already settled in the chair opposite her desk, his pen and pad ready.

"Last evening I felt someone walking over my grave." She was comforted by the gentle kindness reflected in his eyes. For years they had been more like uncle and niece than business partners.

"Look Taryn, these past weeks have been rough on all of us, you more than the rest of us. Unfortunately, my research so far has only come up with legal avenues to pursue once we've identified the culprit. After all these years, I've come to trust your intuition. Anytime you tell me about a gut reaction, I listen. Now, what has you preparing for death?"

"It's like carrying an umbrella so it won't rain. Best to be prepared."

"I can drink to that!" Arthur took a good swallow of his drink.

"First, paperwork. As my official and only attorney, I want some minor changes made to my will. Here I've marked up the current copy of my will, power of attorney, and healthcare directives."

She watched as he studied each and every one of her edits knowing that she would accept his advice, wherever it led. "Your father would be proud of you. You know that, don't you?"

Her smile was the first in several days and filled with the warm thoughts of her father. She loved both of her parents, but it was different with her dad. He understood her dreams. Her mother just smiled with pride and gave her permission to go where her dreams took her.

"Just reading your estate would make him strut around the room like a preening peacock."

Taryn could see her dad doing just that, and it released some of her tension. She knew Arthur had also been on edge from the arrival of that very first FYI missive. It was his joy at her accomplishments that reminded her of the importance of preparing legal documents. It wasn't a morbid task; it was simply being practical.

"OK. Your financial status is currently approaching one hundred fifteen million dollars in addition to the value of your partnership in 4G Investments. Your personal holdings are invested in real estate and a portfolio of stocks and bonds, which I might add is a galaxy away from the first statement I prepared for 4 Girls Babysitting." He laughed at his understatement. "That twelve hundred dollars was a fortune to you and Linda, Ellie, and Kathy."

"You coached me in more than stocks and bonds. When I was in my sophomore year in high school and had saved for college, it was your suggestion that I partner in the purchase of a piece of land back in Dunkirk for $250. That little syndicate you put together did very well when it was sold to the local gas company for a new power plant."

"And that investment tripled in less than one year."

"I did better each time you suggested I invest in one of your syndicated activities. Arthur, why didn't you share that with the girls?"

"They didn't need to make…what did you say? Oodles and oodles of money? I didn't think they would approve the risk you took to build up your personal portfolio."

"Even Jesse was shocked to learn that not only do I own one fifth of 4G Investments, but a couple of apartment buildings, a commercial garage, and part ownership in a national food chain."

"Did you make the fortune you sought?"

"Well beyond my dreams. Funny though, after the first million dollars the money didn't mean anything. It was just a way to keep score. I knew that my investments were in your capable hands and only read your quarterly reports. I never looked at the day-to-day fluctuations or news reports that impacted earnings. I do that for a living. I guess it was no longer important personally."

"I see you've added Dunkirk Hospital to your charitable donations."

"They were wonderful to Mom when she was fighting breast cancer. I'd visit and instead of seeing a balding grey-faced woman, she had me drive her around visiting women she had been taking her chemo treatments with. I watched her share a book or laugh at a photo of them at the hospital. She gave them something to smile about. And her doctor supported these excursions financially and emotionally."

"Why did you add Melissa Lynn Horn to your bequests? Isn't she well off herself?"

"I know if I give money to Melissa, she can add it to her scholarship fund for inner-city girls. So far it's a small contribution to the future of a dozen young girls. I'd like to see her efforts expanded. Without education I couldn't have achieved what I have."

"And Jesse? I see you enclosed a sealed letter."

"He gets everything else, all but what I've left Linda, Ellie, and Kathy. I wanted him to have memories of those especially happy times we've shared. I will also have a photo album to accompany the note. Hopefully that will be done next week. But if something happens before then, you will know to look for it in my office safe."

"You know you haven't updated your succession agreement for the firm since it was written a decade ago, at the formation of 4G Investments and before you married Jesse. It should be updated."

"You're right, Arthur. The problem is that I doubt whether Ellie, Kathy, or Linda would want to take over as managing partner of the firm. Jesse might wish to serve as an advisor knowing that you, along with Linda, Ellie, and Kathy could out-vote him if necessary. But when we've discussed my job, he has always said it wasn't something he'd want to be tied down to."

"What would you want to happen? This is a theoretical question, Taryn. I know how upset you are about the recent spate of mysterious mail. But still, should any of the girls predecease you, each have opted to return shares to your control with profits distributed to their families. You never made a decision."

"Because I see it as my creation. All mine." Stacking the papers into one pile, she nodded. "OK. Can we write Jesse in as temporary managing partner taking direction from you and the girls, while they all decide whether to liquidate 4G or partner with another firm? Let the decision be theirs…acting with your counsel of course."

Looking at her most trusted advisor, she saw that his hair was greyer than in the past. Where did time go? "Arthur, I could name you my successor. You are a partner, and I didn't build this firm without your sage support."

"Taryn, I thought I had retired a decade ago but couldn't resist the temptation to see where you would go when forming the firm. The fun of working long hours is working alongside you. No, let's leave your solution as it is. We can trust Jesse and the rest to do what's best."

"Fine. A decision made. Now I can forget it."

"I will write up a preliminary document for you to review. We can finalize it in a day or two. Do you want me to share this with the others?" *Succession without her. Unimaginable but under the circumstances necessary.*

"No, let's keep this between the two of us at least until we settle our crisis. I'm having dinner with them but doubt they will be thinking of succession when we are celebrating launching our new business."

CHAPTER 24

With a hug and kiss to her forehead, Jesse took his wife's things and pushed her toward the bedroom. "Now financial genius, mother of my child, take a hot bath, dress in that silky jumpsuit I love, and get yourself back out here."

"What happened to your card game? I hadn't expected to see you until much later."

"Oh, Jack cancelled so we rescheduled. I called Bobbie, and she said you were on the way home. So I stopped by the pub and picked up a couple of steak salads for us."

Surprised by the unexpected order to get cleaned up, Taryn simply nodded and headed for the bedroom. What a perfect respite to a tension-filled day. A good long soak will help place thoughts of news clips and preparation for death on hold.

Watching her go, Jesse's worried frown returned. The same frown he'd been wearing since he learned his wife was the target of a vicious campaign of fabricated lies. Adding to the mystery, today he'd spotted a complication in the draft of 4G's quarterly report. This time it wasn't Joseph the Thug Baldino. It was either a mistake or an anomaly.

"Sweetheart, I can't thank you enough. I feel refreshed and almost relaxed. You are a genius."

"No, I am just beginning to know you. Sometimes when you come home from the office, there is a little wrinkle between your eyebrows. When I hug you or refocus your mind away from work it disappears." Handing his wife a glass of club soda, her latest drink of preference, he saw her hesitate.

Smiling, Taryn walked over to the sofa and sitting on his lap said, "So Daddy to be, let's talk about schedules."

The gleam in her eyes restored Jesse's humor. "Ah. Like redecorating the spare room here and another in Connecticut?"

"I saw Serena briefly at lunch, and she thinks we have about six months to get everything ready."

"Everything? Maybe we should have Kathy give us a schedule. She's been through this three times," he replied.

"Well, I had a nice long chat with my mother this afternoon, and aside from the books she plans to send on diet and what to expect, she said that she and dad were so very excited, they couldn't wait to be grandparents," Taryn said, smiling as she remembered her mom's nonstop advice to her only daughter.

"Instead of a weekend in the country, why don't we go shopping," Jesse suggested and was rewarded with a huge kiss.

As she hugged Jesse close, she whispered, "Furniture, paint, and wallpaper."

"And little baby clothes? By the way, am I going to have a son and heir or daughter?" Jesse asked.

Taryn saw a bit of nervousness in his question. "Do you have a preference?" Leaning back to get a better look to see how important his question was, she worried that she wouldn't be able to give him the baby he wanted. "Jesse, let's not ask the sex of the baby. That way we won't be focused on dresses or baseballs but on a healthy new life."

"My sensible wife. And I can live with that," Jesse said ending the conversation with a deep heartfelt kiss.

"The most important thing is that the baby be healthy. So, my love, you are under orders to follow Doctor Jesse's instructions. A relaxing bath each evening, followed by my special expectant-mother massage."

"And after that," Taryn teased.

"Why don't we just see what happens?" Jesse folded his wife in his arms. "We're going to be parents. I never even dreamed...we hadn't planned it...I mean wow!"

CHAPTER 25

"How in hell did you get into this fix?" Melissa said as she watched her friend collapse into a chair. "When you stopped by my office to ask for my help, you told me you needed to solve a problem. This is more than a problem."

To the outside world, Taryn Cooper Walsh was the epitome of cool. She knew that investors wanted their financial advisors to be competent and unemotional regardless of circumstances. Yet here she sat in her perfectly ordered and inviting library a wreck, unable to understand how she had gotten herself into this predicament.

"This isn't some social prank, Taryn. This is criminal and will cost you and your company dearly. Am I to understand that things have gotten even worse?" Melissa asked.

"I know, Melissa. I thought if you, Jesse, and I could go over what's happened so far, we'd be able to solidify a plan."

At that moment Jesse entered the library with a tray of drinks. As she waved a glass of club soda away, Taryn tried to keep her mind focused. "Melissa, has anything like this happened to anyone you know? You meet so many more people than I do." Taryn reached for tissue and blew her nose. "I'm sorry. How could you know anyone this evil?"

"Well, I have nightmares that one of the two men I've crossed swords with will come back to haunt me."

"Melissa, you and Jesse are the most honorable people I know. In all our time together, you've never even hinted that you've had problems of this kind."

"We can go into that at another time, but if it makes you feel better, there is one old mafia demon who haunts me. He threatens me simply by being a large stockholder. I checked him out and can't figure how he's stayed alive, let alone out of prison."

"Mafia? United Chemicals Corp has a mob enemy?"

"I doubt he's an enemy of the corporation. He gets a hefty return on his investment. He is, however, mine. Look, Taryn, we aren't discussing my problems at the moment. We have to develop a plan to uncover the person behind this campaign. If these news clips are leaked, they will ruin you."

"Melissa, I don't expect you to play detective. It's not like you have a lot of free time or that this is a simple profit -and-loss problem."

"Well, I certainly understand covert. If I didn't I'd be out of a job. Listen to me. I may have certain resources. Our worlds aren't that different. We both deal with lawyers, accountants, bankers, employees, and clients. Let's put our heads together and draft a plan. We can adjust it as we go. OK?"

Breathing more regularly, Taryn took a pad and pen and handed both to Melissa. "Here, I'm in no condition to do much else at the moment. Maybe you can ask me questions, and I'll try to be clear with my answers."

"I have one or two underground contacts that might be able to shed light on who could be behind this scheme, at least find out how it is being implemented. Don't look surprised, wife of mine! Your husband travels in a variety of worlds, legal and not quite kosher. Where do you think I get some of my information to help people avoid financial scams?"

Distraught, Taryn got up and began pacing around the library. As Jesse moved over to the bar to get a glass of wine for Melissa, she stopped and blurted, "I received another envelope the other night." Near tears, she continued, "It was left with the doorman." Taryn needn't look at her husband; she could feel his anger. "I waited to tell you both together. I'm scared witless. Why is this happening to me?" As she looked pleadingly at Jesse, she mumbled, "I had more important news to share with you."

"I just want to shake some sense in you," Jesse said. "Can't you get it through that shut-down mind that I, no we, want to help you?" Jesse turned to Melissa, "You see we just found out that Taryn is pregnant."

"Well, that is good news," Melissa cheered and raised her glass in a silent toast.

"Well, there's more," Taryn said in a flat cold tone of voice. She could see her bit of news frightened Jesse and Melissa as well. While she had been dealing with these mailings for more than a month, Jesse and Melissa had only begun to consider her plight. At a gut level, Taryn knew time for waiting had run out.

Melissa took a sip of her wine and then focused her attention fully on her friend. Taryn watched Jesse settle in a chair opposite, his eyes never leaving her face. The room settled. Now that her latest news was out, she sat back down, ready to tell them about its contents, and the newest delivery received this morning.

"I arrived at the office at my usual time this morning and found a manila envelope sitting on my desk. How it got there is anyone's guess because at seven, I'm usually the only one in. Anyway, what I found was a compilation of all those little news clips I've been receiving with the same salacious insinuations. I over charge my clients, I steal from the company, I use insider information to capitalize on my trades, 4G launders drug money. The worst was a copy of the latest, and it chilled me to the core. As I said, this time it had been left with the doorman. It said that 4G's problems were impacting my health. I remembered being so frightened I feared for my life. For someone to write about the way I look could only mean that I'm being watched. Even worse, they knew enough about me to know where I lived."

"Taryn, look at me," Jesse demanded. "Be more specific so we can figure this out."

"Look, you two," Melissa began. "Are those items from the envelope spread out on that table?"

Looking toward the library table that usually held an assortment of publications important to both Taryn and Jesse's professions, Taryn nodded. "I've been sorting through those boxes and files all evening, and I can't find any link to me or the business."

"Let's recap. You went to work at your normal time and found the envelope, and then what did you do?" Melissa asked.

"I had a full day of meetings, so I had to put the envelope in a drawer. No, that's not exactly right. I locked it away in a little safe in my credenza."

"Did you show the contents to anyone? Bobbie maybe?" Jesse asked.

"Are you kidding? Of course! She has been in on this from the beginning."

"Were there any new people visiting the offices? Strangers who might have overheard something either you or Bobbie said?" Melissa asked.

"No. I had a roadshow session on a promising new medical device seeking funding. It went from noon to two, and then I came back to the office."

"Honey, did you meet anyone new during your meetings? Anyone who might have hinted that they were aware of this campaign to ruin you?"

Looking at her husband, Taryn started to tear up once again. "How could I do this to you? Your readers will think you married a crook."

"Taryn, stop it," Melissa ordered. "I need your critical thinking. Focus. You didn't do anything. Someone else either thinks you did or feels a hatred for you that has been building for some time. Just think. This was a carefully planned plot. It took time to create the misinformation before releasing it in drips and drabs. This person, whoever he or she is, hasn't out and out accused you of anything. Instead the person merely suggests you haven't handled yourself in an ethical manner. But the information smacks of insider knowledge. And you tell me that Bobbie hasn't found anything online. So far this has been a campaign of terror, with the miscreant avoiding crossing the line into illegal activity. Importantly, you haven't been approached by a blackmailer."

"That's very good, Melissa. When I research a column, I can no longer rely on the Internet, especially Facebook. I triple check everything. Once when I thought I had a reliable source, it turned out to be false. The person didn't even exist," Jesse said.

"Jesse? You never told me about that. Was it your insider-trading piece?" Taryn, now worried for her husband, had returned to her no-nonsense self.

"I'm just saying that all that stuff may be no more than a vicious smoke screen. So we have to suspect you crossed someone. Although knowing you, I can't believe you could," Jesse said.

"That's a good place to start. OK. Taryn, take me back to the beginnings of 4G Investments. I want to know who was in the original group. Are they still associated with you and the firm? Did you ever have a fight with anyone of them or later one of your clients?" Melissa asked.

Taryn walked over to one of the room's bookcases and pulled down a well-handled volume. Returning, she opened it and pointed to a photo. "The three girls in this photo are my best friends. When we were eight years old, we formed a babysitting service and named it 4 Girls Baby Sitting. Then when we began to expand and earn more money, we started to invest our earnings. That is where I got the idea to form 4G Investments. They are my partners, my lifelong friends, and the foundation of today's hedge fund."

Studying the photo, Melissa saw four cute, clean-scrubbed faces. Pointing to something in the background, Melissa turned the book around. "Who is this strange-looking girl? Also part of your babysitting business?"

Sitting on the arm of Melissa's chair, Taryn looked at the photo and frowned. "Oh, that's Nancy Lou Harris. We hired her during that first year but let her go in the second year."

"And? Why did seeing her bother you?"

"Well, I doubt it's anything. We were never close. But in senior year of high school, Nancy dropped out for most of the term. I saw her briefly after she returned, and she wasn't very friendly. In fact I got the feeling she hated me. I attributed it to having dropped her from the group. That can't be it. That was ages ago."

"Do you know where she is now? Anyone who would? I think we should at least look into her life," Melissa said.

"Honey, could you think of anyone else back then that we should look into? I have a few contacts who might be helpful. Maybe I can dig something up. If you can't think of anyone, I am afraid we have to look a bit farther afield."

Before Jesse had finished speaking, Taryn slowly pulled herself to her feet, and taking a deep breath, walked back to the bookcase. "Look, Melissa, you are my dearest friend. But there is a secret I've kept for almost twenty years. Linda, Kathy, and Ellie aren't even aware of it." With a quick glance to Jesse, said. "Sweetheart, I've never even told you. I just wanted to forget the entire episode in my life. I'm only going to share this if you both promise never to repeat it. Never. Swear?"

Seeing her husband go pale and Melissa nod in agreement, she made the decision she had been dreading for years. "My first job was with Gibraltar Investment Bank. It was the year I completed my master's. I remember being excited about beginning my career at a small firm where I was sure I would gain wider exposure to investment banking. Well, I'd been there about a year when the managing partner called me into his office and said he was going to entrust me with a very special client. Before handing me the folder, he made me swear not to reveal anything in the folder or any future interactions with this client. Of course I would never divulge information on any client. It's not done. Anyway, I thanked him for his trust in me and returned to my office to review the file."

Taryn, standing in front of the bookcase, stepped onto a small ladder and reached for a book on the top shelf. Hugging the book to her chest, she faced them, hesitating before continuing. "The account was for a mob boss, handling his offshore accounts. The size of the transactions was abnormally large for someone of my inexperience. At first, I wondered why I had been chosen. Then, after a closer inspection of the file, I knew that I was being tested. If I took over this account, my life would never be the same. If I didn't, my work at the bank would remain inconsequential at best."

Still hugging the book, Taryn reached for Jesse's glass, wanting a sip, but knowing better, she placed it back on the table, while both her husband and Melissa sat silently, waiting for her to continue.

"It was something out of a crime novel. If I became their representative at the bank, I would be going down a path…what is the expression? To perdition?" Looking at the horror on Jesse's face and seeing a puzzled look on her dear friend, she handed her the book. "Go ahead, Melissa, open it."

Melissa looked at a worn cover of a Bible, and on opening it found a pocket in which lay a small notebook. Looking to Taryn and getting her approval, she removed it and began to read the handwritten notations. "Shit. You copied the entire file? Names, balances, and bank account numbers."

Taryn gave Jesse a quick look, and seeing concern, but no anger, she resumed her pacing. "Yes. The next morning I walked into the managing partner's office dressed in my college skirt and sweater set trying to look as young and innocent as possible. Handing him the file, I remember saying I am afraid this is way over my head, sir. I appreciate your faith in me, but so far all I have done was record activities of the other partners. I've never actually advised a client on their investment portfolio. I would be afraid of letting the firm down."

"Did he buy it?" Melissa whispered.

With her arms hugging her body she nodded. "I was a good actress. And you know, all you have to do is dress the part and most people usually buy anything you tell them. Anyway, I never heard another word about it and a year later left to join an accounting firm."

The cozy library was deathly still, each wondering if the author of the scheme to ruin Taryn was somehow related to this mob account.

"Where in hell do we go from here?" Melissa wondered aloud.

"Don't jump to conclusions," Jesse said. "Taryn, have you ever heard from that partner or anyone from this firm after you left?"

"No. Though I live in dread of this ever becoming known. My official profile begins with my job at the accounting firm. Anyway, the bank was dissolved after this man's death a couple of years later. So I thought that finally my secret was safe."

"Did you cross swords with anyone at the accounting firm?" Melissa wanted to know. "Maybe someone else was aware of Gibraltar's secret and is using it against you. Or waited for a better chance to get even for something you may have done while working at that firm."

"Well, there was a Jack Meloni, who had been at the firm over a year when I arrived. He wasn't too pleased when he found out I was to begin working directly with clients and due to my senior position of responsibility had a larger salary. Additionally, after one year I would be eligible for stock options based on my billings. He hadn't reached the grade where stock options kicked in."

"OK. If this Nancy Lou, Gibraltar Investment Bank, and this Meloni are the only possibilities we have for the moment, Melissa, why don't you start with Nancy Lou and Jack Meloni; I'll see if I can find information about Gibraltar. And honey, I think I should have a chat with Arthur. I am sure he is trying his best to figure things out at his end. From what you have told me, he has been conducting his own search for this lowlife."

"Good idea. I'll let Arthur know you will be in touch."

Melissa replaced the notebook in the Bible and handed it back to Taryn. "I need to think this through. We need a plan and don't want to alert this creep before we're ready to pounce. Why don't I come back tomorrow after work? In the meantime Jesse and I will see what we can turn up." Turning to Taryn she gave her a solid hug. "Don't worry, you have two people who love you and know a thing or two about disinformation campaigns."

Hugging Jesse, Melissa said, "Tomorrow." Grabbing her tote and handbag, she let herself out of the apartment. *I wish I had a Jesse in my life. He's a rock. It would never occur to him that Taryn was anything but innocent. I just hope this pressure doesn't harm the baby.*

Melissa sat in the car as her company driver took her out to Sands Point, Long Island, and the home she cherished, not only for it being the first home she had ever owned but because it represented a private world away from her professional life. She had agreed to help her friend. And it was imperative that no one in 4G

Investments or any of her clients become aware of the situation. So far, only Taryn and her small circle that included her husband, Arthur, and now herself were aware of the danger brewing.

Stepping out of the limousine, she saw that Evelyn had left the downstairs lights on. "Thank you, Martin. I'll see you at the usual time tomorrow." Closing the car door, she paused to breathe the fresh night air with a hint of salt from the Long Island Sound not more than one block away. She could see the twinkling navigation lights in the distance and wondered how she'd ever been brave enough to move away from her cosseted life in Manhattan. Taking a moment to feel the quiet, she squared her weary shoulders and headed into the safety of her home.

"Thank you for waiting up, Evelyn. I can lock up." What would she do without the very efficient older woman? Evelyn was the previous owner of the elegant two-story Tudor house. At the time Melissa had closed on the house and was handed the keys, Evelyn made an unusual request. "Ms. Horn, I wondered if you would be interested in an arrangement where I become your housekeeper. In return, I could continue to live and take care of this house. It was where I came as a bride and lived with my husband Herbert for over forty-five years." Smiling to herself, Melissa remembered thinking that it was a wonderful idea. Being without family, she knew the large five-bedroom house would feel empty. The arrangement had been working successfully for almost eight years, during which she and Evelyn had become good friends, almost family.

As she stretched out on the velvet chez lounge, Melissa decided she required some kind of profile to better understand the kind of person behind Taryn's problems. The first thing in the morning, she'd call her friend Sylvia, a criminal psychologist. With a clearer picture of the type of personality attracted to this sort of activity, she would be in a better position to question suspects. Was it a man or woman? What other tactics might be employed? What were the possible motives?

So far Taryn had been receiving news clippings suggesting that her firm engaged in a variety of unethical practices. Then there were more personal attacks hinting at a cheating husband and poor health. Next she'd have to find out the source of the fake newspaper clippings. And if anyone other than Taryn had received copies. Thank God Taryn's troubles were only threats. The frightening part was they were escalating, and it was too early to determine how far they would go.

I have to help her any way I can. I owe her. She was there in the past warning me of an enemy inside my company, and I've just figured out where to begin.

CHAPTER 26

"Good Morning, Mrs. Hammond," Melissa said, greeting her executive assistant. "I have to make some changes in the week's schedule. Give me a couple of minutes before we get started." As Melissa entered her inner sanctum, her mind shifted to the late-evening conversation with longtime mentor and friend, EF Haynes. He not only convinced her that she was entirely capable of assisting Taryn in tracking down the perpetrator behind the terror provoking news clips but would also keep her dear friend on balance as they began to investigate the acts of malice confronting 4G.

Right, dear friend, and as you so aptly reminded me, I usually search for the essential motivations of any person I'm studying. Her mind turned to her confrontation with Fallon. Knowing who her antagonist was had made resolving the problem pretty straightforward. However, in this case, the identity of the person behind the threats was the big unknown. This seems to be a personal attack. The clippings refer to her marriage and her honor. First suggesting that her husband isn't faithful. *If that's even likely!* Then to suggest she would be so unethical as to launder money for the mob. *Really!*

Hearing Mrs. Hammond approach snapped Melissa back to the business of her day: running an international corporation, managing a staff of primarily men, assessing reports from her field operations, reviewing sales figures by division, checking proposed marketing campaigns, and watching the bottom line to ensure continual growth of the company.

Seeing her assistant squint in the bright morning light, Melissa rose to adjust the window shades behind her desk. "Thank you for the coffee. I don't think my mind will work today without your special brew," she said, taking her first sip of what would be many before she left for the day.

"Ms. Horn, your schedule is pretty tight. Is there something I should be aware of?"

Considering the gray-haired woman sitting opposite her, Melissa realized that this one person not only trained her when she first arrived at the company but was equally assistant and executive manager of her business life. A paragon of principles, Mrs. Hammond enabled Melissa to sail through each day, surviving any bumps that turned into pot holes before they caused damage.

"I reviewed our usual schedule of daily meetings and wondered if for this week we could invite my entire executive team to one morning briefing? That would free up two hours each day to move up some of the other items on the agenda."

Mrs. Hammond nodded. "However, when you began scheduling these meetings, you said that each man seemed more relaxed when you met one-on-one. That as a group they seemed to touch on the imperatives, not the subtleties of a particular situation."

"Yes. It seems when men gather as a group, it's a team sport. Individually the discussions are more frank. However, I need to find time between eleven and one each day for an independent project. This one time, they will just have to adjust."

"And the changes?"

Melissa sat quietly for a moment, at first not sure how much she should reveal. The decision made, she nodded before replying. "Mrs. Hammond, I am trusting you not to divulge what I'm about to share." Melissa knew that Mrs. Hammond not only had her trust but returned it a hundredfold. "I know you don't share our business with others; it's just that this isn't United Chemicals business."

"Of course. My loyalty is to you, as always."

"Never doubted. So here it is. I am helping a friend track down someone out to destroy her firm. That friend is Taryn Cooper. And to that end, I will need the name of that little man you hired to follow Fallon a couple of years ago. He not only kept us informed but also kept his silence."

"Jimmy is the son of an old friend of mine and would do anything for me. But he won't come here. You will have to meet him at a bar on the west side. It's not, however, the kind of place I'd consider safe for someone, let me say, with your appearance and style."

"Didn't you know I'm a chameleon? Wear horn-rimmed glasses to discuss money and contact lenses for business luncheons. How about my pulling my hair into a bun and wearing a simple sweater and slacks?"

Laughing with Mrs. Hammond was a treat. She would have to find a way to enjoy her company more often. *Maybe a private luncheon, just the two of them.* "OK, would you give Jimmy a call and ask him to meet me at eleven this morning? Let him give you the address of his chosen spot. Then contact the executive team and tell them that the week is a heavy one so would they bring their issues to a nine a.m. meeting today. Oh, and be sure to give them my apologies for the short notice. Let them know that if we could make some meaningful decisions as a team, they will have more time to implement their plans."

Mrs. Hammond had been taking notes. Melissa knew that she would have those two things accomplished within minutes of returning to her desk.

"Another thing. Do we have a young wizard, someone we can trust to give me a private lesson on social media?"

"There is a new gal, just graduated from Stamford. She seems to work pretty much alone. Maybe it's because she's new. But then again, she may just be shy."

"How would you know she is a loner? Did you visit her work area?" Mrs. Hammond's knowledge of the organization's employees was a constant surprise.

"No, of course not. But I saw her when she came to the company for her final interview. I was impressed by her no-nonsense corporate demeanor. A reminder of myself when I first applied for a job with Mr. Foster all those years ago."

"Find out if she would be willing to meet me at four today. Also, tell her what I have in the way of computer equipment in case she needs to bring anything with her."

"Anything else?"

"That's about it for now. I will try to keep my other activities limited to the two hours between eleven and one each day. I realize this isn't your job, but Ms. Cooper is a very special gal, and I would like to help her if I can."

⇒⊹⇐

Forty-third street near Ninth Avenue had seen better days, and the Kearney Bar and Grill fit in with the well-worn block. Melissa remembered that this was the area of the city that during the twenties was home of the fearsome Westies, an Irish gang that ran that part of the city.

Dressed all in black—sweater, slacks, and a fitted leather jacket—Melissa entered the darkened bar with sawdust-covered floors. As she removed her sunglasses, she spotted Jimmy sitting alone off to one side in a booth and caught his signal to join him.

Taking a deep breath, she walked slowly toward the slip of a man in a crisp blue shirt and chinos, noting that aside from the bartender, they were the only people in the room.

Melissa could feel her heart beating so fast that she thought it could be heard. She didn't fear Jimmy, but seedy bars made her nervous. An early college experience scared her off entering dark, boozy-smelling places like this one, unsure of who and what she might encounter. Some twenty years ago, Melissa and two girl-friends wanted to experience a bar on the wrong side of town, a place that none of their friends would dare visit. What had started as an evening adventure turned into a nightmare when a fight be-tween two local boys broke out inches away. With the sound of glass shattering, the two men rushed one another using beer bot-tles as knives. Thinking she was going to be slashed, Melissa and her friends moved as far away from the fight as their table allowed. Thankfully, before blood was drawn, a big bruiser of a man broke it up, taking each boy by the shirt collar and rushing them out the door.

Melissa regained control of her thoughts and held out her hand to the middle-aged man. "I'm glad you could meet me on such short notice."

"Sit. Mrs. Hammond swore that you won't cause me no trouble. Don't look so scared. I don't bite."

"May I call you Jimmy?"

"That's my name."

"I asked Mrs. Hammond to get in touch because I need to have you follow someone discreetly. All I want to know is if anyone is fol-lowing her. If so, I'll need a photo." As she handed Jimmy a picture of Taryn, she added, "It's important Ms. Cooper not see you."

"She's a looker. Boyfriend trouble?"

"No. I think it's something more serious. Obviously I can't go to the police. We don't have any evidence. But Mrs. Hammond asked you to do something similar for me a few years back, and what you discovered was most helpful."

"That old dude? Boy, was he ugly."

"He still is," Melissa replied. At the barkeep's approach, she said, "I'll have a glass of whatever beer you have on tap. Can I buy you a refill Jimmy?"

"Sure. The same, Kieran."

"Anyway, I am most interested in knowing if she is being followed from the time she leaves home in the morning to her return home after work. If you can start tonight, it would be appreciated. Then we can meet here at the same time Thursday. Will that give you enough time?"

"Sure if she has a tail."

"OK. I'll pay you the same as last time. In cash."

"That's all? You don't want me to tap her phones, follow the tail? Anything?"

"Well, if you spot anyone following her, yes, take a photo. But that's all. I don't want you to contact her in any way."

"OK. Thursday, here."

"Jimmy, if you have any questions just give Mrs. Hammond a call. She can always find me." With her beer left untouched, Melissa left a twenty on the table. This time Jimmy offered his hand, and taking it, she rose and left.

The afternoon flew by. The reports she had requested from her executive team had kept her so busy that when Mrs. Hammond buzzed to tell her that Jeanne Thomas, her four o'clock appointment had arrived, it took a moment to switch her train of thought away from United Chemicals to Taryn's problems.

"Send her in." Stacking her files off to the side of her desk, Melissa rose to greet the young woman. Not knowing what to expect, she was surprised to see a plainly dressed, extremely pretty brunette no more than five feet tall with a boyishly slim figure approach. Somewhere in the back of her mind she thought Jeanne Thomas would be a T-shirted, horn-rimmed-glasses-wearing nerd. *You should be ashamed of yourself for stereotyping this young woman.*

"Welcome, Ms. Thomas. Please take a seat. I appreciate your agreeing to bring me up to speed on social media, a world totally foreign to me."

"I see the latest in computers so I don't think you will have any trouble. It's like learning a new culture with its own language."

"Well, I need a bit more than the basics found in *Online for Dummies*." Seeing the young woman's puzzled expression, Melissa made an instant character judgment to trust her.

"You see, Ms. Thomas, I want to know how a computer could be used against someone. I'm not worried about security or being hacked. I want to know how to plant misinformation and distribute it via the social media. More importantly how to prevent something like this from happening."

"You mean if someone wanted to make up something, how could they disseminate it to the online world?"

"In a nutshell, yes."

"Why don't you tell me what this is about? You have my promise not to share what you tell me, or what I discover, with anyone else."

"Right. A friend of mine has been receiving photo copies of news clips that we haven't been able to verify as having appeared anywhere. They arrive at unexpected times in a plain envelope and have 'FYI' scrawled on the top of the page in black ink. But each clip appears as if it had run in a specific newspaper…also something that we haven't been able to prove."

"Well, Ms. Horn, first let me first show you the feared Facebook site and how someone can covertly post information and share it with the world. Even if that hasn't happened, this is one site that doesn't vet authenticity of the person or information broadcast.

Another little thing they don't advertise is that users sign an agreement that gives Facebook ownership of everything posted on their site."

"You mean anyone could make up a name and post anything true or not? I'd heard this was possible, Ms. Thomas. Can you show me how it's done?"

Melissa had been so involved in the tutorial that Mrs. Hammond's appearance surprised her. "Ms. Horn, it's approaching six, will you be staying? If so, I'd like to alert security."

"I think we are almost finished here. I should be able to leave around then." After Mrs. Hammond left, Melissa looked at the young woman seated at her side, focused on her desktop computer. "Ms. Thomas, I think I have a better understanding of how an on-line site like this works. Frankly this opportunity for abuse scares me. I appreciate keeping your instruction straight forward and not trying to embellish it in geek-speak. May I call on you again, if I need anything more?"

"Absolutely…err"

"Yes? Is there something else?"

"I have a book written by a forensic specialist who worked for the government on internet fraud. You might find it a good introduction on how hacking and falsifying information can be done."

Looking at the young women's serious expression stopped Melissa from a breezy dismissal with a simple thank-you. "Then you think my friend will be attacked on the Internet?"

"At some point the perpetrator may wish to up the ante. Since it's relatively easy to make false claims online…that might be the next ploy."

"Yes, I would like to see that book, Ms. Thomas. Now that you've introduced me to the criminal side of social media, I'd better learn what this expert has to say."

"Ms. Horn, if I could see the original message, I might have additional ideas."

"Well, there hasn't been anything found online. My gut tells me you are probably right—that could be the next step in this harassment. At least I will have a better idea of where to look and what we'd be facing."

"I'd be happy to help if anything turns up."

"Mrs. Hammond, please give Ms. Thomas your information and let me know if she needs anything else." Looking at the young woman, Melissa extended her hand. "I want to thank you for taking on this challenge. I'll be in touch if anything new crops up."

After the usual end-of-day ritual of bringing Mrs. Hammond up-to-date, Melissa placed a research report in her briefcase. On second thought she removed it, knowing that the evening ahead with Taryn and Jesse would run late and prayed that they would make some progress toward resolving the pending crisis.

CHAPTER 27

The ringing phone was picked up by Bobbie, who answered and then handed the receiver to her boss. "It's Reggie Farmer, said it's important."

"Yes, Reggie."

"Ms. Horn, did you send someone to speak to me about investing in my research?"

The young man's worried tone, not to mention his news, had Taryn sitting straighter in her chair. "Reggie. What's happened?"

"This man arrived at the door of my lab. No warning, just walked in and started telling me that he had heard about my research into inflammation and wanted me to know he thought my work was important. He went on to tell me that he suffered from high cholesterol and believed that he would be better able to control it if he could reduce his inflammation. Apparently it's over two hundred and eighty; that's dangerously high."

"Reggie, other than me and my partners, have you discussed your research with anyone new?" She was holding her breath. The thought of a competitor learning of their interest in Reggie was an unexpected complication. Until all the legal papers were signed, Reggie was a free agent.

"You mean other than the university? No!" he whined. "I told you how this has to be kept secret. I'm not the only one working on identifying the triggers that make a normal process run amok. You promised me you'd keep this secret."

"Reggie, we've kept that promise. I am as nervous as you are about leaks. Can you remember how you responded?"

"I just stared at him. Then asked how he heard about my work. He was kind of vague, saying that he'd heard a couple of students talking when visiting the building…something about visiting with a friend on the faculty."

"Did he say where he was from? Did he give you his name, leave his card?"

"Nope. Nothing."

"How did you get rid of him?"

"I said that I was still a student and not prepared to take any next steps until I received my degree. You know, it's funny. As interested as he seemed, he took my reply calmly. Sorry, I didn't ask for his card, and he didn't offer one. But he did ask me to call him Adam. You know, Ms. Cooper, I want us to work together. I don't need this hassle. I'm nervous as it is."

Breathing a bit easier, Taryn tried to reassure the young man they were there for him. "Reggie, listen carefully. We haven't spoken to anyone about your work. Somehow it came to this person's attention. Let me handle this. We'll find out who leaked it. Just let me know if anything equally strange comes up. I'll handle things from here."

Reviewing the latest problem, Taryn hoped that the clips weren't related to Reggie's unexpected visitor. The person who approached Reggie was probably out for profit. The first one to lock up a new medical discovery made millions. The clips were another matter entirely, and it was time to bring them to the attention of the group.

⋘ ⋙

"Something has come up, and it's time to share the bad news." Holding up her hand to stop the questions before they came tumbling from Kathy and those she could see forming in the minds of Ellie and Linda. Taryn now regretted not having brought the clips to their attention earlier. They had always worked together. Why did she feel that this time things were different? Maybe because the clippings were directed at her and had nothing to do with the others.

The conference room was deathly still. All electronic devices were placed face down on the table as the women waited for her to continue. "For the past several weeks, I have been receiving mockups of news clips; copies are in these folders," Taryn said as she handed them around. "Take a minute, and after you've absorbed the evidence, I'll fill you in on what's been done so far." Taryn picked up her cup of coffee, but too nervous to drink, set it back down. *Time to lay off the caffeine.* What would they think about how she was managing the company? Clearly someone thought her unscrupulous.

"But this is slanderous," Kathy cried out.

"Impossible," added Linda, slamming the folder on the table and pushing it away. "In fact if I were back at the public relations agency, we'd be launching a campaign of damage control."

"But you aren't, Linda," said Ellie, her soft voice emphasizing the importance of the problem facing them. "This would destroy not only 4G but all our lives. Years of hard work. Reputations we fought hard to build, and finally proving that women could handle investments as well as the men's clubs."

Taryn didn't know how to continue. This was weeks later; she should have brought them in when the first clip arrived.

"Jesse, Melissa, and I met last evening to review those missives. Unfortunately, until last night, I'd kept this between Bobbie, Arthur, and myself. While we each made our lists of questions, checked files, and Bobbie searched newspapers and online social media, we haven't been able to get a lead on who or why someone is out to destroy me."

"Not just you, Taryn, all of us. And don't forget it," Linda said.

No longer able to sit still, Taryn began pacing around the conference table. "So far we haven't come up with anything."

"What does Jesse think about this?" Kathy asked. "He's pretty good at puzzles."

Just thinking of his reaction about being left out brought a tear to her eyes. "Ah…I only told him a couple of nights ago. He didn't take it very well." A sudden twinge had Taryn place her hand over her abdomen.

"Ellie, do you know if we incurred the wrath of a client?" Linda asked.

"No. We did have one or two leave 4G, but it was for other reasons. Not that they thought we were crooks. And we have continued to attract new investors from several universities looking to diversify their endowments," Ellie offered.

"Melissa asked me if there might be someone back in Dunkirk who is malicious enough to cause us trouble. She thought a visit home might turn something up."

"You know, Taryn, I visit regularly," Kathy said. "Mom and Dad love seeing the boys, and I miss my mom's cooking."

"I loved her brownies," Linda said. "She even gave me her recipe."

"Well, I couldn't think of anything to share with Melissa other than our strained relationship with Nancy Lou," Taryn said. "But she was just strange, certainly not evil."

"That oddball!" Linda remarked. "Remember how she was always showing up, like she'd been invited?"

"Mom worried when she just arrived for our sleepover. She had only heard us talking about her but never met her. When I complained, Mom said I had to be more charitable because she had a rough life what with her mother working all day and out drinking all night," Taryn added.

"Why not check on what happened to that football player. Buddy something," Linda said. "Wasn't there some rumor about them in high school?"

"Ian Mayer," Ellie corrected. "Good idea, and if we come up with another angle we'll let you know."

The voices around the table were bringing up a variety of names and stories from their time at Dunkirk High. Ellie, Linda, and Kathy were the social ones. She had been busy with babysitting and her job as a hospital aide. Trying to picture each of the people being discussed was confusing the issue. How could some kid back in school even know what she did for a living? Or where she lived? Taryn decided that they would do better without her input. At this point she was too close to the problem. Anyway, she had a business to run. Rubbing her right temple to ease a growing migraine, Taryn picked up a pen and began writing a new list…one of the people she remembered from Dunkirk. It didn't take long to write four names and wondered how many more Ellie would have come up with.

"Well, back to business, ladies. We have 4G Ventures to launch," Taryn said as she rose to return to her office.

CHAPTER 28

"I'm glad we aren't meeting at the office. Taryn has enough on her plate not to be reminded of this growing crisis," Arthur said as he led Jesse to the dining room of the Harvard Club, his preferred location for private business conversations.

"Did she fill you in on our meeting last evening with Melissa?"

"Enough to come up with some additional thoughts you and I could work on. First let me tell you of a new wrinkle that came to our attention earlier this morning. You know that we are in the process of working through the legal requirements to launch a venture capital business?"

"Yes, and I think that as usual my wife has hit on a winner. Scouting new science before it becomes mainstream will not only enable her to build something of value but energize that brain of hers. I don't think she loves the in-and-out trading as much as she first did."

"Especially when the rewards have been dwindling along with an increase in government scrutiny." Refolding his napkin instead of placing it on his lap, Arthur continued. "Anyway the scientist

Taryn is excited about, Reggie Farmer, is working on identifying the mechanism for controlling inflammation. The worrisome bit is that Reggie called this morning to tell her that someone from a competitor had approached him to enquire whether Reggie would accept them as a major investor."

"How in hell did word of 4G's interest in Reggie's work leak? What did he do?"

"The kid adores your wife and said he told the guy he wasn't interested. But he didn't say anything about his relationship with 4G. Apparently Reggie is as paranoid as we are."

"But his science hasn't been proved. What would this other firm gain by backing Reggie at this stage?"

Arthur couldn't help smiling. Sitting a bit more relaxed and having taken a sip of his drink, he looked at the younger man, someone he'd grown fond of. "I guess you haven't read of the recent situation in pharmaceutical firms. Research is increasingly more costly. So now they are hunting for the next big breakthrough, like Reggie's. Once 4G gets going, the first step will be to organize Reggie into a company complete with board of directors, and issue limited shares of stock for Reggie and the directors in lieu of salary."

"I get that. But this hasn't happened yet. What would this stranger gain now? And how in hell did he find Reggie?"

"He's playing the long game. Buy cheap, and when it's time, sell to a big pharma. It could earn shareholders upward of five hundred million dollars."

"Whew! A bigger ball game than the one I report on. But how would someone find Reggie? He's still in school for Christ's sake."

"Right. The only people outside of us who would be aware of Reggie and 4G's new business would be our attorney. He's been drawing up the contract between 4G and Reggie." Arthur took another sip of his drink to swallow his anger. "Here is where it gets interesting. A bit of checking, and I found that this person who contacted Reggie is Adam Matthews, the roommate of Laurence Swinburne…our trusted attorney."

"Hasn't 4G been working with Swinburne since the beginning? Why would he betray a client, especially one as lucrative as 4G?"

"Well, roommate in this case is a euphemism for lover. And before you ask, I know this because they are frequent guests at 4G events. I guess I'm really old-fashioned, but seeing two men together acting more than fraternally sends signals. So I have always paid special attention to Swinburne and up until now never had cause to worry."

"Are we looking at a bit of pillow talk?"

"And a very devious lover."

CHAPTER 29

"Thank you for seeing me, Mr. Meloni. I just have a couple questions for my summary of Ms. Cooper's time with Reed, Reed and Whyte," Melissa said as she sat in a stiff wood chair opposite the thin man in his late forties.

"You said that you were writing an official profile. Are you a reporter? I don't speak with the press."

"No, simply compiling a corporate backgrounder at Ms. Cooper's request. It was her feeling that as a woman, I would be more objective."

"And just how is she planning on using this information?"

"As you are probably aware, Ms. Cooper serves on several corporate boards, and on occasion they need a brief résumé of her experience."

"I see. How may I be of assistance?"

"Were you with the firm at the time Ms. Cooper joined? Were you colleagues? Did you work on the same accounts? It will be helpful if you could provide me with your title at that time and original date of employment."

"I don't see how that would be of any help."

"I'm sure you understand that I will need to place her history in chronological order." While Melissa kept a serene presence, Meloni was sitting a bit more stiffly in his oversized desk chair.

"Which corporation will be receiving this information? If it is a client of this firm, I'm afraid I won't be able to comment."

Melissa had been studying Jack Meloni's reactions to each of her questions noticing that he shifted his eyes away from hers when avoiding a question. Outwardly he was all charm, providing hardly any information other than to confirm that Taryn had once been employed by the firm.

"I am certain that the corporation is not a client of your firm. However, this is a time-sensitive matter, and I will be submitting my draft for Ms. Cooper's approval at the end of the week. The reason for my question is that it has come to my attention that you've been overheard speaking ill of Ms. Cooper while she was with this firm."

"What are you driving at?"

"Just that this is a warning to never mention her name again." Melissa noticed that the charm had worn away, leaving an arrogant, frightened little man.

"Ms. Horn, not that it is material to your report, but whatever you think I said, it couldn't have been possible. You see I took a month break about the time Ms. Cooper joined the firm. Therefore, we only worked together for a little more than a year. That should suffice as verification that she was a member of this firm."

As she pretended to make notes on a small pad, Melissa needed to know if he was behind the campaign to ruin Taryn. "Mr. Meloni, I understand during this break of employment, you were traveling back and forth to Canada. Were these trips by car?"

If she had hit him with a cream pie, the slick young man couldn't have appeared any whiter. "I have a report from the Windsor border station that you had been held on several of these trips for carrying prescription drugs."

"Yes, they are extremely attentive to possible smuggling activities. And I had been carrying several weeks' supply of Oxycodone."

There it was again, that shift in eye contact. She could almost see him shrink into his chair. "One more item, I believe the car you drove had been confiscated due to its four doors being packed with street-grade narcotics."

"Just what are you insinuating? That I smuggled drugs?" The vitriol in his voice might have scared her if she hadn't been expecting it. Her goal of throwing a scare into Jack Meloni was working. She had his attention at last.

"Let me make myself clear. I have proof of your brief incarceration in Windsor, and if you should ever again even breathe Ms. Cooper's name, I will hand the report to your father-in-law. I believe he is the remaining named partner of this firm." It was years of dealing with intimidating men playing her for a fool that enabled her to deliver the take–no-prisoner threat.

"What do you mean? I've never mentioned Ms. Cooper's name. As you have probably gathered, she wasn't someone I enjoyed working for."

"Let's keep it that way. Now, I'll take my leave knowing that you and I have reached an understanding." With that Melissa rose to her full six-foot height and with a cold stare boring into the unsettled man, left. *He's too weak to be the culprit. Back to the drawing board. Shit!*

CHAPTER 30

"Thank you for coming downtown and meeting me for lunch. I'm swamped at the office, trying to get through management-team meetings and proofing the shareholder's quarterly report due at the printer tomorrow. There just doesn't seem to be enough hours in the day. Jesse, I envy your freedom. You work at home and can pretty much control your day. I only wish."

"Melissa, I'm on deadline. This latest project is a really big deal for me. It will break me out of the narrow world of financial advice columnist into a larger field of influence. I don't want to argue about who is busier. I just know we have to get to the bottom of this before Taryn crashes. She's been amazing, going to work every day pretending that nothing is wrong. And if that weren't enough stress, she is experiencing daily bouts of morning sickness."

"How are you doing...with the pregnancy? Experiencing any symptoms?"

"Very funny. I'm so nervous that I keep stroking Taryn's belly just to make sure she's really carrying my baby."

Seeing the approaching waiter, Melissa gave the menu a quick glance. "Hi, Robert. My usual salad and coffee. Thanks."

"And you, sir?"

"I'll have the Cobb salad and coffee. Make that decaf."

"OK, let's share notes. I've enlisted the services of a formerly valuable contact to follow Taryn and see if she is in fact being followed. I spoke with Jimmy earlier, and he said he couldn't find anything suspicious. This means that whoever is plotting against Taryn is privy to information gained in a more devious manner. Those new clips run too close to home for it to be a stranger."

"I agree and that frightens me even more." Jesse reached for his glass of water, concern written on his wrinkled brow. "I guess you told him to be discreet because she didn't say anything about being followed. That would terrify her, especially if we hadn't alerted her in advance."

"You don't know the half of it," Melissa replied. "As for the strange Jack Meloni, I learned that he had a grudge against Taryn's success, but while he's guilty, it's not of these clips. He's been smuggling drugs in from Canada, and when I called him on it, he backed down. I left threatening that if he ever spoke of Taryn, I'd turn the information I had from Canadian customs over to his father-in-law."

Melissa pulled a notepad from her briefcase and handed it across the table. "Here's my research into Taryn's high-school senior class. I've been looking for people she was friendly with, including that Nancy Lou Harris. I've checked off the names of people I've located so far, including the dozen kids she was closest to." Melissa reached across the table and pointed to the unchecked names of Taryn's lawyer, investment banker, marketing specialist, and printer. "These still need attention. I just can't seem to find the time."

"You can leave these to me. I met with Arthur, and while there may be a cause for further investigation into the lawyer, Swinburne, we believe a recent leak of 4G plans was an accident of opportunity. It's not likely that he's responsible for these news clips."

Surprise lit Melissa's face. "And…?"

"Arthur and I met to discuss possible business contacts who might have some reason to ruin 4G. Anyway, that morning Taryn received a call from Reggie who told her he'd been visited by someone interested in backing his research. Arthur seems to think that while it led back to Swinburne, it wasn't him. As for the banker, Stephen Harrington, he's squeaky clean. And until the paperwork is done, marketing and accounting aren't part of this need-to-know group."

"And you both think Swinburne told a competitor about Reggie and his research?"

"Yes and no. It looks like Laurence Swinburne has a secret lover. Arthur said he may have unknowingly left papers or information out for someone to see."

"Now that is interesting. Do you know the name and home address of this woman?" Melissa asked only to see Jesse smiling. "Jesse, this is serious."

"I agree. It's just that this person is an Adam Matthews, and he lives with Laurence."

"Ah. And we don't know if he's connected to the FYI clips?"

"Right. But Reggie told Taryn his visitor's name was Adam."

"What if I have Jimmy, a man of unusual talents, follow this Matthews and photograph everyone he meets outside of work. Do you know where he works?"

"Here are his business and home addresses. I would love to know what your contact uncovers. I've met both men at 4G events, and they are so upright that they look like magazine ads for Wall Street's finest."

"That brings us to the unexplored topic of Taryn's childhood in Dunkirk. Jesse, what do you know of her hometown and high-school activities? Her friends? I may be whistling into the wind, but I think this campaign could go back that far. The only oddball in those photos she showed us was this Nancy Lou, and she didn't look very bright."

"You know my wife. She doesn't share anything personal. It took me a year of dating before I even knew she had a babysitting service at the age of eight. Do you know anyone trying to impress a boyfriend not sharing this major bit of history?"

"I suppose she didn't think it was important. You know those board meetings we attend? Well, she shreds seasoned men when they try to slip one by us. If it wasn't so serious, I'd break out laughing. But men are such sensitive creatures; they don't take kindly to being embarrassed." Melissa was surprised to see Jesse blushing. "You do know you are a *paragon* among men. And, along with your wife, a favorite of mine."

"I'm not accustomed to such flattery," Jesse said and touched the rim of his water glass to the rim of hers. "And you are a favorite of mine. So back to business. Enough stroking, we need to be in attack mode."

"Have you been to Dunkirk recently? Or even before you were married?" Jesse nodded, so Melissa rushed on. "Anything out of the ordinary? Who did you meet? Childhood friends? Stories that now might seem relevant?"

Placing his elbows beside his plate, hands on either side of his head, Jesse took a moment. "Melissa, her life wasn't ordinary. Her parents are solid, upper class members of the community. Her friends are the same three she founded 4G with. No stories of accidents, either physical or emotional in nature. Other than her driven, shutdown way of dealing with emotions, there's nothing to tell you."

"Shut down? I would say careful. You know Jesse that the world treats smart women differently. I learned early in life to hide my intensity and focus on getting ahead. One time way back in grade school, when I slipped, I was treated as a freak. I never made that mistake again. You learn when to let loose and when to fly under the radar."

"Now that you mention it, Taryn's ability with numbers would appear freakish to normal people. And if I remember the story correctly, she had a similar incident in preschool when she already knew her numbers and could add and subtract. She said the teachers started to treat her differently. All except for Linda, Ellie, and Kathy. They didn't care."

"Then I guess you are about to take a trip with Taryn back to her past. Make it a weekend, and visit the Coopers. Have your wife take you to some of her old haunts. Go to dinner with one or two of her high school friends. I know men don't gossip but try. Hopefully you'll learn a secret or two."

"Damn it, Melissa. I just told you I'm on deadline. Just because you have the title CEO doesn't mean you can delegate responsibility to me. I don't work for you. Remember?"

Melissa froze with embarrassment as the nearby table stopped all conversation to stare. With a deep breath, she stiffened her spine, and switching into formal mode, she turned to the diners and smiled. "My brother and I seem to have forgotten we weren't at home. Please accept our apologies." She signaled for the waiter. "Robert, will you please refresh the adjoining table's drinks and place it on my bill."

"Of course, Ms. Horn. Right away."

"Hey, I'm sorry," Jesse whispered, once he had her attention. "The way you handled my outburst makes me feel like a worm. We aren't enemies. Just trying to protect my wife."

"You're right," Melissa responded knowing full well that Jesse was refocused on the problem at hand.

"Look, my inquiries are mainly online and with a few phone calls to trusted sources. Maybe I can check off a few more names on that list. I could make a call and encourage my mother-in-law to divulge some family secrets."

Reaching over to squeeze Jesse's hand, Melissa confided, "In business I'm considered a cold-eyed bitch. Since I don't have a personal life outside you and Taryn, bitch seems my normal demeanor. I shouldn't have inflicted my dictatorial self on you. Forgiven?"

"You aren't being fair to yourself. Public scenes are bad form for me as well. I'm just frightened this miscreant is going to escalate from threats to physical violence. I'd die if anybody hurt Taryn."

"Do you think we can meet at your place tonight? That way we can share what we've found with Taryn."

"She's got a dinner thing; maybe she can switch it to drinks. I'll ask. I'll have dinner ready. A huge salad with shrimp, OK?" Picking up his cell, Jesse punched in his wife's office number. "Hi, honey, can you switch your dinner to early drinks instead? Melissa and I want to share our early discoveries with you. I'll have dinner waiting."

"Of course. It's only with Sam and our auditor. A conversation best handled in person. I should be home by eight. Will that be all right?"

"See you then." Ending the call, Jesse gave Melissa a thumbs-up. "Eight tonight."

Melissa glanced at her watch and then looked down at her half-eaten lunch. "Oops, have to rush." Reaching for the bill, she pulled out her credit card. "Don't worry about this. Invite me to another one of your little dinner parties. I haven't had such an enjoyable evening in years."

Brushing Jesse's cheek with a quick kiss, Melissa turned to the adjoining table, pleased to see that they were deep in conversation. Apparently their earlier blowup had been forgotten.

After removing their dinner plates, Jesse poured coffee for himself and tea for Taryn. "Look, honey, we've filled you in on preliminary findings. Melissa and I tend to think there is something in your past that may have triggered this creature's attack."

"What would you think if you and I spent a couple of days visiting Dunkirk? Maybe staying with your parents?" Melissa suggested in a soothing tone.

"What is going on in that complex mind, Melissa? My parents don't know anything about this."

"Don't get riled up, Taryn. We just thought that you are too close to things. I had thought of joining you, but then we thought it would seem less serious to your parents if you and Melissa made a casual visit. Since Melissa doesn't really know your family, she might be able to get them to reminisce about some old high-school friends and uncover some gossip or even a secret. It would help narrow down our search."

"My parents would love to have us." Thinking out loud, she said, "They'll want to talk about the baby." Then refocusing on the reason behind the visit, she looked at Melissa. "I don't want them worried, understand? They are to stay in the dark about this."

"Won't they be focused on the baby? Melissa asked.

"Yes. And I look forward to sharing that with you all. But, maybe Melissa, you could trigger a lost memory. I'm not very good at looking back. I seem to always be propelling myself forward. Ellie once said that if I kept rushing through life, I'd miss it."

Breathing a sigh of relief, Jesse was glad his wife took to their idea, and more importantly that Melissa had relented and agreed to go instead of him. "All right, ladies, how about a hot fudge sundae?" The laughter sounded good after a tense evening where food was the least on their minds. "Taryn, think of it as nourishment for our son and heir."

"Or daughter," Taryn teased.

"How about one of each?" Melissa piped in, enjoying the lighter mood. "I can't wait to see how quickly he or she learns to add two and two."

Blushing and patting her barely expanded stomach, Taryn relaxed knowing that Jesse and Melissa had her back.

CHAPTER 31

"Bobbie, did you get plane reservations for Melissa and me?" "Right here," Taryn's assistant replied, handing her boss tickets and a car-rental confirmation. "I've ordered a car service to take you to the airport. He's scheduled to pick you up at three."

"Thanks, Bobbie. Please let Ms. Horn know your arrangements so she will be ready. She mentioned that she had an appointment nearby and would meet me here. Hopefully I can clear up this desk before we have to leave."

The ringing phone had Bobbie reaching across Taryn's desk. "Ms. Cooper's office." With the handset held out to Taryn, she said, "Its Ms. Foster."

"Yes, Linda. I expected you back this morning."

"I stayed an extra day to speak with a local construction-management firm about the complexities and costs of building a new office complex."

"Complex? I doubt we want to be that aggressive at this stage. Just something for Solo Pharma's needs and a bit extra to rent out to cover some of the costs."

"Right. Well, he said that for somewhere between fifteen and twenty million dollars we could build a sixty-thousand-square-foot building, of which only twenty thousand would be slated for the Solo Pharma lab. It would be a three-story basic structure but built with future expansion in mind."

"We do own that property. If he thinks it's a good location, would he be willing to provide some sort of proposal for consideration?" Taryn asked.

"Yes. In fact he said the property was perfectly situated, being located off a major highway. Another thing, have you ever considered investing in a real-estate investment trust?" Linda asked.

"No, can't say I have. How would that fit with our venture-capital investments?"

"I was discussing our needs for Solo Pharma, and the construction-management representative mentioned that his firm had just finished building a site devoted to medical and scientific clients," Linda explained.

"I don't understand. How does that impact us?"

"Taryn, it seems there is a huge rental market for small independent laboratories and medical testing facilities. These laboratories require specific infrastructure that would be costly to install for someone renting a bare-wall facility. Well, this group invests in those properties and rents to medical-imaging equipment firms and other medical-testing laboratories, that kind of thing. It occurred to me that if we could become an important investor…"

"Clever, and you thought we could consider a similar business opportunity for the new Solo Pharma facility. And maybe offer 4G's clients another avenue of investment."

⇒ ⇐

"Hello, Ms. Horn. Ms. Cooper is expecting you," Bobbie said as the elegantly dressed woman entered her office, thinking that even her overnight bag probably came from a designer.

"Yes, Bobbie. However, I'm a bit early and wondered if you had a few minutes to answer some questions about that first news clip incident?"

"Ms. Horn, you know I would do anything to help Ms. Cooper, but I don't know what I can add to the information I've already shared with you."

As she set her handbag on the corner of Bobbie's exceptionally organized desk, Melissa nodded, and pulling up a nearby chair, she sat next to Bobbie. They weren't strangers, often speaking when one or the other had information for Taryn.

Bobbie seemed anxious but not near the hysterical woman Melissa had met the day she had first questioned her about the series of mysterious mailings.

"You were very thorough, Bobbie. It's just that since then I've wondered about a few details that weren't quite clear. For instance, are you the one who usually finds these envelopes? And have you been checking the social media for anything not directly relating to 4G? Maybe something about Taryn or even one of 4G's clients?"

"I am usually the one who gathers the memos and mail and bring it to Ms. Cooper. Oh. Just a minute."

Melissa watched as Bobbie opened a bottom desk drawer and withdrew the tablet. "Originally this was a gift from my husband, and I planned to use it for shopping and staying in touch with my sister in Wisconsin."

"Is that what you are using it for now?"

"Oh no. When I showed it to Ms. Cooper, she asked if I had used the tablet previously. When I told her that it was brand new, she instructed me to purchase a replacement and keep this one here, just in case…"

"Just in case you found something posted?"

"Yes. But so far, thank God, nothing's appeared on either Facebook or Twitter. Just those newspaper clippings that somehow find their way to our office."

"Bobbie, how could something addressed to Ms. Cooper arrive on your tablet? Wouldn't this person have to send it to her directly?"

"Ms. Cooper doesn't have a personal Facebook or Twitter account. She uses her computer for correspondence on a secured site and the Bloomberg terminal for research." A small smile lit the woman's face. "She's a bit old-fashioned. Maybe it's just a woman's thing, but she handwrites her notes to friends and business associates. I love that about her."

Melissa had never thought that something as simple as a handwritten note would engender such personal feelings. On occasion she wrote notes to people, but only personal friends to wish them a happy birthday or other event. Not for business acquaintances or employees. She'd have to think about that in her own universe. A way to show her appreciation to those in her inner circle.

"So you are the one with the Facebook account?"

"I guess she thought that if someone wanted to reach her and couldn't find her personal information in Facebook, they'd search the company website for a listing of officers. I'm listed as executive assistant. And I do have a Facebook account."

Melissa saw evidence of Bobbie's loyalty by the smile when mentioning that she, not Taryn, was listed on the firm's website.

"In fact when this all started, I opened a new Facebook account with my maiden name. I don't have more than twelve "friends," so it was easy to redirect them to the new home page. But…"

Melissa's intuition told her Bobbie just thought of another glitch. "But? Bobbie, what just crossed your mind?"

"Well, when I tried to delete my previous Facebook account, I couldn't. On checking further, I was told that if I chose to close it, they retained ownership of all my information." Looking over to Ms. Horn, she asked, "Isn't that illegal?"

"If my mind serves correctly, when you signed the agreement to use Facebook, that was in the agreement. You might want to reread that agreement and check into their privacy settings. Just in case."

Melissa couldn't help feeling for the young woman. No matter how careful she probably was in the office, she forgot about protecting her own privacy.

As Melissa rose, she gave the young woman a warm smile. "Don't worry, Bobbie. We are going to shut down this odious individual and restore sanity."

"Promise?"

"Absolutely!"

⇒+ +⇐

"Mom, Dad, I'd like you to meet Melissa Lynn Horn, a close friend and colleague." As Taryn hugged each of her parents, Melissa followed her introduction with warm handshakes.

"I can't tell you, Mr. and Mrs. Cooper, how long I've wanted to meet the parents of this unusual woman. Smart, modest, and someone I can count as a trusted friend."

"Enough, Melissa, or you'll have me blushing."

"It's our pleasure to welcome you, dear. It's Beverly and Bennett, please." Ushering them into the living room, she added, "Of course we couldn't be prouder of our daughter, even if it's only her father who really understands what she does for a living."

Knowing something of Melissa's early life and strained family relationships, Taryn was glad to see her quickly warm to hers. Following them into the living room, Taryn saw that her mom had set out her best tea service with a spread of cheeses, olives, smoked sausage, along with bread and crackers.

"May I offer you a drink, Melissa? I believe I have most everything," Bennett Cooper offered.

"Daddy, she's a single malt drinker like you and me, also with two cubes. But make mine water."

After Bennett had served drinks all around, Melissa raised her glass. "I'd be honored to make a toast." Seeing that she had their attention, Melissa said, "To the grandparents to be, Beverly and Bennett." Amid laughter and several sips, Taryn watched her friend settle into the sofa, relaxed and enjoying herself. While this was to be a fact-finding mission, she still wanted Melissa to get to know her family. Her friend once confided that her own family was ruled by her forbiddingly strict father and her mother who cowered to avoid his displeasure. Not for the first time did Taryn think herself lucky having the loving and supportive Beverly and Bennett for parents.

"So, Bennett, Taryn followed in your footsteps and became an expert in finance," Melissa teased, once the excitement died down.

The room again echoed with warmth-filled laughter. "I wish that were the truth. But you see while I worked, Taryn along with Kathy, Ellie, and Linda were learning at Arthur's side. I believe you've met him?"

"And he thinks of himself as your surrogate. Always on the lookout for anything that might hurt them," Melissa said.

Taryn watched her friend quickly blend in with her family's conversation and caught an occasional comment directed to her mom, seeking a bit more information on something Beverly had said. Talk during dinner included sports, the local election, and the social gossip from the country club.

When Melissa began to chat about how she admired Taryn's business success, Taryn jumped in. "Mom, this pot roast is delicious. I miss your cooking."

Oops, Taryn thought looking over to her father and seeing his "I know you're hiding something look" as he folded his napkin and placed it next to his plate. "Is there anything you want to share, Cookie?" Even the use of her childhood nickname couldn't get Taryn to fill the silence that followed. *Shit!* With her knife and fork set on her plate, no longer able to keep her stomach quiet enough to finish, she silently prayed that her news wouldn't scare her parents. "Well, I guess there is no way to avoid mentioning another reason for our trip."

"You mean other than trying to find the author of those damaging newspaper clips?"

"How…?"

"Arthur gave me the cliff notes version. So why don't you just fill in the blanks. Cookie, there isn't anything I wouldn't do to help. By now you should have known I'd be here for you."

"Now, Bennett, let your daughter tell her side of things," Beverly said. "It won't help if you interrogate her."

Tears filled Taryn's eyes and only will power kept them from spilling over. "It's so hard to admit that someone hates me enough to want me destroyed."

"Beverly, Bennett, I know Taryn has a hard time sharing problems, but fortunately she has Jesse and Arthur who would do anything to protect her. As for me, I am still not sure how I can be of assistance, except that I am an outsider and as such may catch some bit of information that can help uncover the person behind this scheme. Maybe my not knowing anyone from Dunkirk, some story or bit of gossip could provide a clue to resolving this crisis," Melissa said, momentarily directing attention away from Taryn.

"You know when the girls were young, they ran a babysitting business?" Beverly asked.

"A bit. What can you tell me about that time?"

Beverly settled into her story, as she began telling Melissa a treasured family memory. "The four girls talked some of their grade-school friends into working for them. I think that first year they had four employees." As she giggled, Mrs. Cooper shook her head. "Employees at eight years old? Now that I think of it, I realize I didn't raise a girl—she was born full grown."

The following laughter broke the tension. Taryn wondered what her mother would say next.

"The following year they invited another four to join the group. I was so proud of them. Each of the girls they worked with came from good homes…all except for Nancy Lou Harris. Her mom drank and ignored her daughter. My, my, if you could see how she dressed. That girl needed someone to take her shopping. If the color wasn't wrong, the style was. I'd see her at the house and want to take her under my wing. But of course I couldn't."

"Funny, I don't remember that about her, Mom. I guess I never paid attention to Nancy Lou's clothes. But she did have a weird personality. One minute hanging around us and the next gossiping about what we wore, where we went, and how she was one of our best friends."

"That's the girl in those photos you showed me?" Melissa asked.

"Yes."

"Beverly, can you tell me anything else about her? Maybe a boyfriend? Or a job she may have had? If she still lives in town? We've been having trouble trying to locate her."

"Let me see. Taryn, dear, didn't she go out with that football star? Ian Mayer?"

"Yes, for a while. But he dumped her senior year."

"Beverly, do you know where Ian is today? Taryn, we could pay him a visit. You know chat about old times? Maybe he can tell us how to find Nancy Lou. Then we might clear up a few missing pieces."

"He's working for his dad's foreign-car dealership over on Genesee. I believe he married a girl he met at the University of Buffalo, and they have two daughters," Beverly said.

"Great idea, Melissa." Taryn turned to her mom, trying to change the subject. "Mom, did you make that fabulous chocolate cake I love?"

"Of course. How could I not welcome you home without baking your favorite dessert?"

As she passed around plates of cake, Taryn sneaked a peek at her father. "Dad? Something else on your mind?" She was troubled to see him deep in thought. This was her problem, not his.

Knowing him as she did, she should have expected him to want to help any way he could.

"You might say. What makes you think your enemy is someone from Dunkirk? I've lived here all my life. As president of the bank, I know most everyone in town. On the whole, we are a civilized community. I don't know of any scandal that would implicate you? So out with it."

"Bennett, Taryn, along with Arthur and Jesse have been looking into clients and associates of 4G and so far haven't a clue as to how this person can pepper these clips with information that while, patently false, are too close to Taryn's business and personal life. As an outsider I thought that maybe there was a connection to something or someone here in Dunkirk."

"Mom and Dad, it's the only avenue we've yet to explore. I'm sure there's no one from Dunkirk involved. But Melissa is right. We have to check into every person and place that is connected with my life."

"Well then, in addition to checking Ian, why don't you speak to Mr. Brown at the town pharmacy? The kids use to gather at his soda fountain after school. He once told me he had enough gossip to create a comic strip about their goings-on," Bennett offered.

"Shall we adjourn to the living room for coffee?" Beverly said, inviting everyone to the living room. "I want to know more about my daughter's plans for her baby."

"I'm counting on Mom to help me answer what I expect to be an encyclopedia of questions from my husband," Taryn quipped, as everyone laughed. "Anyway, how about a game of bridge? Melissa plays. And maybe with her as my partner, I can win a game or two from you two masters."

CHAPTER 32

Shiny, brightly colored cars were lined up like the dance line of Radio City's Rockettes, in front of a one-story glass-and-chrome building. A tasteful Mayer & Son Auto sign floated above the entrance.

"Greetings, ladies." The handsome, business-suited adult version of Dunkirk High's football star held open the passenger door. Getting out of the driver's side, Taryn leaned over the roof of her Lincoln and gave him a big smile. "It's been a long time, Ian. Still handsome, I see."

"Taryn Cooper? Well, I'll be. What a beauty you turned out to be. I should have waited for you to grow up."

He's certainly turned into quite the charmer, Taryn thought. "Ian, I'd like to introduce my friend, Melissa." Ian promptly, and not too subtly, gave Melissa a through appraisal, followed by a wink.

"Is there some place we can chat? Maybe go over to Brown's for a soda?" Taryn asked.

"Wish I could, but the best I can do right now is take you into my office. Follow me, ladies."

Taryn watched as Ian passed his secretary and asked her to get them coffee. If she weren't mistaken, there might have been a bit more than an employer-and-employee relationship going on. It wasn't what he said; it was the way the girl, almost half his age, frowned as the two women followed her boss into his office.

"Mom told me you went into your dad's business, and since Melissa hasn't been to Dunkirk, I thought I'd introduce her to its high-school all-star."

Taryn noticed he'd bought her praise as his due. *So the leopard hadn't change his spots.*

With coffee and chatter accomplishing nothing, Taryn decided to bring up the reason for their visit. "So, most everyone left Dunkirk after high school?"

"Most went on to college. A few stayed."

"How about your old girlfriend, Nancy Lou? Whatever happened to her?"

"Funny you should bring her up. She stayed in town and went to community college for two years and after graduation disappeared."

"You mean moved away."

"No, Taryn. Disappeared. I run into her mother every once in a while at Benny's Diner, and she has no idea if Nancy Lou is alive or dead."

"I hope nothing's happened to her. You know she worked for our babysitting service."

"She mentioned you were friends when we were dating. But I didn't know that."

"Will you look at the time, Taryn? We promised to pick up that prescription for your mom," Melissa interjected.

Rising, Taryn shook Ian's hand. "It has been fun catching up."

"Don't forget me if you ever need a car." Ian's easy reply showed why he probably sold a lot of cars.

"I won't. Of course you will give me a friendly discount."

"My aim is to please the prettiest girl in Dunkirk High. Good seeing you again, Taryn. And you, Melissa."

⇒⊦ ⊣⇐

The apartment was just the right temperature, nearing sixty-six degrees. Cool enough to keep an overactive mind from melting the writer's body. There was a hole in plans to continue the campaign of fright, followed by destruction. When completed, the need for revenge that had eaten away and prevented finding love, laughter, and simply peace would be gone.

With phone in hand, the number connected. After a bit of social chatter, it was time to get to the reason for the call. "And, while you are at it, can you get me details on the clients who left 4G? You know… was it a problem with fees or dissatisfaction with the return on their investments? Anything you can come up with should be a great help."

"That might take a bit longer. Those records aren't easily available. How soon do you need this? Wasn't the information about that kid at Johns Hopkins enough?"

"You know me. My readers want puzzles in each of my plots. How can the hero save the fair damsel if there isn't some threatening crisis?"

"I'll get back to you when I have something. I wouldn't want to disappoint your readers…or miss that scrumptious four-star dinner you are going to take me to when this manuscript is done."

"Great. I'm counting on you." Finding Adam had been a godsend. His resourcefulness, susceptibility to flattery, not to mention bribery with champagne, vintage wines, and dinners at New York's finest restaurants were cheap at any cost.

With plans for another series of rumor-inspired mailings swirling around in the author's mind, the schedule of activities was filling in quite nicely. Soon the details needed to complete the balance of false news items would be written and ready for mailing. "Ah wine. No, I think it's time for tequila."

CHAPTER 33

M elissa, totally uninterested in Taryn's guided tour through downtown Dunkirk, sat silently, trying to remember if anything Ian had mentioned would suggest that Nancy Lou was behind Taryn's problems. Disappeared? Alive or dead? How would they go about finding out?

"Taryn, you know we should find out if Nancy Lou left town and her present location. Any idea how we might do that?"

"Well, if she died it would have appeared in the newspaper and then Mom would have seen or heard about it. We could check the local church. If memory serves she attended Sunday mass faithfully. It was one of the reasons for her not being able to babysit on Sundays."

"Let's stop by the church and see if she still attends mass."

⇒⋅⇐

"Father Donnelly, I wonder if you can help us. My name is Taryn Cooper Walsh, and this is my friend Melissa Horn. We are trying to locate one of my childhood friends who was a member of your parish."

"Are you related to Bennett Cooper?"

"Yes, Father. I'm his daughter."

"In that case you're like family. I've had occasion to visit your father at the bank. He was always sympathetic and generous. Follow me; the records are in my office."

The dark Victorian furniture included a large round table off to the side of the room. Bookcases lined two walls, and the velvet sofa looked well used. Father Donnelly placed two volumes on the table. "I don't usually let people go through these books. But they contain records of the birth and marriages in my congregation."

"Thank you, Father. We appreciate your trust in us."

Taryn and Melissa reviewed the marriage records from the years of Nancy Lou's presumed high-school graduation to present. After an hour of comparing dates and names, Taryn closed her book. "This isn't getting us anywhere. There is no Nancy Lou of any kind in these records."

"Actually it has. We can now assume she is probably not married." Melissa sat back and gave her friend a satisfied look. "Now, let's try and track her movements since high school. Didn't Ian say she went to community college? That should be our next stop."

⇥⇤

"Mom, would you mind if Melissa and I stayed until Sunday? We need a bit more time tracking down some information."

Beverly Cooper couldn't be more delighted. She hadn't spent as much time as she would have liked since her only child married. "Of course, dear. And I am sure your father would be happy to hear what you've uncovered. We both are very worried about you." Hugging her daughter close, Beverly couldn't hide a sniffle.

"Mom, it will be all right. Promise," Taryn said as she patted her mom's back in comfort.

"Good," Beverly replied, her composure restored. "How about lunch? Ever since your dad retired, he expects his meals scheduled. Lunch promptly at noon, tea or drinks at five, and dinner at six-thirty p.m."

"But you usually lunched at the club with your friends or went shopping in Buffalo. Does he expect you to stay home just because he retired? Did you stop meeting your friends?" Taryn saw a mischievous smile break out on her mom's face, something she couldn't remember seeing before.

"Actually, we've come to an agreement. If I'm going out with my friends, I leave him his lunch. It took some getting used to, but he's adjusted rather well. In fact, he's a wiz at peanut butter and jelly sandwiches."

Taryn's father came home shortly after. "OK, young lady, what have you two dug up so far?" Bennett Cooper said as they sat at the oval dining-room table and passed around the platter of chicken salad.

"Right to the point, Dad? Nothing's changed," Taryn replied with a giggle.

"Dear, why don't you let them eat and save the interrogation for coffee?" Beverly interjected.

"It's all right, Beverly. I think Taryn and I could use some of Bennett's wise counsel," Melissa said softening the mood. "Actually, Beverly, we took your advice and visited Ian Mayer who said Nancy Lou had disappeared from the face of the earth. On a hunch, we visited Father Donnelly." Turning to Bennett, Melissa said, "He asked to be remembered."

"And, Dad, we looked through the church records of marriages and still no sign of Nancy Lou."

"Why is she your primary suspect? While I didn't know the girl, isn't that a bit far-fetched?"

"Dad, I wish I knew. She is the only one on our list that we can't verify. No address or occupation. This is such a small town that alone seems pretty suspicious. If we can at least locate her, then we can rule her out as a suspect. Yet, I can't think of anything I ever did to make her want to ruin me."

"Taryn, let's look at this situation like a puzzle. All the blue pieces go into one pile, the green in another, and so forth," Melissa suggested.

"Clever girl," Bennett said.

"In this case people who may know something about your business and personal life fall into the following groupings: clients, business associates, competitors, social acquaintances, and friends," Melissa said. "During our visit we can at least explore friends from Taryn's childhood."

"Arthur and Jesse have almost completely ruled out business associates. My friends, aside from you and Jesse's pals, are Kathy, Linda, and Ellie. Ellie has contacted our clients and all seem satisfied. That would leave competitors, and aside from a mysterious investor approaching one of our clients, there hasn't been even a hint from that quarter," Taryn said, unaware that her father was staring at her.

"Cookie, there may be something you've forgotten," Bennett began. "You came home from school one day extremely upset. Your mother was off somewhere, and after I settled you down, you told me about an unpleasant scene in Brown's pharmacy. Do you remember?"

"Sorry, Dad, I don't. What did I tell you?"

"You said you had overheard one of your clients complaining about Nancy Lou ignoring the two boys she babysat. That all she did was watch television, and the boys disliked her so much that they found ways to torment her."

"That's why we dropped her from the babysitting service. That couldn't have upset me." Chewing her chicken salad into paste, Taryn suddenly looked up, eyes wide and mouth still. "Oh! I remember something else. Maybe that's what had me so upset."

"Taryn, is it about Nancy Lou?" Melissa asked.

"Yes. Wait." As Taryn swallowed her salad, she turned inward trying to recapture that day during senior year in high school. "We were seniors when I met Nancy Lou at Brown's. She told me that she had been away for six months studying in Italy. I remember thinking that odd since she didn't have the money for a trip of that kind and later at lunch in the school cafeteria mentioning it to the girls. I told them that I had heard she was really in Buffalo at a home for unwed mothers."

"And you didn't share that with anyone else?" Melissa asked. Taryn shook her head. "Did you see her after that?"

"Only once. I ran into her at Brown's a few weeks later. She had changed. The easy-going girl I remembered was curt and stared me into silence. Had no interest in accepting my greeting and evaded any attempt at conversation." Taryn looked up. "That couldn't be behind all this. It was an off-hand remark. I wasn't stating a fact."

"Do you know what happened to her?"

"No. Mom used to keep me up on the local happenings, but she never mentioned Nancy Lou."

"Cookie, do you think that was the incident I remembered having upset you?"

"Oh, Dad. I would hate to think I had been the source of spreading that story. I didn't even know if it was true. The girls and I were obsessed with college applications. You know me; I don't live in the past. I'm always preparing for the future."

"Yes, dear. I always knew where you were and what you were up to. If I didn't get a call from Linda's mom, it would be Kathy's or Ellie's wondering where you were. We still laugh about how serious you all were, although we wished you were thinking about boys and clothes, like we had at your age. Instead here you were crowded in the dining room discussing your babysitting clients and making money, as if you needed to," Beverly said, smiling remembering her memories.

"So, no knowledge of what's become of her, and now a possible personal grudge? Here's what we have to do," Melissa said. Taking out her phone, she began making a list. "First, we need to go to the community college and see if they have any record of her current address. We can also check her major and that may give us a lead on a possible career."

"Ladies, why not check the alumni office and see if she sends an annual donation to the college. They might have more recent information," Bennett suggested. "If she does, then ask if she makes her donations by check or credit card. If check, see if they will give you the bank routing number, and I will track it down and get you a name and location of the bank."

"We can call the college now. It's Saturday, so someone may still be there," Taryn got up and rushed to the phone, and then as she was about to dial, she looked up as Melissa handed over her cell phone.

"Here's the number and address," Melissa said. "Let's just drive over."

Taryn looked at the handset, bewildered. The only time she used a landline was at the office. "Right, Melissa. Thanks."

CHAPTER 34

"Adam," Abigail said, followed by sharing of air kisses, a ritual of the socially superficial. "I am so glad you were free tonight. I just had to see you. I hope you don't mind my having you all to myself."

"Abigail, if it were anyone else I would. You know Larry would join us if he could. When you called, I asked him to meet us here. Unfortunately, he's under the gun at work so probably won't be home until after ten."

"Oh, the poor boy. I hope it isn't trouble."

"No. He's a genius. I'm the slacker. It's just that one of his clients is on deadline. You know what those are like."

"Deadlines, and the threat that if I don't make mine, my agent will skin me alive. In fact that is the reason I had to see you tonight. A deadline and my plot is in trouble. You know what a dummy I am when it comes to finances," Abigail complained.

"Not so dumb. Wasn't your last contract with your publisher for twice the previous one?"

"Tut, tut. Jealous? Wasn't your last year's bonus with the bank the one that purchased your forty-foot sailboat?"

"I have your usual table ready, Mr. Matthews. Follow me." The head waiter led Abigail and Adam to a back corner booth in their usual meeting place, a French restaurant on a side street in the sixties. A bit out of the way and frequented by people wishing to not to be seen by their regular business associates.

"Don't you look fab! New dress? The color is perfect for your coloring. I wish I had your peaches-and-cream complexion. I'd play it to the hilt," Adam said.

"Oh, you flirt. You bring out the best in me. And I did notice your new hairstyle. Longer in the back makes you look like the hero on the cover of one of my romance novels."

Drinks had arrived—their usual waiter knowing their order had set two martinis with olives in front of them and returned shortly with menus.

"We will need some time before we order, Carlos." Left alone Adam raised his glass in a toast. "To friends."

"Friends," Abigail responded and then leaned across the table, drink forgotten. "Now sweetie, here is my problem. I need my character's investment firm to have a small but significant failure but don't know enough about the business to describe it."

"Well, do you want her. I assume it's the same character we've spoken about before, to survive?"

"Yes, but mortally wounded. Then I can get a sequel out of it. My new contract you so love to tease me about has me writing this book as the first of a two-parter. It seems they sell better and offer a possibility down the road to be repackaged as a double volume. So I'm about to wrap this book up and need a dramatic event to tie the plot pieces together."

"Well, you certainly have several problems scattered though out this one. It seems to me that the only area you haven't covered is the failure of one of the funds."

"Ooh, I like that."

"I know of a client who is closing down a couple of their funds. I can't give you the details, but if you order me another drink my caution might slip."

With her well-manicured hand raised, Abigail signaled the waiter for another round of drinks. "Sweetie, could you explain to my somewhat limited mind what that would mean to this firm?"

"Well, the hedge-fund business had been rather dicey lately. If there was a hint that they were closing a couple of their funds that could be significant."

"And the damage?"

"Well, if it was due to investors withdrawing money, it would not only be a financial hit for the firm but a major hit to its reputation."

"Did I ever tell you that I love your mind? It's so colorfully deceitful." Laughter followed, and Adam began to boast about his latest business success in finding companies for the bank's private investor group.

While Abigail pretended to listen by smiling at the right times, she was busy drafting her latest missive in her mind.

CHAPTER 35

Ellie, Linda, and Kathy were seated around the conference table, listening to Taryn's report in total silence. "So you see, Melissa and I did learn something in Dunkirk. But nothing that gets us any closer to identifying the source of these mailings. And we still haven't been able to track down Nancy Lou Harris. Kathy, you remember, she hardly said anything of interest, and if we hadn't invited her to join the babysitting service, we'd probably never have spent any time with her at all. It wasn't as if we were close friends."

"Ms. Cooper," Bobbie said from the doorway, "your dad's on the phone. Do you want me to transfer it in here?"

"Yes, Bobbie. Please."

"Dad? You are on speaker. I'm here with the girls. Did you learn anything about the check's routing number we got from the college alumni office?"

"Yes, it comes from a bank in New York City. But I doubt that will be of any help because all I have is the name of the institution and a list of its branches. In this case all the branches are in New York. Sorry, that's the best I have been able to do."

"At least we now know Nancy Lou is likely alive and living in the city. That narrows the search."

"I'll send you the listing of branches. Maybe one of the locations will trigger something or someone to follow up with. I sincerely doubt any bank will provide information on one of its customers. I know I wouldn't."

"This will help. Thanks, Dad. Love you." Seeing the girls each mouthing a greeting, she added, "And the girls say hi."

"Please give them my best."

"Dad's information confirms one thing. We may still be able to locate Nancy Lou. As for the rest of our Dunkirk information, Melissa and I also stopped by the college admissions office. Their records showed Nancy Lou completed the two-year program and that she majored in English literature. We saw a copy of her yearbook in which she said that she wanted to write romance novels."

Ellie's unaccustomed interrupting surprised the group. "Taryn, do you think she became an author? I love romance novels and have probably read all the popular authors, but I've never come across a Nancy Lou Harris. I know I'd have mentioned it if I had."

"You've been addicted to those since high school, Ellie. And you just gave me an idea." Taryn dialed her home number. "Jesse, can you do us a favor?"

"Sure. I'm taking a break."

"Don't writers have some online directory that locates authors and agents? Would you look up Nancy Lou Harris?"

"Sure…hold on." Looking around the table, Taryn saw what looked like hope written on each face.

"That's odd. Nancy Lou Harris's last update was twenty-four years ago. She's listed as a writer of self-improvement articles primarily for women's magazines."

"Is there an agent mentioned?"

"Nope. There's no phone or address either. She's just listed as a freelancer."

"Thanks, sweetheart. I'll fill you in tonight. Love you."

"Sorry to bother you again," said an agitated Bobbie Klein.

Taryn looked up in surprise seeing her assistant anxiously holding an envelope in a plastic-gloved hand. Long days, last-minute changes, nothing threw Bobbie off her stride, except finding these white envelopes.

"This was in the afternoon mail," Bobbie said.

With a resigned look, Taryn took a deep breath. "Bobbie, will you bring me a pair of gloves? Then let's see what your little gift has to say."

Bobbie had come prepared, and entering the room, she handed her boss a new pair of plastic gloves. Taryn looked at the expectant faces of her lifelong friends, and taking the envelope from Bobbie, she slit it open. "Let's see what dishonest incident I'm guilty of now."

"Taryn, you didn't do anything, Kathy said, as Linda and Ellie nodded in agreement. "This is probably more lies from someone targeting you for ruin."

The now familiar page with FYI scrawled on the upper left corner of a photocopied news clip looked identical to the previous ones. Taryn cleared her throat before reading it aloud. "4G is set to close down one if its funds. Is that due to a new round of client withdrawals?"

The silence in the room was electric.

"Bobbie, would you get Melissa on the line?" Taryn said, pleased that at least she sounded in control.

Bobbie quickly dialed in Melissa Horn's office number and the room waited for someone to answer. "Ms. Cooper, if you don't need me, I'll go back to the office."

"Sure, Bobbie. I'll see you later."

While she waited for Melissa to get on the line, Taryn, thinking aloud said, "You know, this is the fifth such message that has contained elements that no one outside our small group would be aware of."

FYI

"Taryn, have you been followed? Is your office phone tapped? Has your laptop been hacked? I can get a friend to check, and if there has been a leak, maybe he can trace it," Ellie said.

"Arthur does a sweep of all office systems regularly. In addition, my guy has placed alerts on each of our office computers and updates me of any breaches," Linda said.

"Melissa," Taryn said. "I've got you on speaker and am with Ellie, Linda, and Kathy. I'm calling because I've just received another too-close-for-comfort news clip." As she read the text to Melissa, Taryn thought this had to come from one of 4G's independent contractors. Lawyer, accountant, broker? She'd run this by Arthur, then Jesse, after the meeting.

Melissa's voice was heard clearly over the tabletop speaker. "Yes, and I may have a way to track down our leak. Can you, Jesse, and I meet after work?"

"Sure. I'll call him now. Six at our place." Taryn clicked off the phone and her mind returned to the puzzle of Nancy Lou Harris. As she drummed her fingers on the table, she remembered her conversation with her dad about meeting Nancy Lou in Brown's. "Will each of you try to remember anything from school that would suggest Nancy Lou has some grudge against me? Maybe she said something to you that was a bit odd."

"Still worried about Nancy Lou? Why? She wasn't evil. Just a bit of a nuisance," Kathy said.

"I know, but why would she drop off the face of the earth? Especially if she had nothing to hide? That's the one thing that keeps coming back to me," Taryn said. "Enough. Now we have to find the 4G leak. I'm going to speak to Arthur. Call me if you get any fresh ideas."

Taryn got up to leave, noticing that no one stopped her, each lost in their own thoughts.

As soon as she returned to her desk, Taryn phoned Arthur. "We had another FYI special delivery. Jesse, Melissa, and I are going to

175

meet at my apartment this evening at six. Our latest mailing says we are losing investors. I'm furious. We're doing better than most firms our size. And we're signing new clients. I asked Ellie only a few days ago if anyone was unhappy. She said we lost a couple of clients but not for any reason connected with our performance. Is my office bugged?"

"Calm down, Taryn. I'll call our specialist and have him sweep the offices tonight."

"Arthur, I'd feel better if you'd join us at six p.m. I know Jesse would appreciate it. I certainly would. Next to Ellie, you know each of our clients better than I do."

"Certainly. But I want to be here when the offices are checked for bugs. So, look for me closer to six-thirty."

Relieved that the people she trusted would be there to offer their ideas and assistance, Taryn began closing down for the day. It would be a stressful evening, and her stomach was already protesting. She opened her desk drawer and took out a couple of soda crackers. As she nibbled, Taryn's thoughts turned inward and patting her stomach felt a bit calmer. Her mom's suggestion to keep the crackers nearby had helped.

⇥ ⇤

Romance novelist? Mmm…let me check my notes. Ellie, as meticulous in habit as in her appearance, pulled her reading diary from one of two living room bookcases. She had been keeping a record of every book she'd read since high school. Her entries included both fiction (written in green) and nonfiction (written in blue) and had a couple of sentences on plot, style, author's background, and an asterisk if she liked the work of an author enough to read another of their books.

OK—no Nancy of any kind listed. Let's see what I've written about each of the authors. Reviewing each notation marked in green brought a favorite novel by that author to mind. While not having a photo-graphic memory, Ellie did have a passion for romance, and usually one book by each author had imprinted itself in her memory. In fact some books she'd reread seven or eight times…those times when she couldn't get to sleep. By rereading a favorite book, she could fall asleep when her eyes grew tired and not be pulled to find out what happened next.

That's funny! I had written something about each author but don't have even one personal note about Abigail Lang. All I've written were the titles of books I gave a five-star rating. Puzzled, Ellie needed more information. She'd kept all books she'd given a four-and five-star rating. The rest she'd donated to her local library. Ellie looked for authors whose style was similar to Abigail Lang and pulled a book by three different authors and one by Abigail Lang from the shelf.

Well, well. All book jackets, except for Abigail Lang's, featured a small photo and brief bio of the author. Abigail Lang's book cover was a dramatic photo representing the hero and heroine on horseback, but when she checked the back cover, Ellie found a simple listing of her previous books along with excerpts of reviews by notable romance authors and book reviewers.

CHAPTER 36

Having just hung up from sharing the author listings with Taryn, Jesse was jarred by the ringing phone. "Yes?"

"No pleasant hello?"

The shock of Sharon's cloying voice drove thoughts of Taryn's problems out of his mind. "Sharon. What now?"

"I haven't heard from you even though I gave you a whole month instead of days to get back to me."

"I guess you found another sucker to pay your debts."

"Well, in a manner of speaking I have. So this time, prick, you are going to do me a favor, and it isn't money. You are going to take me to a financial dinner."

"You are certifiable. Why would I go near you?"

"Because, my dear ex-husband, I have told this man I'm going to marry how nice a divorce we've had. And, of course, how important I was to starting your career."

"And I'll tell him about going into hoc to get rid of your scheming ass."

"I don't think you will, sugar pie. You see, the man I'm interested in is your wife's attorney. It wouldn't look good for him to know what a louse you've been."

Should he tell her that her next money pot is probably gay? No. It's more fun for her to figure that out for herself. In his smoothest voice, he advised, "You don't need me, Sharon. Show him that you need his sage advice. Flatter his brains. I'm sure you know how to do that. Anyway, you have other charms. You don't need to drag an ex-husband with you."

"Don't you want to know where I got the money?"

"No."

"From Charlie. He always liked me."

"The same man you cheated on me with? Figures." Nothing his ex did could surprise him.

"You left me alone night after night, studying!" she screeched. "Charlie was there to cheer me up."

"So you reunited for money? You do realize what that makes you," Jesse said.

"Shut up!"

"Anyway Sharon, you're now his problem. Don't call again." Hanging up, Jesse's laughter spilled over. This is the best form of revenge. And I didn't have to do a thing.

Work forgotten, Jesse grabbed a sweatshirt and headed for the gym. His fast jog around the track was fueled by the bubbling of laughter, lightening each and every step.

CHAPTER 37

"Holy shit!" Staring at the wet stringy hair, wrinkles, and dark circles under her eyes, Abigail saw herself as she appeared throughout high school—an all-beige visage with no outstanding features.

After three flu-ridden days, the shower was meant to revive her. She had to begin work on her next novel. Instead, the face staring back from the misted medicine cabinet mirror was one she had been avoiding ever since leaving home to make it big in Manhattan.

The shock had her envisioning bits and pieces of her teenage life. Sleepovers at Taryn Cooper's house. Sharing sodas after school at Brown's with the girls. Being known for getting top grades in all her classes, except for gym. But that didn't count because she was one of the in-group.

And that party senior year. Accompanying Ian, celebrating the last football game of the season. For the first time in memory, her mother had given her enough money to purchase a new dress at the local department store. And along with the money was her left-handed compliment that she never believed her daughter would attract anyone, especially not the high-school hunk.

With thoughts of that evening fresh as yesterday, Abigail envisioned her younger self—having felt like a princess, everyone complimenting her on her dress, and afterward the steamy evening in Ian's car. The evening was also special because for the first time she had been partying with Ian Mayer's friends. They were the school athletes. Ian, the star quarterback. He always said he hadn't wanted to share her with anyone. He was afraid that his teammates would try to take her away from him. But that evening Ian had stayed with her, and she had felt so very special.

Reality returned when she remembered the abrupt way the evening had ended. It was after midnight when Ian let her off at her house and gave her his news. What was it he said? "Nancy Lou, we're through. I've got a scholarship to Buffalo and am going to have a new group of friends. I can't have you hanging around."

Hanging around! Someone to fuck was what he meant.

Wrapping herself in a big terry robe, she tried to still the ghosts that still haunted her twenty years later. What she needed was something to help remember all her successes.

Going to her bedroom closet, she reached up to the top shelf and pulled down her senior yearbook. As she thumbed through pages of candid photos of high-school plays and football games, she noticed that aside from her senior-year portrait, the only other picture of her appeared with the staff of the school newspaper. *Well, I was editor three years in a row.* Where were all those photos at lunch in the cafeteria, surrounded by the ever-popular Cooper and her friends? At football games cheering the team on. Throwing the book on the floor, Abigail retreated to her overly large upholstered chair.

I was part of Taryn Cooper's tight circle of friends. We went everywhere together. Then they just dropped me as if I never existed. Come to think of it, we never double dated. Ian kept me all to himself. Was Cooper after him? Is that why she dropped me from the babysitting business? I needed the money. Damn it. Didn't she know that I didn't have a rich daddy to buy my school clothes?

Come to think of it, everything changed in senior year. I was shunned. Laughed at as if they thought I couldn't hear them calling me town trash.

Well, now she was Abigail Lang, the successful author of romance novels living the life of one of New York's rich and famous. She remembered that first royalty check for $25,000. It was more money than she ever thought she'd see at one time.

Money helped her turn dowdy Nancy Lou into sophisticated, slim, and mysterious Abigail Lang. Her first major expenditure was a plastic surgeon who, with medical magic, refined her puffy features into a face of sharp cheekbones and defined jaw. The new face was further enhanced by compulsive dieting and exercise so that her once size twelve was now a fashionable size six.

Then her mind focused on the worm in the apple: Taryn Cooper. Fear had changed Nancy Lou from a regular outgoing teen to cloistering herself away from others. She could still feel the shame of becoming pregnant and having Ian's baby. Not that she had ever told him to man up and marry her. Not after he two-timed her with that tramp of a cheerleader, Brenda.

No one would have known about the baby if Cooper hadn't been overheard by Barbara Brewer the class gossip. She would simply have returned to high school after delivering the baby, tell everyone she had been studying in Italy, and resumed her activities. But instead, that bitch ruined everything when she overheard Cooper whispering to her friends that I hadn't been in Italy, but in Buffalo, at a home for unwed mothers.

The liquor cabinet called. The tequila shot accompanied her memories flashing before her like clips from an old movie. A second shot couldn't dim the pain of having been pitied and shunned by the very people who had been her friends.

She marked that event as the beginning of her retreat into the safety of her own private world. Instead of trying for a scholarship out of state, she lived at home working at the local restaurant and attending night classes at the local community college. The day she received her diploma, she fled Dunkirk leaving Nancy Lou behind.

The intervening years had been focused on building a career. While writing her first romance novel, she paid her rent writing for a neighborhood paper, and on occasion, for the women's magazines. All her articles featured self-improvement themes, most of the research based on her ongoing efforts to attain perfection. Hands down, her best creation was Abigail Lang, the mysterious romance author adored by millions of readers. As dazzling a creation as she was, fear of her past shame becoming known drove her…privacy had become an obsession.

Life would have continued being the best invention in her creative mind, until ten years ago when she had learned that Taryn holier-than-thou Cooper had opened a hedge fund. At first she had been amazed to see the name of someone she had gone to school with featured in the *New York Times*. But with each milestone Taryn Cooper reached, Abigail's anger grew. When she'd read that Taryn had married, the dam burst. How does she deserve to find love, let alone a husband?

Taryn Cooper was queen of Dunkirk High. Ian had always followed her with his eyes, even before he dropped her cold. Then she dropped her from the babysitting service. No longer invited her to sleepovers or Brown's for sodas. Well, too late. What mattered was that someone she had considered to be her best friend had ruined her life.

Enough! The campaign was in play. Her plans detailed on spreadsheets, itemizing the dates and timing of each phase of the roll-out. Another tequila shot and she relaxed, smiling like a Cheshire Cat. Revenge was after all just like plotting one of her novels.

The ringing phone brought her back to the present. "Yes?"

"Abigail, it's Samuel."

"And you want me to dress and meet you at the Mandarin?"

"Not today. I'm calling to read you the latest sales figures for your recent title."

Shit. If he's calling and not scheduling an expense-account lunch, it must be bad news. "Yes?" She asked, silently worrying that her career was on the wane.

"Well, book sales are off by five percent. We commissioned a focus group. The results suggested that your sex is all fire and no sensitivity."

"Sensitivity? Have you read the fan mail? They love my books because I give them lots of raw passion. It's something missing in their everyday humdrum lives."

"Look Abigail, you are scheduled to deliver your new manuscript later this month. Why not reread it for sensitivity?"

"Are you telling me my contract is in jeopardy?"

"Of course not. Abigail, you know how important you are to this company. Your books are the central display in book stores and airports across the country. I am just saying that maybe you need to adjust the sex by adding more love."

"As a man you would know how women think of sex?" She had calmed down, knowing that in Samuel's case as a man nearing eighty, he was limited by his age and the death of the love of his life, his wife of almost a half century.

"I've enjoyed being your publisher for these past dozen years. I've read and enjoyed each and every relationship between a man and woman you've created. Just think about this, please. I am in the midst of planning a marketing budget. Before I feel comfortable about spending our usual sizable amount, I want you to take another look at love and passion and then sex. Then the marketing team can prepare the appropriate copy."

"I'm just tired, Samuel. This flu has gotten me down. I will reread and reconsider everything you are and are not telling me. Promise."

"Very good. Get well. We need you."

Abigail knew Samuel wasn't going to be a problem. She'd change a word here and there, and he'd be happy. *What I need is inspiration, like watching a really soppy movie.* The rack of old films contained favorites of the thirties and forties…when sex was implied, not shown. Perfect, she thought as she pulled down a DVD of *Queen Christina* with Greta Garbo and John Gilbert. "Ah! That and a bit more tequila will restore my creative juices."

First, a trip to the bathroom. To her delight, Abigail was looking back from the mirror. The panic had subsided. Her career would be fine. Her soul-tormenting anger would be avenged. It was justified. *A life for a life.*

CHAPTER 38

Taryn had invited Melissa and Arthur to the apartment to continue discussing the looming crisis. She knew that Jesse had been in touch with both and wanted to know the status of their efforts. Had they found a leak at 4G? Were they any closer to finding the person behind the disturbing news items?

"I found a link between Laurence Swinburne and Adam Matthews. A friend of my vintage has seen them together at a couple of the more private gay clubs. Anyway, he assures me that Laurence is totally smitten with Adam to the point of allowing him to charge all food and drink to his account. The man makes a six-figure salary, plus bonus. He certainly can pay his drink bill," Arthur reported.

"This is the first positive link into the Laurence Swinburne-Adam Matthews relationship," Jesse said with relief. "Now, Arthur, how do we make sure Laurence is as innocent as you believe?"

"Melissa, do you, in your wide universe of acquaintances, have any familiarity with this circle of New Yorker?" Jesse asked. "I certainly don't."

"Right, but you work at home so how would you even know if one of your contacts was straight or gay?" Taryn giggled.

"Jesse, I am one of their favorite escorts," Melissa's amusement evident in her reply. "Why would I care if a business acquaintance was gay? He won't hit on me. He's usually cultured, intelligent, and knows the best restaurants. Hey, this is New York. Anyway, who cares?"

The four friends had been nibbling on appetizers since 6:00 p.m. when Taryn decided to take a break. "Look, just chat among yourselves. I'll go into the kitchen and see what I can whip up in the way of real food."

"No, please have pity," Melissa begged.

Laughing at the shock on his wife's face, Jesse got up, gave her a deep kiss, and pushed her back to the sofa. "Not to worry, I thought ahead. Pasta all around. Is that all right with you, Arthur?"

"Yes," Arthur and Melissa said in unison.

"Ha-ha," Taryn replied. "I got the message when I first learned Jesse was a chef disguised as a financial columnist."

Over dinner, Taryn had sat quietly listening to theories and next steps, wondering how to tell them her latest fear, that she was being followed. That every time she left home or the office her skin prickled, even though she never saw anything or anyone out of the ordinary.

When the dishes had been scrapped clean, coffee sat cooling in half-finished cups and silence echoed around the room. Taryn watched Melissa reviewing her handwritten notes, while Arthur and Jesse were focused on some inner debate.

"Jesse and I have to take Laurence out for drinks," Arthur announced. His outburst returned everyone else to the task at hand. When Taryn was about to jump in, he shook his head. "This is a man's thing, Taryn. I personally need to know if the attorney I've worked with for the past decade is taking drugs or changed in any way to make him capable of turning on 4G. We are one of his most important clients and pay him a hefty fee for his services as well as his discretion."

"How can we continue to have him represent 4G when his lover is being cavalier with our very livelihood?" Taryn asked.

"Taryn, don't rush to conclusions. Laurence may not even be aware of Adam's duplicity. And if I am any judge of character, he won't be pleased when he learns that his partner is dishonorable. Remember, Adam not only tried to undermine 4G by approaching Reggie and offering to invest in his research, but if he is the leak, his actions could ruin Laurence's reputation as a trustworthy attorney. Leave it to Jesse and me."

"Then what am I supposed to do?" Taryn cried. "It's my life, reputation, and business on the line. I can't just sit quietly and wait. Not when I think I'm being followed." Taryn, surprised by her outburst, sat hugging her arms, trying to protect herself from her newest fear. "There, another mystery. I'm a target even in my own home. How else would they know where I lived if I hadn't been followed?"

Taryn saw Jesse give Melissa a nod. "Taryn," Melissa said reaching across the table to clasp her hand. "You were followed for a couple of days last week. But I was the one who hired the tail."

"What?" Taryn almost screamed. "Why?"

"Jesse and I met to share our thoughts and discussed the possibility that someone was following you. We were worried about your safety. I know someone who helped me with a difficult situation and asked him to follow you and photograph anyone he thought suspicious. He wasn't to approach you or let you see him. Just to see if you were safe."

"And?" Taryn asked, once again all business.

"And no, you weren't followed. But why not follow Adam and see who he meets when he isn't with Laurence?"

"I like that idea," Jesse said, his eagerness shared with the others.

Melissa took her pen and crossed that item off her list. "This time I am going to request photos of anyone Adam meets after he leaves the bank. It's a long shot if Adam is always with Laurence. But I think it's worth a try."

"You're leaving me out of this decision, just like my not being capable of joining you men at lunch? Like some lame-brain!" Taryn grumbled.

"Taryn, stop it now!" Jesse snapped. "Melissa's contact may just find the missing link. And Arthur wasn't being patronizing. He merely believes that getting Laurence to talk freely at lunch would be easier if you weren't there. You can't help in either situation, and you know it."

Taryn needed to take back control. So far, the evening's conversation was driven by everyone else. "I was going to call Susan to begin work on a marketing campaign. Of course, only after all of our papers were filed, and Laurence had officially registered us with regulatory agencies. When this latest FYI arrived, I held off," Taryn said. "The fewer people who are aware of our activities the better. And if 4G does begin to lose clients, well, we won't need Susan's skills, will we?" Taryn snapped. "But damn it you are all treating me like a weakling," she cried.

"Taryn Cooper Walsh. I've know you since you were eight years old, and you have never in all that time given up on anything. Now is not the time," Arthur declared.

Arthur's rebuke found its mark. Taryn knew he was right, but he made her feel like a kid. It echoed of something her father would have said after she had gone too far. Deflated, she sank more deeply into the sofa, trying to hide her misery from the others. Unaware of the now silent room, Taryn was surprised when Jesse picked her up and held her close. Feeling safe his arms released her defenses and with it tears.

Melissa closed her eyes. It was too private for her to witness. Then leaning over to Arthur, she whispered, "I'll call you tomorrow once I've engaged my contact to follow Adam. Maybe for now, we can work together. Jesse and Taryn need to have time to just be a married couple with a family on the way."

"Agreed. For Taryn it's no longer just business. Now that she's pregnant, she needs to lean on Jesse to help her navigate both parts of her world," Arthur added.

⊨ ⊨

The apartment was quiet. Jesse had tucked his wife into bed and prayed that this latest upset hadn't caused harm to her or the baby. Dimming the bedroom lights, he was about to leave when Taryn stopped him.

"Sweetheart, would you mind sitting with me?"

"Oh, Taryn," Jesse moaned, rushing to her side. Hugging her close, he whispered, "I'm here." Pulling back and studying his wife for a clue to her state of mind, he saw a new resolve, a look he knew meant full steam ahead. Whatever had gone on in her mind from the time she broke down in tears to now had been a journey of courage. He wanted to support her. Fight *with* her. But definitely not leave her to fight alone.

"Jesse, I am not quitting on myself or the firm. I'm just over-wrought, probably helped by raging hormones. Arthur and Melissa think we may have a lead to identifying the source of the leaks. Until Melissa gathers proof, we can't move forward."

Taryn saw Jesse's love and strength. "In the meantime, I am going to finalize the new firm's structure, identify potential investors, and begin to draft a marketing approach."

"That's the fighter I married," Jesse said, and hugging her tight, he noticed her color returning along with the determined set of her mouth. *It was a quick recovery*, he thought, *after her earlier mood of self-doubt.* In all their time together, he could count the number of times he witnessed a breach in his wife's iron will on one hand.

"And if that isn't enough work to distract you, I know a few ways to help."

It didn't take much for Taryn to fall into Jesse's kiss. He was hypnotic. The taste of his lips always elicited shivers.

"Please don't stop." As Taryn's arms wound around her husband's neck, she moved her hands and with the softest of touches felt his body move to place his sensitive spots directly under her fingers.

"When you kiss me like that, I'm mindless." Taryn's mouth became greedy for more.

Once shed of his clothes, Jesse stretched out, his bare body pressed into his still-clothed wife. With a slight adjustment in position, he gently unbuttoned her blouse, reached for her bra, and having unhooked it, he moved the cloth aside. The sight of her full breasts drew him to touch, caress, and hunger for the feel of her against his bare skin. With a practiced tug on her slacks and thumbs hooked on the waist of her panties, Taryn lay exposed to his gaze. "Oh, so beautiful." Lightly stroking both breasts, he placed his mouth on a nipple and began to suckle. Hearing Taryn's uneven breathing, Jesse leaned back, kneeling over her quivering form, and with soft brushing of his fingertips resumed caressing her breasts. "I am going to have to share these soon. I wonder if I'll mind."

Taryn pushed Jesse over on his back. "It's all your fault. So if it bothers you, maybe you should prepare for the future?" She laughed as Jesse repositioned himself on top of his spirited wife.

"What a good idea." His suckling led to stroking over her rounded stomach, followed by a fluttering of light kisses and whispering his love to the baby she carried. As his fingers moved downward, touching, circling, and caressing the soft hair hiding her passageway from sight, Jesse leaned in with his mouth, first tasting, and following with his tongue flicking in and out, taking his time in exploring her growing moistness. No longer languid he entered his wife and began his slow in and out strokes, elated by her rousing excitement. With her eyes closed, Taryn began a slow circling of her hips, increasing in pace that matched his intensity. Lost in emotion they moved with increasing rhythm, their growing heat leading to ultimately attaining release. Breathless, limbs entwined, Jesse watched his wife as her limp body melted into his. What had his life been before this enigmatic nymph? He was going to make sure that no one would harm her or their growing child.

CHAPTER 39

"Jimmy, thank you for working so quickly. I never thought you'd be able to find Adam Matthews and follow him so closely."

Melissa was once again visiting Jimmy at his office in Kearney's Bar. She had made a quick visit only three days before with instructions, a photo of Adam Matthews, supplied by Arthur, along with his home and business addresses.

"He's an easy mark. You might want to take a look and see if you need anything more?"

"Right. I guess I am afraid of what I'll find."

Opening the envelope, Melissa found several eight-by-ten photos of Adam with Laurence Swinburne at one club after another. "This is a usual night on the town?"

"So it seems. This guy can't stay out of the gay-bar scene. Although in his case, he favors small, discreet watering holes."

One photo was of a cocktail lounge where Adam sat with a well-dressed woman wearing the latest Carolina Herrera suit. Melissa knew that particular suit because she had stopped by her favorite boutique and tried it on. The style, not to mention price, placed

Adam's companion in the upper tier of New York's wealthier inhabitants. Studying the photo for clue as to who this person was, Jimmy reached over and handed her a name and address.

"How? You followed her?"

"You already knew where to find Matthews. I thought this could be important. It was the only woman he saw all the while I followed him. The rest of the time he was with his boyfriend. After they left, I asked the bar tender if she was a regular. He said not a regular; she only came in when meeting Matthews."

"Did you happen to find out anything else about this mystery woman?"

"Her name is Abigail Lang, and she writes those pot boilers."

Little nerves coursed through her as Melissa remembered something about Nancy Lou's college year-book entry. Didn't she say she wanted to write romance novels? Could it be the missing Nancy Lou transformed herself into a noted romance novelist?

"Jimmy, here is a little extra. For your creativity and speed. I appreciate your help in this little matter. Really." Melissa stood and shook Jimmy's outstretched hand, and with a smile, she turned and left the bar. Once in her car, she phoned Jesse. "Are you available? Can I stop by now?"

"Of course. Do you want me to call Taryn to join us?"

"Yes, and Arthur if he can. See you in a few minutes."

<hr/>

"Ellie, do you have a few minutes to stop up?"

"Sure, Jesse. Do you want me to stop by and pick up Taryn?"

"Good idea. Tell her that Melissa is coming over with her associate's report."

Thirty minutes later, Taryn rushed into the apartment and threw her handbag and briefcase on the hall table. Hearing Jesse's and Melissa's voices, she headed for the library with Ellie close behind. "OK, what did you find out?" Breathless, Taryn stood, waiting for someone to tell her why she rushed home at midday.

"Ellie, Taryn, let's go to the table. I want to show you the photographs Jimmy took. His assignment was to follow Adam, but bless his heart, he also followed someone Adam met."

Melissa spread a dozen photos on the table, and Taryn and Ellie handed them back and forth after studying them. "What am I supposed to see?" Taryn asked.

"Does the woman look even a bit familiar?" Melissa saw Ellie look to Taryn, eyebrows raised in question.

Neither seemed to recognize the stylish woman in deep conversation with Adam Matthews.

"I think this is your missing Nancy Lou." Melissa's voice while low sent vibrations through Taryn.

"How can you be so sure? This is a very attractive woman, well dressed and certainly seems self-confident. Nancy Lou was the exact opposite," Taryn said.

"Do you have a name?" Ellie asked.

"Yes, she's a popular romance author, Abigail Lang."

"Shit," was Ellie's unaccustomed response.

"Ellie?" Having rarely heard Ellie curse, Taryn was more worried than shocked. "Do you know who Abigail Lang is?"

"Yes. You know that since high school I've kept a diary of each and every book I had ever read, even partially read. My notations also include a bit of information on the authors. That's just in case one was going to appear at a reading of their latest book."

"And?" Melissa asked, hoping Ellie had more than verifying a name for them.

"And the publicity associated with each of these authors usually tells something of their backgrounds...all except for Abigail Lang. It seems that someone decided to keep her likeness and personal history a secret, probably thinking it would create an air of mystery that readers of romance novels all love."

"There isn't even one photo?"

"Nope. The other night when I couldn't sleep, I reviewed my diary and each of the authors of books I've read. There was nothing in her section except a listing of previous titles. So when I got to the office today, I did a search on her publisher's website, and in all the publicity they posted, there wasn't one scrap of personal information on their famous author."

"You wouldn't have cursed because of not finding anything about someone we hadn't even known about. What else bothered you?" Jesse asked.

"I thought I had made a mistake when reviewing the list of her books. I made a note that she mentioned the Kimmelweck. Taryn, you know that was my favorite sandwich roll in school. I've never even heard it mentioned outside of Dunkirk."

"This couldn't be a coincidence. Not with Adam being one of her friends. If Laurence talks in his sleep or leaves papers out for Adam to see, that would explain how those news items were so close to the truth," Melissa said.

"OK, keep this to yourselves. Arthur and I still have to meet with Laurence. Maybe he knows something about Abigail." Turning to his wife, he could see she was itching for a fight. "Honey." Not getting her attention, Jesse placed his hands on his wife's shoulders, forcing her to look at him. "Patience. Now is not the time to go off on your own. Without proof we can't let anyone know what we suspect. So why don't you, Melissa, Arthur, Ellie, Linda, and Kathy try and figure out how we can pressure this *creature* into stopping her campaign to destroy you before it becomes public."

"You're right, Jesse. With Ellie's fondness for drama, Linda's for organization, Kathy's online research capabilities, and Melissa's legal background, we should be able to develop an airtight defense. I mean attack!"

CHAPTER 40

Knowing Laurence Swinburne's love of a good steak, Arthur had booked reservations in a quiet area of Spark's midtown restaurant, requesting a private table for three. Arriving early, he greeted Jesse, and they were directed to a corner booth off to one side of the main dining room.

"Arthur, I've been going over and over this in my mind and haven't a clue how to proceed. I only know the man socially, and conversation, while pleasant, certainly hasn't given me any insight into him as a man or attorney."

"Don't worry, Jesse. Just back me up. I remember what to do after all those years when working for Taryn's father at the bank. He trained me to listen and drop a word here and there to get the client talking. Bennett Cooper was a genius at this, and usually the person revealed more than he or she intended."

Arthur and Jesse stood and shook hands with a well-tailored Laurence Swinburne as he joined them at the table. With Arthur and Jesse having already picked up their napkins, Laurence slid into the center seat in the corner booth.

"Gentlemen, this is a pleasure. A man's luncheon. I assume that this is on the 4G's expense account," Laurence said, with a twinkle in his eyes. "I am looking forward to enjoying a medium-rare rib eye and all the trimmings and of course your company," Laurence added.

The waiter handed menus all around and asked for their drink orders.

"I'll have a Heineken," Jesse said. "A glass of your house red," Arthur added, and seeing Jesse's surprise, he said, "I don't usually drink at lunch but since we are all men, I am making an exception." As Laurence ordered the same, the mood of conviviality continued.

Conversation resumed after a brief look at the menu, each man already knowing what he wanted to order. Arthur signaled the waiter over. "I think we're ready. Laurence, why don't you start?"

"I am looking forward to your rib eye, medium-rare, creamed spinach, and a salad with your Roquefort dressing."

Arthur noted their quarry was in a social mood. *So far so good.* "A sirloin, medium for me, and just the house salad."

"And I'll have the baby-lamb chops, medium-rare, and creamed spinach." Jesse handed his menu to the waiter, and sipping his beer, he looked to Laurence. "I know Taryn would love to see me wearing a shirt like yours. She sees you in your Savile Row's finest and comes home to an aging high-school athlete."

"Ah, women and fashion," Laurence replied as he took out a leather note pad no larger than a business card, and pulling out a small gold pen, began writing. "Here is the name of my sales rep at Paul Stuart. Tell him I sent you." Handing the card to Jesse, Laurence gave him a once over. "Your suit doesn't look like it was purchased by an aging athlete. If I were to guess, it was custom-made here in New York."

"Caught. But I didn't pick it out. My wife insisted I dress for one of her business functions and took me in hand."

"You are a lucky man. While she is a client, she is one of my favorites. Polite, easy on the eye, and has been loyal to this lawyer from the beginning."

"Easy on the eye?"

"Yes, I may have other interests, but it is more pleasant to work with attractive people. Don't you think so Arthur?"

Arthur chuckled. "I totally agree with you, but I have the edge where Jesse's wife is concerned. We go way back."

"I know you are the silent partner in 4G, but ten years isn't way back," Laurence said, and was startled as both Jesse and Arthur broke out in laughter. "What am I missing?"

"She was my client when she was eight years old." The stunned expression on Laurence's face was priceless. "I am afraid you are a new-comer to her fan club."

After the meals were served, conversation over the sound of knives cutting into fork-tender meat revolved around the local politics. Arthur, taking advantage of Laurence being well sated with food, set down his flatware. "Jesse, don't you and Taryn have an anniversary coming up?"

Jesse noted the slight change in Arthur's expression, not quite flinty, but definitely firm. *Here we go.* "Yes. Our fifth is coming up in three months. You know Arthur, with everything going on with the baby, this may be the only time we can really do a blowout celebration."

"Baby?" Laurence asked.

"I hope you won't say anything for a while. Taryn is a bit superstitious. She wants to keep it private until at least her fifth month."

"Of course, but how absolutely marvelous. That will certainly change your lives."

"Weren't you married once?" Arthur asked.

"Not very happily, I'm afraid. So children would have been the very last thing on my mind."

"I'm sorry. Were you married long?" Jesse, not knowing the man, was surprised to learn he had once been married.

"Yes and no. Long in aggravation and short in time. It was while I was in law school, and the pressure of wanting to not only graduate close to top of my class but hopefully with honors had me totally focused on myself. Jane thought I should be focused on her."

"You have my sympathies," Jesse replied, thinking of his own first-marriage problems.

"Well, that and other things made me take a real good look at my life. Did I want to live it encumbered with wife and family, or did I want to experience all that my hard-earned salary would provide? Coming from very modest means, I was drawn to a life only available with money."

In the few times he'd talked to this man, there was never anything personal mentioned. Not sports he played or followed, nor theater. Nothing except the world of business. "And a successful career you've earned with plain hard work," Jesse added.

"Yes, but I do have my friends. I must say they aren't nearly as demanding as a wife."

Jesse thought, *not yet. Just wait until Sharon gets her hooks into you. I wonder who will cry uncle first.* "Arthur, I think I am going to have dessert. Laurence, could you find room and join me?" Jesse said, wanting to change the subject. He wasn't planning to share his personal history with a man yet to be identified friend or foe.

"If they have that scrumptious chocolate dessert, count me in."

"Working at home I usually have a sandwich for lunch, so I am glad Arthur asked me to join you two. Since all my professional lunches are with women, you and Laurence are making this a special treat," Jesse said.

Arthur, sipping his coffee, was pleased that Laurence had mentioned his earlier marriage. "You know, gentlemen, I was thinking that Jesse should arrange for a private anniversary celebration at their home in Connecticut. Taryn wouldn't have to know about it. Since she's gearing up for the new venture, she'd want to stay in the city. And Jesse, didn't you tell me you have a new project?

Couldn't you use that as an excuse to move up to the country for a few days?"

"I really don't want to leave Taryn right now, but by then she will be nearing her eighth month, and should be a bit more settled. So, yes, I could run up for a couple of days," Jesse replied and looking at Laurence, he noticed a bit of interest. "You know, if a wedding anniversary doesn't remind you of bad times, Laurence, why don't you plan on joining us? Bring a friend. I don't think we would have more than," looking over to Arthur, "say a dozen people?"

"That would be wonderful. What a welcomed invitation. Imagine, a happy marriage. I would enjoy celebrating yours."

"Something else, Laurence," Arthur said. "I've been hearing a bit about 4G from the oddest people. We have worked together since the beginning and know all the same people connected to our new venture. Would you have any idea how these people found out about our new business plans?"

Unaware of Arthur's change in tone of voice, Laurence sat amiably considering his question as he swallowed his last mouthful of dessert. Focused on its flavor, Laurence replied, "I can't imagine anyone in my office would dare share information about a client. Arthur, you've met my executive assistant, Gerald. He's the definition of safe and secure."

"Wasn't he an attorney with the army?" Arthur asked.

"Yes, during Vietnam."

"How about socially?" Jesse asked.

The table grew strangely quiet as Laurence put down his dessert fork and turned inward. Arthur and Jesse sat still, anxiously awaiting his response.

"Maybe you left some papers out and someone took a quick read?" Jesse suggested.

"Come to think of it, I did bring the registration papers home. I wanted to review them before sending them to Arthur. You know, give them a triple read."

"When was that? The information I have goes back almost two months," Arthur added, keeping an even tone.

A startled look crossed Laurence's handsome features, followed by a quick intake of breath.

"This is serious, Laurence. You know there can't be anymore leaks until we are ready to announce the venture capital launch," Arthur said more firmly than during the earlier relaxed conversations. It had a chilling effect on the table. Jesse grew quiet. Arthur remained focused on Laurence, waiting for his reply.

It took Laurence time to absorb the information, and taking a sip of his coffee, he came to some conclusion. Shaking his head and looking directly at Arthur, he knew that somehow he had been the source of the information.

"Don't you live with Adam Matthews?" Arthur asked, pressuring the visibly shaken man.

It was as if all the starch and polish in Laurence's appearance melted, his composure along with it. "I would have thought that was a secret known to very few."

"Look, your sexual preference is your choice and no one else's business," Jesse said in a show of sympathy for a secret that could damage the man's professional reputation. "It doesn't matter to any of us which way your eye is focused."

"No, Laurence, we are here to tell you that you have misplaced your trust in Adam." Coming from Arthur, the senior member of the group, added a gravitas to his distressing information.

"Adam," a startled-looking Laurence whispered. "I have always known him to play at the outer edges of ethical business practices. Sort of a cowboy in banking. But he's never cheated, stolen, or embarrassed me."

Arthur reached out and clasped Laurence's forearm. "Did you know that he approached Reggie Farmer to solicit him as a client?"

Shock at this news had Laurence speechless, his eyes widening in surprise. "Adam wanted to cheat one of my clients? He knows how long I've worked with you Arthur, and that you and Taryn are favorite clients of mine."

"How did he find out about Reggie, Laurence?" Arthur questioned, demanding an answer.

The stricken man sat with head bowed over his plate, then looked directly up at Arthur. "Along with the registration papers was the outline of Reggie's research. I swear that when I bring work home, I always lock it away." Looking down, he whispered, "But not that time."

"What are you going to do?" Arthur asked in a somewhat softer tone. "This impacts your personal life as well as your professional reputation." He felt sorry for the man, now assured he had been duped.

"I am forced to end my romantic relationship…no, my association with Adam Matthews…tonight."

"Can I suggest that you wait? It's Friday—maybe confront him on Monday? By that time we will hopefully have been able to stop the leak," Arthur said.

"Laurence, were you aware that Taryn had been receiving threatening notes? Arthur and I are about to confront the source of these threats. We are pretty sure Adam isn't the one behind this scheme. He is, however, the source of the information contained in these mailings. You can't let him know we are aware of his behavior. Will you keep our secret a bit longer?" Jesse pleaded.

"I have trusted you as our business associate and as a man of honor for more than a decade. I can see that all this is troubling but now you understand why Jesse and I had to bring it to your attention. When this is resolved, we'll get together just the three of us to celebrate the ending of this crisis for you and 4G," Arthur said.

That seemed to have added strength to the man's resolve. He sat up and with gratitude in his expression. "I appreciate your support and devastating honesty, Arthur. I am the man you have trusted all these years…just a fool in the one area of my life."

"Will you wait until Monday before confronting Adam?" Arthur asked.

"Yes. We're supposed to leave tonight for a weekend at the beach. I couldn't go now. Never. I'll plead an upset stomach. Adam will express regrets, but knowing him, he will go without me."

CHAPTER 41

"Thank you, Linda, for inviting me to stay over. Imagine, no dirty faces to wash or people to pick up after." Kathy sipped her second glass of wine.

The chuckles hid the seriousness of the gathering of lifelong friends. Chinese take-out devoured, wine glasses refilled, and Ellie, Kathy, and Linda began pouring over the snap shots each had of their days in Dunkirk.

"Ellie, I can't believe your organization. You have a photo album for each year from third grade through senior year," Linda exclaimed. "And this was way before Shutterfly."

"How else was I going to remember our changing hairstyles, school events, and summers at the pool? If I look back, all I remember is babysitting and dreary meetings with Arthur."

"Well, the news is that Nancy Lou, now Abigail Lang, is probably our culprit. How can we prove it? What did we ever do to make her our enemy?" Linda asked.

The apartment's bell signaled the arrival of the group's missing member. "Taryn, what's taken you so long? The food is almost gone." Linda greeted a weary Taryn as she shed her coat, handbag, and briefcase."

"For once, I'd like to see you without that briefcase," Kathy remarked. "You have to stop working long hours and enjoy your life. Speaking of which, how's Jesse?"

It felt good to be with friends. As she accepted a plate with a mix of Chinese leftovers, Taryn asked, "Linda, do you have a scotch? No, forget that." She patted her expanding waistline. "Just a reflex thought of a bygone habit."

"Before you arrived, we were trying to figure out what we've done to put Nancy Lou on the warpath. Especially now since according to our resident romantic, her novels have made her rich. And those photos Melissa had taken show a woman of substance, or was that the title of a book?" Kathy chuckled.

Settled with the plate on her lap, Taryn looked wearily at her friends. "Look, since these crazy notes began arriving and targeting me, I have tried looking into the past. For the life of me, I can't figure out what's gotten her so riled up."

"Let's start at the beginning. Didn't her father leave before we got to know her? That would mean she was raised by a single mother from age seven? I remember it was before we invited her to join us in babysitting," Linda said.

"Her mother was no dream. I remember my mom gossiping on the phone, and she was saying how she would see Nancy Lou alone Sundays in church and how much she wanted to tell the priest to talk to her mother. When she got off the phone, I asked her why she wanted the priest to visit her mother. She told me that Nancy Lou's mom worked as a waitress at the local restaurant and partied hard whenever she had the chance. Mom doubted she had anything to do with her own daughter since she was born," Kathy revealed. "Being a parent is a full-time job. And my boys are good. Rambunctious but really good kids. I can't imagine any one of them raising themselves."

"But what did I do?" Taryn cried. "Am I mean? Do I scream? Did I cheat her out of babysitting fees? What?"

"Maybe you didn't do something," Linda said. "Maybe it was something she thought you did?"

"Calm down. Getting upset isn't good for the baby or helpful," Kathy advised.

"Ice cream, anyone? I need chocolate to recharge," Linda offered, and a chorus of yeses rang out, smiles brightening previously serious faces. Returning with four heaping bowls of chocolate fudge did the trick.

"Taryn, how long has it been since you indulged in a rich, gooey bit of heaven?" Ellie teased.

"You laugh, but our freezer reminds me of Brown's soda fountain's list of flavors. Jesse loves his pecan praline." Lifting her filled spoon, she said, "I'm with Linda; chocolate any way I can get it."

"Wasn't it rumored that the family relied on an uncle in Buffalo for financial assistance?" Kathy asked, bringing the group back to the evening's topic.

"Yup. He worked the docks or something," Ellie answered. "But wasn't it also said he was connected?"

"Connected?" Taryn repeated.

"As in mob," Ellie replied.

"Mob? Buffalo? Then he would be in position to protect Nancy Lou if her mother wouldn't or couldn't," Linda said. "Funny, I remember she showed up at a party during senior year in a pretty dress. Since her clothes always looked like they came from the church bin, it was nice to see her look normal. Do you think her uncle paid for it?"

"Wait a minute. Wasn't it after that party that she broke up with Ian?" Taryn asked.

"No, he broke up with her," Ellie corrected. "I remember seeing her after that. She was totally devastated."

"Hey, do you remember a rumor in senior year that Nancy Lou had a baby? Wasn't that about the same time?" Linda asked.

"Sort of. Do you think Buffalo's somehow connected? Do you think if it was true that when she was pregnant, she'd gone to see her uncle? If she needed a place to hide or an illegal abortion, he'd be the only person she might trust," Linda suggested.

"Taryn, Ellie said baby, not abortion," Kathy corrected.

"I don't remember her looking pregnant but do remember we may have mentioned it," Ellie offered.

"Fuck it!" Taryn exclaimed getting up and going into the kitchen for a glass of water. The group sat stunned. Knowing she had to process her thoughts before sharing them, they waited silently for her to rejoin the conversation.

On returning Taryn dropped down in her chair. As she looked to each of her friends, she felt utterly shamed. They had lived more than three decades together, closer than sisters. And she was probably the reason behind this crisis. "I remember something. You have to help me figure out if this is the source of Nancy Lou's hatred." Seeing only support, she gathered her thoughts.

"It was toward the end of senior year, and I had met Nancy Lou in Brown's drug store. She looked thinner and a bit more grown up. I said something like, 'Hey, Nancy Lou, where have you been? We missed you at school this year.' She stopped placing items in her basket and gave me an ice-cold look."

"What did she say?" Kathy asked.

"She said, 'I've been away at school. I didn't realize you'd miss me after you exiled me from your little group.'"

"I remember thinking I didn't want to rehash our not having asked her back to the babysitting service. After all, that happened five years before. But apparently Nancy Lou carried a grudge."

"Oh, Taryn," Linda said. "Don't you remember how all the kids treated her when she came back to school? I know you had mentioned that she might have been pregnant, but we would never have shared a rumor like that with anyone else."

"I remember hearing that Nancy was telling kids she'd been studying in Italy. But everyone knew it was a lie. Nancy Lou traveling when they knew money at home was tight?" Ellie added. "Come to think of it, that was when she shrank from everyone. She must have known the kids gossiped about her because they quit talking when she passed by. Once I overheard some of the kids saying that Ian only dated her to get in her pants."

"That would have been a double whammy. Pregnant and a slut," Linda remarked.

"OK, gals, we need to find out how to get to this Abigail Lang. We have her address but that won't help us find out if and how she produced those damn news clips," Linda said.

Taryn took out her phone and called the one person who seemed to be getting close to the source of the 4G leaks. "Hi, Melissa, do you have a minute?"

"Sure," Melissa replied.

"I'm with the gals, and we remembered something from school that might be the reason behind Nancy Lou's disappearance and reinvention as Abigail Lang. What we need is some inside information…maybe contact someone who works for her? Someone who watched as she produced those mocked-up copies of the *Clarion*'s column? We know they are fakes. Bobbie hasn't found even one mention of any of these items in the paper or anywhere online," Taryn said.

"OK, let me contact Jimmy again and have him follow anyone entering her building on a regular basis. I'll get back to you."

CHAPTER 42

Melissa sat as instructed on the park bench amid a cluster of tall plantings. It wasn't a place she would have chosen because at dusk she would be hidden from the rest of the park's visitors. Thankfully that was a full hour away.

Since Jimmy's photo was taken on the run, she wondered what the mysterious contact would look like. He was only able to learn that she worked for Abigail Lang. Melissa wanted to know if she cleaned her home, did her shopping, or worked as her secretary.

At her instructions Jimmy watched the apartment building, and spotting her leaving at the end of the day, he handed her Melissa's note. It simply said that she would like a few moments of her time and listed her first name and cell number. Greatly relieved that this stranger called less than an hour later, Melissa felt that it may have been more than curiosity that led her to make the call. First, she had to be surprised by Jimmy's approach and then a stranger wanting to speak with her had to be suspicious. Melissa thought that if circumstances were reversed, she probably wouldn't have made the call but if sufficiently curious might have asked Mrs. Hammond to check the number.

In a tentative, low-pitched voice, the woman wanted to know how she learned that she worked for Abigail Lang. Melissa, in as tactful manner as possible, explained that she was interested in speaking with someone who knew about the author's writing schedule. And when that seemed to pique interest, she went on to say that she was prepared to make it worth this woman's time. Surprisingly, she hadn't been asked what she meant by making it worth her time or what Melissa wanted to know. And after agreeing to conditions including she was to be alone and had to meet at this secluded location, they set up the meeting for the same afternoon.

"Were you followed?"

Looking around to locate the owner of the gravelly voice, Melissa was momentarily at a loss. She wasn't going to converse with someone she couldn't see. "No." Melissa settled back on the bench, waiting for the voice to materialize. No boardroom had ever made her as nervous. Business had rules, a formal set of procedures. They didn't include meeting a stranger in this secluded spot. But if she was going to help Taryn, she was prepared to see this through. This meeting was the first break they'd had since learning about Abigail Lang.

"Nice coat," said a fortysomething woman as she sat at the far end of the bench. "I'll bet it's a designer's."

Looking at the stranger, Melissa noted the sparse gray hair, thick glasses, and indeterminate body hidden under a bulky raincoat. Something out of the '60s idea of a well-brought up woman. Neat and not flashy.

"Are we here to discuss fashion?" Melissa said.

"Touchy. You're the one who wanted to speak to me. Why?" was the sharp retort.

Melissa, using the same business tone when wanting to disarm a potentially difficult associate, said, "Well, you see I am a fan of Ms. Lang and interested in learning more about her work."

"Why not call her?"

"She's known for keeping a very low profile. I thought speaking with someone who knew her would give me an idea how to reach her. By the way, how are you and Ms. Lang associated?"

"I'm her secretary," was the surly reply.

"How interesting. Will you tell me about her schedule? It's getting late, and I am sure you have other places to be."

"Impatient, aren't you?"

Melissa decided confrontation would only get this stranger's hackles up. Men were easier to read. They simply stated the obvious in a threatening voice while standing over you and with a lot of finger pointing assumed you'd cower. This person chose sarcasm; so far it wasn't mean or threatening, more like a protective mechanism. "You seem like a loyal person. So what would you think if your employer was engaged in potentially criminal activities?"

The abrupt lifting of her gaze, followed by the nervous shifting of her feet, indicated that this stranger knew something. Time for the direct approach. "Look, I am going to share some sensitive information on the understanding that it will stay between us." Seeing the woman's nod was encouraging. "I have a friend who has been receiving newspaper clippings containing damaging and false information. I was hoping you could help me find out why someone is threatening ruination of my friend and her firm."

"Why would I do that? I don't know your friend."

"Maybe you would like to help us catch this blackmailer?"

"Blackmail?" was a startled reply. "Are you trying to tell me this is about money?"

"Not necessarily, but none of these news clips have appeared in the paper, so we think it is going to lead this person to demand a huge sum of money to make it go away. This situation is defaming an honorable, hard-working woman. We don't know why or how far they are willing to go."

"And you think I can help find the person behind this scheme?"

Opening her handbag, Melissa pulled out a copy of one of the FYI pages. "Does this look familiar?"

The strange woman seemed to consider this while Melissa waited in silence, noticing that she took her time in reading its contents.

Silence, a readjusting of her position on the bench, and finally looking directly at Melissa, she said, "OK. I work for the person behind this scheme. Recently she let me know how little she thinks of my years of working long, odd hours as her assistant. Well, I have value. Just ask my family. The stress of taking her crap, of maintaining her double life, treating me like an indentured servant—not someone with a MFA." With each statement the force of her voice increased.

Whatever Melissa had expected, it certainly wasn't the eruption of an angry woman.

"Yesterday she told me that the manuscript I've worked on for the past three years was crap. That witch has given me bleeding ulcers."

"And you want revenge?"

"I want her to suffer as she's made me suffer."

Melissa had been trying to maintain eye contact, but the agitated stranger was entirely focused on her own issues with Abigail Lang. The words that had tumbled over one another sounded as if they'd been repeated many times before. On the surface she looked like an aging woman in her late forties, but dressed like a young girl, complete with a velvet headband, and a pleated skirt showing below the hem of her coat.

"Look, I'm sorry you have a difficult life. Maybe we can start again. I'll begin by telling you my name, Melissa Horn. I am also a friend of Taryn Cooper Walsh, and we believe your boss is out to destroy her."

"I recognize you. You're sort of famous you know. Anyway, I agreed to meet you because Ms. Romance is ruining my health, and now you are telling me she's possibly engaged in blackmail?"

"If you work as Ms. Lang's secretary, you may have seen this newspaper clip before. All I am trying to do is identify the author of this information. Anything you can share with me will be appreciated." Melissa said in a coaxing tone. She didn't want to threaten or scare this angry woman. She needed to enlist her help.

The strange woman stared directly at Melissa. As if she had come to some important decision, she softened her tone. "I happened to find a file in my boss's drawer labeled FYI. It contained photo copies of clippings like that one. The clippings were on mastheads she had me Photoshop for her. I was curious, so I read them. Each featured Ms. Cooper and how she was stealing from her investors."

Not believing her luck, Melissa waited for the woman to continue. After an uncomfortable silence, she said, "Well, you know who I am. May I have your name? It makes discussing things easier, don't you think?" Melissa watched the woman's pasty, makeup-free complexion now devoid of expression.

"What do you need my name for? Are you going to call the police? I'm not the one threatening your friend," she spat. "Well, lady, I'm just going to walk away and let your friend's life go down the drain. I didn't agree to meet you to get put in jail."

"I'm sorry. Did I say something to make you think I was out to harm you?" For the life of her, Melissa hadn't expected to trigger such an extreme reaction, and she reached for the woman's coat sleeve to keep her from leaving. "Please, understand. I am not going to call the police. I am only seeking information to help my friend. You must believe me."

"Ruth," was a mumbled reply.

"Ruth? That's your name?" Seeing her nod in agreement, Melissa continued. "Please sit with me, Ruth. We can discuss this situation calmly. I promise that I will never let your name become connected to what you tell me."

Ruth pulled a well-worn manila envelope from her tote bag and once again retreated into silence. Melissa wanted to grab it from her hands but could only sit by, watching as she tapped it against her knee.

"I carry this everywhere. It's is my insurance policy. I've copied all the news clips and a list of my employer's various contacts as protection. It was bad enough to have her throw my manuscript in my face. I needed to have something to throw back at her. Now you are telling me that simply by making up the mastheads of that newspaper, she is involving me in some illegal scheme. My sainted boss cheats me out of overtime pay; I've even seen snatches of phrases from my work appear in one of her manuscripts, but nothing as evil as what you are telling me."

Opening the envelope, Melissa saw the familiar clips that had been sent to Taryn over the past month and a half. But the photo and dual identity of a famous romance writer was a complete surprise. It was a glamorous publicity photo. According to Ellie, this woman never appeared in public to promote her books. A quick glance at the half dozen names, and Melissa spotted Adam Matthews along with the name of a well-known publisher."

"Ruth, is this Abigail Lang?" Seeing her nod, and careful to keep the excitement out of her voice, Melissa continued, "I need to speak to her. Can you set it up?"

An enraged Ruth jumped up and screamed, "You're no different than my boss. You conned me. Led me to believe I wouldn't be involved." Then, to Melissa's shock, she grabbed the envelope and hit her across the face with it. "Now you want me to introduce you to my boss? Are you crazy? I knew not to trust you. She has an uncle in the mob. She'd have me killed," she screeched.

Melissa sat speechless, rubbing her smarting cheek, and watched Ruth storm out of the park, crushing the envelope as she fled. Melissa knew she'd never be able to contact Ruth again. "No matter," she mumbled. "I have the information we need—the name of the villain out to destroy Taryn and proof she created the false news clips."

She needed a moment to calm her excitement before picking up her phone to bring Taryn up to speed. *Finally, the rat is cornered.*

"Arthur, Melissa just called and told me she met with Abigail's secretary and confirmed that Abigail Lang and Nancy Lou are one and the same. She also found out that Ruth, her secretary, was the one creating the mastheads but didn't know Abigail used them for her FYI mailings."

"We will have to consider how we treat this information, Taryn. It could create problems if this Ruth were to let this information leak."

"Another problem," Taryn responded.

CHAPTER 43

"Are you ready, Taryn?" Arthur asked, noticing not for the first time that she kept circling her stomach with her hands. Finally drawing her attention, Arthur was reminded that Taryn would shut out the world if business required some action or decision.

"Yes. Will Laurence agree to meeting Nancy Lou in his office for what I expect to be an unpleasant showdown?"

"Ah, Laurence. I returned with him to his office Friday after Jesse and I had met him for lunch. That lunch during which we dropped the Adam bombshell. I feel really sorry for him. Anyway, we sat and reminisced about the growth of his practice, of 4G's, and how life was even better than we dreamed as young adults."

"You are very understanding, Arthur. I didn't know how to reach out to the man. Maybe being nearer his age inspired confidence. We were pretty tough," Jesse added.

"A man learns something by the time he's reached fifty. Especially if he's a success in his profession. Anyway, he opened up about accepting his homosexuality and the necessity of hiding it from his peers. Apparently after he had been married a couple of months, the decision to stay in the closet began to tear him apart. He talked a bit of the duality of keeping it out of his professional life and trying to be selective in his choice of partners."

"And now Adam," Melissa commented. "I wonder if your news was a complete surprise. I went to school with a man who only a year or two after graduation told me about his similar path. Thank goodness the stigma is lessening."

"Anyway, he thinks that inviting Abigail to his office Sunday midday, while Adam is out of town, would provide a neutral setting with attorney-at-law undertones. That and his friendship with Abigail could be helpful in setting the stage."

Jesse was considering Laurence in a new light. He liked the man he met at lunch. Maybe he'd reach out in friendship at future 4G events, not just greet him as his wife's plus one.

"He told me that he had planned to go home Friday and pack for a weekend at the beach. Instead he would tell Adam he wasn't well and was sorry he couldn't join him."

"Wouldn't Adam stay home to make sure he was taken care of?" Taryn asked.

"Apparently not. He said that Adam would always choose his social life over staying home."

⇌ ⇋

"Abigail, I'm alone this weekend and wondered if you would join me for lunch?" Laurence said, speaking into his cell, in the back of a taxi on his way to the office. He agreed to Arthur's plan and had a sleepless night trying to figure out just how to approach Abigail.

"That would be fun. But where is Adam? Sunday lunches are usually with the three of us."

"I'd had a spot of upset stomach and didn't feel up to joining him at the beach. So it's just me. Do you mind awfully?"

"Of course not. I'll dress in my wealthy client's best."

"I'm sure you will be stunning. Anyway, I have some things to clear up at the office, so why not meet me there. I'll have my executive assistant, Gerald Johnson, meet you at the security gate at noon."

"I'll look forward to seeing you in your natural environment. I wonder if you are any different at work than during one of our socially extravagant dinners," Abigail teased.

Laurence wished he had offered Abigail more than a light-hearted good-bye, but he was far from a cheery mood.

Dialing Arthur's cell, he confirmed the arrangements for today's showdown. "Can you, Taryn, and Jesse meet Gerald at the security gate at eleven? That will give us an hour to get ready for Abigail's arrival. I don't know which name you will be using when addressing her, but Arthur, I only know her as Abigail."

On the dot of noon, Abigail Lang, in her latest Chanel suit and accessories, walked to the security desk of the third-avenue office building. "My name is Abigail Lang to see Mr. Swinburne. I'm expected."

As the guard called upstairs, Abigail looked around the empty lobby, noticing a shuttered coffee bar set off to one side. Empty chairs set amid planters filled with leafy green shrubbery that softened the granite hard surfaces of the building. Were lobbies for weekday visitors while the executives worked a seven-day week?

"Ms. Lang, I'm Gerald Johnson. Mr. Swinburne asked me to bring you up to the office." Inserting his key card and swinging the metal gate aside, the ramrod straight man of uncertain age led her to the open elevator door.

"You work on Sundays, Mr. Johnson? I thought I was the only one who worked a seven-day week." Seeing the man smile, Abigail wondered if he too was gay. *What a shame if all the stunning men were homosexual. Maybe that's why my books are selling so well.*

"Ms. Lang is here," Gerald announced while standing to one side, allowing her to enter the office.

Laurence, wearing a friendly smile, walked over to Abigail and gave her an air-kiss over both her cheeks. "I'm so glad you could meet me here. I have something serious to discuss with you."

"Serious?" she asked as she looked around the masculine office and quipped, "Right out of Hollywood. It suits you, Laurence. I may describe it in one of my books."

The smile on Laurence's face was genuine. He really did enjoy Abigail's sense of humor. "Take a seat," he said, indicating that she should take the chair in front of his desk.

As Laurence walked over to open a side door, he announced, "May I introduce you to Mr. and Mrs. Jesse Walsh, you may know Mrs. Walsh as Taryn Cooper, managing partner of 4G Investments, and Arthur Mallory, a partner in the firm."

Not believing what she was seeing, Abigail nodded.

As she walked up to the well-dressed woman who bore only a slight resemblance to the Nancy Lou of their youth, Taryn thought this meeting might not go so badly until she saw the clenched jaw and fingers curl in a fist, "Nancy Lou…"

"It's Abigail Lang," was the curt reply.

"Yes. Mysterious author of popular novels. You are to be congratulated on your success. From what Laurence tells me, your books are in great demand." Whatever Taryn expected, it wasn't a look of hostility.

"Well, well, the princess of privilege in the flesh," Abigail replied as if a cat toying with a mouse.

Taryn hadn't expected a warm welcome and took a few calming breaths before she continued. "I am also aware of your dual identity. That is of course entirely your business." She hadn't meant it to be as dismissive as it had sounded. Still Abigail's only visible reaction was her carefully made-up face tightening into a sneer.

By this time Jesse and Arthur had moved to stand beside her, a show of their unspoken support. "What I want to know is why you have been sending me those ugly mocked-up news items. It isn't worthy of the girl I knew in school. That girl was sweet, kind, and a friend." Taryn's voice remained soft, but firm.

"Worthy? And I suppose you are going to tell me I was your best friend?" Abigail, angered at being cornered, glared at the source of her hatred. "And ruining my life was worthy of you?" she snapped.

"Ruining your life? How would I have done that?"

"I meant so very little to you? Even when you dropped me from that babysitting business, I still counted you a friend."

"And why would you think things changed? Didn't you sleep at my home? We met at Brown's for sodas." Taryn couldn't believe the increasing antagonism from this stranger. Nancy Lou was always kind and mild, nothing like this visage of bottled-up rage. Whatever this woman thought had happened must have been brewing for years.

"Were you even aware that I needed to earn money? That the few dollars I earned each time I watched those brats enabled me to pay for basics like clothes and school supplies?"

The icy tone triggered something Taryn remembered her mother having said. That this woman's mother, in addition to living on a waitress's salary, ignored her only daughter.

With cold fury behind each word, Abigail's tirade continued. "You turned Ian against me."

"Ian? We were just friendly kids in school. I was never interested in him."

"Not only Ian, but the rest of the class." Abigail had settled into a quiet seething.

"Abigail, I still don't understand what I could have possibly done to you that would engender such malevolent actions." Taryn was as mystified now as she had been on receiving the first FYI message.

"Enough," Abigail said, standing up to all of her five foot two inches in height and walked over to Laurence. "What is this setup? I thought we were friends."

This bitter quiet fury forced Laurence to explain. "When I heard about how you pumped Adam for information to then use in creating this campaign against someone I prize as a client, not only for her business but her ethics, I agreed to this meeting to sort things out. I couldn't believe you would do anything so evil and wanted to hear your side of things." He then reached out and placed his hand on her shoulder. "Abigail, we go way back. You must know I don't want to hurt you. Let's sit down and see if we can get to the bottom of things."

As she pulled away and circled the room, Abigail looked at each of the people gathered. "So you want to screw me over…Jesse, the loving husband, Arthur the lifelong advisor, and you, the Princess. As always, Taryn Cooper, people protect you. Who protected me from Ian using me for sex but making me believe I was the love of his life? Who protected me from the catty slurs and hushed voices when I walked by kids I thought my friends? Who protected me by robbing me of my future? Forcing me to create another life to hide from my shame?"

"Just look at yourself," Arthur commanded, moving over to face Abigail. "You are a highly popular romance novelist, wealthy, more attractive than you were back in Dunkirk. You forget I lived there as well."

"Sweet words. What would the officer of the bank know about a fragile girl from the other side of town being mocked, ignored, laughed at just as she was about to begin a life of promise?" Turning to look at Taryn, she shrieked, "I had a full scholarship to Buffalo. Did you know that? Did you know that without that scholarship I couldn't have afforded to go to college?"

"I had heard you got a scholarship and remember congratulating you. But I also know you lost it because you were out of school for six months senior year and had to make it up in summer school," Taryn corrected. "You certainly can't be blaming me for that."

"Don't you remember senior year, in the lunch room, when you were telling your girl friends that I had gone to Buffalo to have a baby?" The venom-filled voice echoing around the room had the men gasping.

"You must believe me that I never meant to hurt you. If I said something like that, it would have been mentioned in speculation and only to Linda, Ellie, and Kathy. It was certainly unintentional."

Abigail, seemingly lost in thought, settled back in her chair. "Well, you were overheard by the class gossip, Barbara Brewer. Remember her? It was probably Barbara who spread the rumor about me and Ian because she wanted him for herself. She wouldn't have known about my pregnancy if she hadn't overheard you discussing it at the school cafeteria. You gave her that juicy bit of gossip she so willingly spread around school."

Taryn was at a loss for words. "Did I do that? Is that what all this is about? I don't remember every saying an unkind word to you or anyone."

"Can we all sit down at the table," Laurence interjected. "Let's see if we can take the emotions down a couple of notches and resolve this situation as adults." Moving over to his desk, he picked up the phone. "Gerald, you can bring in the coffee."

With each settled, coffee sitting mainly untouched, Taryn knew she had to find a face-saving solution. If Abigail couldn't bury the past, her anger and campaign would only intensify.

"Look, Abigail, why did you think your life ended in Dunkirk? Whatever drove you, look where you are now. Would you have moved to New York, worked hard, and become a success? From what I've heard, getting published and building a loyal audience of readers is almost as difficult as picking the right stock."

"Have you ever read one of my books?" Abigail taunted.

With the first smile of the meeting, Taryn shook her head no. "Did you know Ellie is a fan? She's read every one of your novels, some several times. If you remember how disciplined she was, it won't surprise you to know she keeps a diary of her thoughts of each of your books."

"Really? Why?" Abigail asked, curiosity overtaking her anger.

"Well, Ellie feels that making money by moving in and out of investments is a cold way to earn a living. She would rather live in the worlds you create filled with romance."

"Abigail, have you shared any of your clips with anyone? Maybe online?" Laurence asked.

Turning to see his genuine interest, she decided to see what they wanted. "Not yet. I didn't want to ruin Mrs. Walsh, only hurt her like she hurt me. Destroy her goody-two-shoes reputation."

"Then maybe you could agree to stop this and destroy your records. You could move on with your life as Abigail Lang. Isn't Hollywood interested in several of your novels? That might mean red-carpet walks, socializing with the real men portraying your fictional ones."

"Laurence, maybe you could help her negotiate a favorable contract," Jesse suggested. "The west coast thinks authors are simple minded. I should know."

Taryn thought there was nothing more to say. Abigail/Nancy Lou would have to make the first move. The silence didn't help calm her nerves. Feeling the baby move, she looked to Jesse, and taking his hand, she placed it on her stomach.

Abigail saw the expression on their faces and knew that this baby was wanted. Thinking back to her own pregnancy, she at first had thought of ending. But being a good Catholic girl, she gave it away before even taking a look at the result of her shame. Frankly, she never thought of it again. *Dear Father, help me.*

"What do I get in return? I can't return to being Nancy Lou Harris. She's dead. Are you asking for legal retribution? A public apology?"

Horrified, Taryn slumped back in her chair not knowing what to say next.

Arthur saw the frightened girl, not the angry woman. "Abigail, we don't want any of those things. What do you want to make this all go away?"

"Years of shame did spur me to create this new and highly motivated person. I probably should thank Barbara Brewer and the rest of those horrid kids. But this anger intensified with the years. I forgot that Taryn was never anything but straight with me. So when I read about her success with 4G, the old pain reignited my apparently misplaced rage. To me she was a leader among the thieves of Wall Street. And how much I hated her being touted for her success."

"There is a lot of that misplaced anger about finance officers going around. Maybe because people read about the large sums of money we manage. They forget that we make our clients' money, and if we make a bad decision, we lose as well. It's all about trust," Taryn replied.

Abigail felt boxed in. She'd created this mess, all by herself. "Laurence, what do you suggest?" Abigail was counting on his skill as an attorney and years of friendship.

"Why not let Arthur and Gerald accompany you home? Between the three of you, all files both in your desk and on your computer can be destroyed." Looking to Arthur and seeing him smile, he then looked to Taryn, who was mouthing a silent thank-you.

"No legal action?"

"Of course not. That was never my purpose in meeting you. After all we were once friends," Taryn replied.

CHAPTER 44

"That's all of it, Abigail?" Arthur asked.

"Except for my computer folders."

"Let me take a look," Gerald suggested. "That is what I do all day, check for accuracy and hidden files."

"Gerald, aren't you a bit old to be Laurence's assistant?" Abigail asked.

He laughed. "Yes, ancient. He seems to need discipline during office hours especially with organization of his files."

"So you're retired from the army?" she pressed. "Married, family?" Abigail wanted to see if this specimen was a possible lover.

Seemingly ignoring her questions, Gerald suddenly exclaimed, "You forgot a little detail, Ms. Lang."

"Excuse me?"

"Facebook? You have been an active friend."

Walking away from studying the bookcase filled with international editions of Abigail's books, he saw what Gerald was pointing to.

"Can you retrieve her posts? Her circle of friends?" Arthur asked.

"Already done. Let me print out a list of posts to and from her friends."

Abigail wasn't really worried. It was all make-believe. So far she had only opened five false profiles and begun accumulating friends.

With the printed pages spread out on the dining room table, Gerald and Arthur began by isolating Abigail's five profiles from the extended circle of friends. "Ms. Lang," Gerald called out, getting her attention, "We can do this the hard way, or you can explain these postings and people. I don't see one with your name."

"Why wouldn't you have a personal Facebook account but would use five to destroy Taryn?" Arthur questioned.

"You're kidding me, aren't you?" Seeing his puzzled expression, she took a deep breath and sat down with the paper trail of her activities. "First, there is nothing private on Facebook. The firm's philosophy is that everyone in the world should be connected. They sell their lists, and while they claim that all member names remain hidden, it is still a breach of my personal privacy. I haven't spent all these years building a duplicate life to have it come crashing down on me now."

"Does everyone know their information is sold?" Arthur asked.

"Yes, but the computer generation doesn't seem to care. It's only the precomputer generation that refuses to post their innermost private lives for others to read."

"Ms. Lang, the printouts of these five friends. Are these the fake profiles you created for gathering a community of real people to build your extended circle of contacts?"

"Yes. And if you look to each one's page, you will see the number of friends that are now following them."

"And the wider circle shows they have attracted no fewer than forty-four others?"

"Yes. So when I did post one of those news items, it could be shared, spreading the questionable practices of Taryn Cooper to a wider circle of people. At least that was the plan. You can delete everything, even close those accounts if that makes you feel safe." Skepticism was evident on Gerald's lean stern face.

"What?"

"You know very well I will and can terminate your five accounts. But Facebook never deletes information."

"I know, but there isn't anything damaging to anyone. Just gossip, fashion problems, grooming tips designed to keep this group growing," Abigail said. "I haven't posted anything on 4G or Taryn Cooper."

Arthur, wanting to defuse her defensiveness, patted her on her back. "Is this over? Are you sure that you and Taryn, in fact all of us, can put this little situation behind us?" Whether it was his fatherly approach or being faced with the extent of her planning, he couldn't know. Arthur just felt her nod in agreement was sincere.

Abigail looked over to her bookcase and seeing a Romance Writers of America citation, realized her pettiness, and more importantly, she was no longer Nancy Lou of her past. To keep up this campaign would make her a pariah to her fans. One look at both men, and she saw only sympathy. Not recriminations.

"Gentlemen, I am now almost forty-five, and today I believe I have finally grown up. The past got me to where I am today, which if you look around this penthouse, is beyond the imagination of that poor girl from Dunkirk. Destroy everything and with it my past. I am Abigail Lang, beloved romance author. I've earned my fame, wealth, and success."

CHAPTER 45

Melissa was thinking of all Taryn had shared about the meeting with Abigail/Nancy Lou at Laurence Swinburne's office the day before when Mrs. Hammond walked in with a large vase of lilies. "How gorgeous. Who are they from?"

"Ms. Cooper; there's a card."

"Thank you, Mrs. Hammond. I'll take them and place them on my desk." The never diminishing stack of files was quickly placed on her credenza, making room for the almost two-foot-tall vase made even taller by the two dozen stems of pale peach flowers. "Opening the note she saw that it was handwritten and from Taryn.

> I doubt my tears are due to hormonal surges, but due to your generous support and assistance in putting this horrid affair behind us. Jesse is planning an anniversary celebration at the apartment. He has invited several more of his male friends as guests. The invitation will read Formal Dress. This dear friend is meant to show you off to advantage.
> Love always,
> Taryn

The flowers had cleared her mind of business and focused instead on a strangely sad Ruth, Abigail's secretary, who was the link in solving Taryn's problem. She wanted to repay her but wasn't sure just how. Then she spotted the copy of Abigail's latest book on her office sofa. She had read it wanting some sense of the woman. It reminded her of Ruth's own efforts having been spurned.

Picking up her phone, she dialed Jimmy. "It's Melissa Horn, Jimmy. Did you happen to get a last name or home phone for the woman I met in the park? The one you passed my note to?"

Writing down Ruth's home phone number, she said, "Thanks, Jimmy. Let Mrs. Hammond know what I owe you." As she entered the number on her phone, she looked at the clock and noticed it was almost six. *I hope she's home.*

"Yes? Who is this?" the voice was no less angry than when they'd met.

"Ruth, this is Melissa Horn. I wondered if I might have a copy of your manuscript. I know someone who is friends with an agent. And if he thinks it's ready, he will pass it along for her consideration."

"Why would you do something for me? I don't remember leaving you in the best of moods."

"Because I know how difficult it is for a woman to break into a field when she's an unknown. And because you didn't have to meet me or listen to me tell you about my friend's problems."

"But I took the envelope with me."

"But I found out what I needed, and now thanks to your bravery, the problem is all solved. And, I might add, without your name being mentioned."

The silence lasted only seconds. "You would really show my manuscript to your friend?"

"Yes. Would you prefer I read it first and then call you with my thoughts?"

"Actually I would. You see no one other than Abigail Lang has seen it. No one in my writing class. No family members. No one."

"I would be honored to be the first outsider and promise to give you my honest opinion." Melissa gave her the office address and personal e-mail. "If you prefer, you can e-mail it to me."

"Thank you, Ms. Horn. Really. You are giving me hope that someone could think my hard work had value."

⟞⟝

"Laurence, it's Melissa Horn. I wonder if you would do me a great favor."

"Of course, if I can."

"It's a sensitive matter. It seems that Abigail hasn't been too kind to her assistant Ruth Edwards. That when Ruth had shown her a manuscript she had worked on for three years, Abigail tossed it back in her face. But I owe this woman a kindness. So the favor is, do you know someone in publishing that isn't connected with Abigail who would read the manuscript and give an honest critique?"

"I would be happy to give it a read and then, if it's ready, show it to a lawyer in my firm who represents authors. How's that?"

"Great. When I get it, I'll make a copy for myself. I told her I'd read it first. I owed her that. Then I'll messenger a hard copy to you. Thank you, Laurence, from the little we know of each other you are the gentleman Taryn and Jesse said you were."

CHAPTER 46

With his neck feeling squeezed, Laurence wearily shed his tie while walking into the bedroom. The meeting with Abigail had worn him down emotionally and physically. He would need all his energy for the upcoming performance to end it with Adam. His lover's betrayal hurt. At the advanced age of fifty, Laurence finally knew what being in love felt like. Adam had made him happy. For that reason alone, Laurence would strike as swiftly and impersonally as possible, and make the break a clean one.

The open suitcase lay on the chaise in readiness for a last-minute check of weekend necessities for the trip he hadn't taken. A moan escaped as he closed the case and slipped it under the king-sized bed. *Out of sight, out of mind.*

Just then he heard the apartment door open. "Larry, are you here? I don't see any lights," Adam called.

Laurence had been dreading this moment all weekend. It wasn't just the freedom to love a man; Adam brought youth and exuberance into his life. At least until lunch on Friday and learning that he was devious and loose lipped where his career was concerned. As he draped his jacket and tie on the clothes tree, Laurence gave the bedroom a once over, wanting it to be in order. The last thing he would be able to stand was Adam flinging him on the bed for a sexual romp.

"Coming," Laurence called out before walking out into the living room. "How was the weekend? Any new people, parties, things I would have hated missing?"

"Same people, same parties all to raise funds for dogs, horses, and the environment. Nothing your heart is into."

As Adam moved toward the bedroom carrying his weekend satchel, Laurence held up his hand, halting him in mid stride. "Adam, would you like a drink? We have to talk."

"You look terrible. Is your stomach still giving you problems?"

"No, it's my heart." Laurence had poured two drinks and handing Adam a cognac, he gestured for him to sit in the wing chair adjacent to the sofa.

"What's the mystery? You never hand me a drink when I've been away for a while. What have you been up to?" Adam walked over to the stereo and was about to turn it on, something he always did when first entering the apartment.

"Please don't, Adam. I have something very serious to discuss with you. No music. I need your full attention."

Sitting in his favorite chair, Adam lifted his glass in a salute. "OK. You have my undivided attention, Larry. Shoot."

"I understand you tried to solicit Reggie Farmer as new client for the bank." Noticing surprise but not discomfort, Laurence realized that he had given Adam more credit for character and ethics then he deserved.

"Yeah. So?"

"How did you learn of him or his research?"

"Oh, is that what's troubling you? You had his preliminary research on your desk. I had wanted a pen and gave it a quick look."

"You didn't consider that by approaching Mr. Farmer you were compromising me and the trust my client places in me?" Seeing a blank expression at hearing this bit of information, Laurence tried again. "Adam, you and I work in a world that demands trust between client and attorney, or in your case broker. What made you even think of approaching my client's business acquaintance?"

"Hell, Larry, it's done all the time. Anyway, the kid wasn't interested. Is that what's bothering you?"

"Adam, on all those occasions when you met Abigail without me, what did you talk about?"

"Huh? The usual gossip. Why?"

"Did you happen to share tidbits about 4G's activities?"

"Yeah, but I never mentioned the firm. If that's all, I'll unpack."

"Not all by a long shot." The sternness of his tone did what a discussion of Adam's devious actions couldn't. The beautiful young man was finally listening. "I don't think you realize just how serious these actions are. Nor that they placed my reputation in jeopardy."

"Larry, will you cut to the chase? I haven't nor would I do anything to screw with your reputation. What's gotten your underwear in a twist?" Adam swallowed the rest of his drink in one gulp, sat still, and waited.

It was an anathema for someone in their profession to treat a matter of trust so lightly. Laurence knew that explaining the entire situation would be a waste of his time. Further, if he mentioned Abigail's campaign to destroy Taryn, Adam would simply be amazed that she had the talent or ability to be so vindictive. Apparently Adam and his colleagues had a loose definition of trusted behavior.

As he walked to the bar for the bottle, Laurence returned and poured Adam a refill. It was important that he maintain a physical distance and assume the manner of the formidable attorney his clients paid for. "Adam, our relationship has to end right now. I am aware of your other social activities but never felt you would betray me. Your betrayal has destroyed all my feelings for you."

"Wait a minute," Adam cried as he jumped up from the chair. "Are you telling me that some stupid bitch is breaking us up?"

"No, you are. I have paid one month in advance for a room at the club. Of course you are no longer able to charge items to my account. That includes the little extravagances you charge at Paul Stuart. Your personal things will be packed up and delivered tomorrow. In fact, your clothes have already been sent over."

"Just like that? You bastard! No warning? Just cut me out of your life?"

"Yes, but quietly. No one need know anything about why we broke up. As far as anyone we know is concerned, you can say that you got tired of playing the role of the younger stud."

CHAPTER 47

"OK. Let's call Taryn and invite her to a gathering at our first favorite New York City place, that tiny hole in the wall Peruvian restaurant on ninety-fifth, way over almost in the East River. You know, the one with that fabulous chicken, not to mention sangria," Ellie said. The women were gathered in a favorite after-work cocktail lounge, indulging in drinks and catching up with each other outside 4G.

"Oh no," Linda chimed in. "How about that little place downtown with fabulous lobster rolls?"

"We can do better than that. How about booking a private room at La Grenouille? Remember when we launched 4G Investments? We fed our success by indulging to overflowing, in rich dishes and their fabulous crème brûlée?" Kathy said, drooling with every word.

"Ooh. But when? This is only Monday. I know for a fact that she's in high-functioning mode, what with the soon to be released 4G business announcement," Linda said.

"Hey, how about a baby shower with just us?" Ellie suggested. With all expressing delight, she picked up her cell thinking not for the first time how each of them had changed. Who would have thought a grade-school teacher would be in high finance or that her invested net worth would be nearly five million dollars? She could have as many Kimmelwick sandwiches as she liked. But times and city living had sharpened more than her taste buds. It gave her a freedom she'd never dreamed of. Freedom to travel first class, volunteer in faraway locations, and more importantly enjoy these women in an ongoing pursuit of interesting, exciting, and mind-expanding opportunities.

"Hi, Taryn, am I interrupting anything? Arthur told all of us about Nancy Lou and how you got her to drop her campaign of terror," Ellie said.

"Talk away. I was just about to leave for a cozy dinner at home."

"OK. I'm with the rest of the gang, and we want to celebrate so many things but especially the ending of our torment. You do realize that Nancy Lou is also part of our past, and we took those dammed FYI mailings as personal assaults?"

"No. I haven't forgotten how close we were back in Dunkirk. It was like we traveled in a pack. I just thought that for someone to hate that strongly, it had to be directed toward me."

"You always took the punishment but left the kudos for us. Shape up, Taryn. It's time you took a bow as well."

Taryn realized that throughout the years, she felt the burden to protect the rest. After all she was the one that kept getting them involved in one of her business ideas. "Ellie, I stand corrected. And I'd love to celebrate. What did you all cook up? I can hear the glasses clicking as we speak."

"How about meeting tomorrow at La Grenouille, say seven? I'll book a private room, so we don't embarrass ourselves with our hilarity," Ellie said.

"Really? I'd love that. We celebrated opening 4G there and can still taste all those rich, creamy, fattening flavors. Tell the gang that I miss our time together, and now that life is back to some semblance of normal, I plan to change all that."

"We miss time with you…time not measured by the clock," Ellie replied.

"OK, I'll tell Jesse tonight. See you in the office tomorrow. And Ellie, I love you all. Sorry about having been so preoccupied."

CHAPTER 48

"Jesse," Marilyn sang into the phone. "Your new best friend loves the original outline of your teaching plan. And, if that isn't exciting enough, offered to arrange for you to meet with an uber celebrity agent to see if one of his clients would be interested in participating in your video."

"Marilyn that was a quick response. All I've done was outline the sections of a ten-week course. I haven't actually written it."

"Well, he's already paid you for the first installment and wants to see what his money bought. Can you blame him?"

Thinking now that Taryn's 4G's problems had been resolved a few months ago and the looming future family under control, Jesse knew he had to hunker down and give his agent the written script she was asking for. "OK, listen, I'm planning a little surprise for Taryn and was going to hide away at the Connecticut house for a couple of days. While there, I'll finish that script."

"That's my boy. By the way how is the pregnancy going? Is Taryn still experiencing morning sickness?"

"Are you kidding? She's beginning her eighth month and a behemoth." Picturing his wife as she lay in bed, her stomach stretching her nightgowns, he forgot the pressure of his own work.

"I've known you for a long time and never expected the self-contained private man you were to look forward to having a family. You do know your life will never be the same?"

"I'm looking forward to playing with blocks, even dolls if that becomes the toy of choice." As usual, his skeptical agent had him laughing. "You know, Marilyn, I think I work better when I have someone I love to worry about. It focuses my mind and priorities."

"Jesse, I couldn't be happier for you both. You are like a son to me, and Taryn almost a daughter. Except," chuckling, "with my genes I'd never be so lucky to have a brilliant child."

"Not to worry. You will be Aunt Marilyn and can join in the fun. And I just figured out how I'm going to have my wife convince me that I have to leave for the country. I can hear her now, telling me that I must get to work and finish writing my script. Bye for now. I'll get in touch if I run into a rough patch." Jesse continued smiling after he hung up with Marilyn. He was picturing Taryn's delight at the party in Connecticut celebrating their fifth wedding anniversary instead of an intimate apartment gathering she was expecting.

CHAPTER 49

In spite of having to finish the financial video for Marilyn, Jesse had arranged for the local restaurant to cater a barbeque complete with a tent set up on the back lawn of their country home. He'd planned it for the following week, five years to the day he and Taryn married.

From what he and Kathy discussed on those long phone calls for help, Taryn was approaching the last stage and the most uncomfortable part of her pregnancy loomed ahead. He didn't know what he would have done without Kathy's advice on everything from raging hormones to making sure he got his busy wife to get enough rest. *Ha. Taryn rest?* With Nancy Lou out to destroy her, starting a new business venture, and studying new medical advances to identify nascent companies for investment, rest to Taryn meant slow down.

Without Kathy's guidance, Jesse would have dissolved. Together they had figured out that early in her pregnancy, Jesse had to get into the routine of preparing a bubble bath followed by a back rub before bed. And, to his surprise, it not only did the trick, but he enjoyed it as well. But then he never needed an excuse to get his wife naked. And when he wanted to know what she'd need to take to the hospital, he remembered Kathy's laughter. "Are you kidding? Taryn has a bag already packed and waiting at the office and another in Connecticut. If you look at the top of her closet in New York, you will see a third. Did you doubt she'd have planned ahead?"

The guest list was Jesse's biggest concern. Because this was to be a surprise, he couldn't ask Taryn for advice. This was to be friends only. People they enjoyed and shared time and memories with. The problem he had was that while he didn't want business to be part of a personal celebration, their friends were also business associates. He'd put his foot down, no clients, either Taryn's or his. But his agent, Marilyn, had to be invited. Just as Kathy, Ellie, Linda, and Melissa were business associates, they were also friends. Then there was Arthur and his wife, Lorraine. On the personal side, there were Taryn's parents. His had passed away several years before he'd met Taryn.

"Let's see, oh Jack and Marty." Maybe Marty would bring Ellie since they've gone out a couple of times. Wouldn't Taryn love to have someone for Melissa and Linda? I'll ask if they want to bring a guest. It's up to them. I'm not my matchmaking wife.

Jesse picked up the phone wanting to review the list with Arthur. He was going to call Kathy, but then Arthur saw more of Taryn than he did.

"Hi, Arthur, if you have a minute, I'd like to go over the guest list for next month's surprise party for Taryn."

"Shoot."

After reading out the list of people and their possible extra guests, Jesse heard Arthur clear his throat. "You know we did invite Laurence to the party we'd used as a ruse to gain his confidence."

"How's that going? Have you seen him or spoken to him since? Is he still 4G's attorney?"

"I guess Taryn hasn't brought you up to speed. Laurence dropped Adam the day he returned from that weekend at the beach. He'd already packed his clothes and sent them to the club, where he rented a room and paid it up for the month. Told him the rest of his things were going to be packed up and would follow the next day."

"So when Adam arrived, he left? As simple as that?"

"I took Laurence out to lunch later that week, and he said that not only did our bomb shell give him another look at the person he thought he knew, but he'd suspected that Adam hadn't been faithful. And the two betrayals made his swift action easier."

"Man to man, Arthur. Do you like him? Trust him? I felt sorry for the guy."

"Yes, on all accounts. We could suggest he invite a friend?"

"Why not," Jesse said.

"Are you issuing these invites by phone, online, or snail mail?" Arthur asked.

"I know if my wife were in charge they would be handwritten notes. Well, I'm not Taryn. So I thought that since it's not actually a surprise to most everyone, I'd simply pick up the phone. And, with your views on Laurence, I'll give him a call as well. Can you give me his office number? I don't have Taryn's contacts on my computer."

"That's a nice gathering of friends. Don't worry, Jesse, Taryn will be thrilled. Lorraine and I haven't seen her parents in several years. We'll enjoy getting together again."

"As for food, I thought barbeque would be best, but I've made sure there will be enough farm-fresh vegetables available. I've never had a meal with Ellie, Linda, or Kathy and not noticed their attention to salads."

"Call me if you have any other questions. Happy to help out. If you want, Lorraine and I can arrive early, and I'll have my wife take over so you can enjoy the afternoon."

"Arthur, you couldn't have said anything more wonderful if you tried. How about eleven-thirty; the guests won't be arriving until two."

"When I get home, I'll check with my wife and see if you've left anything undone." Laughing, he hung up. With his hand lingering on the receiver, Arthur thought, *Taryn chose as well in her husband as she did her childhood friends.*

CHAPTER 50

An unwieldy Taryn followed the head waiter to a small private room in the upscale La Grenouille restaurant. As she waddled after Ellie and Linda, she couldn't help remarking, "Thank god I haven't lost my taste buds along with my waistline."

Tall vases of lushly arranged flowers decorated the restaurant, promising delights to the eye as well as the stomach. This was one of the city's famed French restaurants, and by seven o'clock, the main dining room was buzzing.

Once settled in a small private room, Taryn took a breath. "I hope you won't mind, but my feet are killing me. I have to slip off my shoes."

At that moment, the door opened, and a waiter entered carrying an armload of elaborately wrapped boxes. "What's this?" Taryn asked as she saw the grins on her dear friends' faces.

"A personal, private 4G baby shower, complete with surprises," Linda said. "Here, open this first." Handing Taryn a thick envelope, they watched her shake it, smell it, and laughingly remark, "It's not bigger than a bread box, but you've got me stumped."

Taryn, taking a knife off the table, slit the flap and was stunned when she withdrew a certificate for one share of stock, to be registered in the baby's name as soon as she was born. I'm rooting for a girl," Linda said.

"Yes," Kathy and Ellie agreed.

"Well, if you don't tell Jesse, it is," Taryn whispered amid laughter. When she actually read the certificate and saw that it was for one share of Berkshire Hathaway Class A stock, Taryn was dumbfounded. "Oh, this is too much. We can't accept this. It's a fortune. Last I checked this is worth two hundred forty-eight thousand dollars," she exclaimed.

"And we wouldn't have it to spend without you. So don't cheat us out of showering our niece to be with a welcoming gift. Who knows? She may turn out to be even smarter than you!" Kathy quipped as the group broke out in laughter. "Seriously, Taryn you placed us on this journey, and we've never found a way to repay you."

"But—" Taryn tried to say before she was interrupted by Linda. "Here, open this one next. See if we are as clever as we think we are."

Linda then proceeded to hand Taryn one gift after another. Each box contained either an elegant article of baby clothing or a treasured toy reminiscent of their childhood including Steiff's famous teddy bear. By the time all gifts were opened, each triggering stories of their shared childhood, the once elegant room looked like the end of a New Year's Eve party.

"Ladies, are you ready to order?" asked the waiter who had brought along a young helper to clear up the torn gift wrappings. After stacking the toys on an upholstered chair, he left as quietly as he arrived.

"Ladies, tonight's specials are on this little card. Let me take your drink orders, and I will leave you to study both menus." Retuning shortly thereafter, he served champagne cocktails to Ellie, Kathy, and Linda, along with a watermelon ice tea for Taryn.

"I'm sorry if I've been out of sorts," Taryn said. "Tonight reminds me that I've become driven, first with our struggle to maintain profitability, and then the Nancy Lou/Abigail mess. Tonight you remind me why we started this business in the first place. Because we enjoyed one another as friends and business partners."

"And?" Linda asked.

"And it was to provide a challenge and financial freedom to do whatever the hell we wanted in life and not worry about how much it cost."

With the delicious dinner winding down, crème brûlée dishes scraped clean, Kathy spoke of the ghost in the room. "We have to discuss Nancy Lou. What she was really like back in school. The girl we never saw, not the one we spoke to when she was around."

"Yes," Linda said. "Why did she focus on you and not the rest of us or the kids who actively shunned her?"

Ellie only sipped at her wine, not really enjoying alcoholic beverages. "I think it was because she placed Taryn on a pedestal. Don't shake your head, Taryn. I watched her follow you around, and if she had any money, which the poor girl never did, she'd copy everything you did and wore."

"We all wore the same stuff. Pleated skirts, button-down blouses, and loafers. What's so special about that?" Taryn asked.

"I guess you never noticed clothes, but Nancy Lou dressed in the same grey skirt and blouse all through high school. Oh, she changed her tops, but aside from a pair of blue jeans, that was the extent of her wardrobe," Ellie said.

"That couldn't have been the reason for the growing hatred?" Taryn remarked.

Linda got up and added more ice to her drink before answering Taryn's question. "Well, we knew she probably needed the money, and you were the one who told her we wouldn't be needing her services any longer. What she earned babysitting may have been the only money she had."

"But I remember telling her we had to drop her client."

"You may have been tactful, but she probably took that another way. Did you ever watch her in school? She always found us. Just appeared as if we'd invited her along," Kathy said.

"Now that you mention it. What were we to her? She was dating Ian senior year, and he had his own group. Why didn't she just hang around with them?" Taryn asked.

The look on Linda's face was one of amazement. "Taryn, you can't be so blind. We were admired, probably envied by some, if not for our comfortable homes, our grades, not to mention the business. What eight-year-olds start a business? Paper route or errands for a neighbor, but not a business with employees. Wake up. You are different!"

"But her actions were those of pure and simple hate," Taryn countered. "In all our school activities, we tried to be fair. None of us were cruel, mean spirited, or picked fights with other kids. Hate was something you read about, not practiced."

"I'd say she deluded herself into thinking she was one of us. Then dating the football star added to her false sense of her place in school's social hierarchy, even though he always saw her alone. But when the rumor she'd had a baby became the topic of conversation at school, along with learning Ian never loved her but just wanted sex, it had to shake her sense of self-worth," Kathy added.

"Even if it propelled her to success as an adult, that fall from grace had to have been an open wound festering since senior year," Linda said.

Taryn remembered Abigail's every word aimed at her during their meeting in Laurence's office. And Linda had just hit the nail on the head.

"Enough," said Taryn. Looking at her friends, she thanked fate for their love and support. They were the true center of her world. "This may be the last party I can enjoy for a while. So no more worries. Let's just enjoy ourselves."

"Here, here," the rest sang out.

CHAPTER 51

S he never felt so much love as the evening before and the unexpected arrival of her parents. It was Jesse's thoughtful surprise to help celebrate their fifth anniversary. They had spent hours talking about the baby. Furnishing of the baby's room in New York and then showing off the bedroom here in the house. When Bennett wanted to know if he was going to have a grandson or granddaughter, Jesse laughed. "She won't tell even me."

"That's not entirely true. I'm just superstitious, and if you don't know the sex of the baby, you will be focused on having a wonderful healthy addition to our family, not disappointed if the baby wasn't the sex predicted by the doctor's tests." Turning to her husband, she added, "Fortunately, Jesse understands."

"I've accepted it," Jesse said. "The truth is you are probably right."

"Well, the baby's room here in Connecticut is lovely, fresh white and yellow with hints of pink and blue. Any baby would be happy in such a cheerful nursery," Beverly said. Then moving over to the bookcase filled with family photos, she brought a small black and white silver framed photo over to Jesse. "Are these your parents?"

"Yes, the only photo I have of us together. I keep it as a reminder of my childhood that ended in my late teens."

"Soon you will be a parent. I'm sure it will help fill that sad place in your memory," Bennett offered.

Jesse had prepared a late-night snack, and the four sat around the table talking. With busy lives, Taryn and Jesse didn't get a chance to visit her parents often. They had a lot of catching up to do.

"So, Jesse, are you prepared for those sleepless nights until the baby becomes adjusted to life in the real world? I've brought you some books with the latest childrearing information," Beverly, the protective grandmother-to-be, said. Through it all, Bennett just smiled. It had been a late, happy family evening.

⊨⊢ ⊣⊨

She was reluctant to leave her cozy bed, when she heard the sounds of people talking, the banging of hammers and couldn't figure out what was going on. Taryn looked over to Jesse, and seeing him sound asleep, got out of bed, and waddled to the window. Curious, she pulled the curtains back and was amazed at the activity flooding the back yard.

The garden was rimmed with pottery planters filled with flowering plants of late summer. She could see those near the house with the rich blue Statius standing tall amid soft pink camellias that were interspersed with green fronds and ivy. The morning sun shone on the bare-backed men erecting a tent large enough to cover half of the back yard.

"Surprise, honey. Happy fifth anniversary." With her mouth ajar, she started to tear up. "A party? And you kept all this from me?"

"Yes, now go and make yourself beautiful. Company arrives at two, but your parents will want a full breakfast and continue quizzing you about my son and heir apparent. I'm sure your mom hasn't even begun to offer advice on the pending event." Seeing her about to correct him, he rushed, "Or daughter and heiress." With laughter and hugs, Jesse gently pushed his overly pregnant wife toward the bathroom.

The afternoon sun was on the wane, and the air filled with the scent of meat being cooked on an open grill. Chatter of over a dozen voices buzzed as people wandered from bar to tables set up in the tent with assorted nibbling food including cheese, baby-capon drumsticks, mini quiche, and bowls of steamed shrimp. The dinner would be served once the meat had finished grilling.

Jesse walked over to Taryn standing in the shade of a large maple tree and handed her a glass of ice tea. "You aren't going to cry?" he asked not surprised to see his wife tear up, a frequent occurrence of late. "It's just that it might have been nice for you to celebrate our fifth anniversary with the shapely wife you married, not this blimp."

Hugging her close, he whispered, "I wouldn't change a thing. You are and will be my love. I've never felt as complete as a man." As he kissed her forehead, he reached down to the extended stomach and as if on cue felt a kick. A smile of pure joy lit his face. "Now, there's your proof our love is growing."

"Hey, you two, I know it's your party, but I'm going to pull your wife away," Arthur said as he gently guided Taryn over to Laurence Swinburne. "I'm glad Jesse invited him. He wasn't the only one betrayed. He told me that he really loved Adam."

"I'm glad he came," Taryn said, "I see he's here with a friend. Do you think Adam is really out of his life?"

"In the short time, throughout all the trauma of Abigail and Adam, I learned that Laurence is a man out of time. He's the stereotypical gentleman who gets on with his life and doesn't dwell on past disappointments or difficulties."

"I envy him. I seem to carry negative incidents with me long after they've been resolved."

"Just wait until the baby is born. Your priorities will shift. You won't have time for negativity."

Taryn gave his arm an affectionate squeeze. "Arthur, is that a promise?"

She was glad that the elegant man hadn't been part of the Nancy Lou/Abigail campaign. She had always respected his legal guidance and was looking forward to continuing their relationship. Holding out her hand, Taryn saw delight on Laurence's face. "I'm so glad you could join us. I think we both needed something to celebrate."

"I was with Arthur and Jesse when they started planning this surprise, and I felt a wonderful sense of the rightness, especially after the difficulties of recent events. You know my romantic history, so you won't be surprised if I tell you how happy I am in sharing this day with two people I admire."

"Oh, Laurence, I can only wish you find that companion. It makes all the difference. I have been accused of matchmaking. Should I add you to my list?"

Laurence bowed his head and looked up with a mischievous grin. "Why not? I know he'd be carefully selected." The laughing trio was soon joined by Laurence's guest. "Taryn, I'd like to introduce you to Clark Hampton. Clark is a new client and will soon be appearing in a television series." Seeing a questioning raising of her eyebrows, quickly added, "I thought I'd introduce him to Melissa and Ellie."

"You're as bad as I am. This should be fun. And thank you for thinking of it." As the middle-aged man with twinkling eyes and suntanned square-jawed face shook hands, Taryn thought he looked as though he hadn't a care in the world. He moved easily, wore his blazer and slacks as if they were a second skin...a man comfortable in himself, not someone trying to impress. "I'm very pleased to meet you, Clark. Please enjoy our little gathering." As she walked off, Taryn headed over to Ellie, where she suddenly stopped. Wonder and fright shared equal attention as she felt a gush of liquid rush down her legs. Reaching out to pull Ellie over, she whispered, "Ellie, get Jesse and my Mom. My water just broke."

⚊ ⚊

It had been a mad dash to the hospital. Jesse, usually calm, lost all sense of logical thought. His planning of months, scheduled list of phone numbers for the doctor, hospital, and police, if needed, were left in the den. It took Bennett to pull him together and guide him over to Beverly and Ellie as they gently helped Taryn into Arthur's car.

Kathy rushed into the house, picked up Taryn's bag from the bedroom and walked over to Linda and Melissa. "Come on, girls. Time to distract the men once Taryn is settled."

"Jesse won't let us near her," Linda remarked.

"Don't worry. Jesse won't be a problem; he'll stick to her like glue. But from what I've seen, we will have to listen to the doctor and nurses and translate to the dazed man."

"I'll stay behind and get things wrapped up. You know, food put away, caterer packed up," Linda said. As she watched Melissa and Kathy drive away, she walked over to the remaining guests. "Well, we have an unexpected announcement. The commotion you've seen is because Taryn's water broke and they are taking her to the hospital. I'll be heading over to join them just as soon as I get things here in order. Anyone who wants to join me is most welcome." As she expected, the announcement was met with one whistle and lots of good cheer.

⚊ ⚊

With Taryn rushed into delivery, her doctor on his way, Jesse was totally focused on following his wife as they negotiated admissions and getting her settled in a room. Meanwhile the waiting room of the local hospital began to fill with family and friends.

"OK," Arthur began. "The best we can do is stay quiet. Jesse will let us know how Taryn is doing."

It wasn't necessary, along with Bennett and Beverly Cooper, Arthur and Lorraine Mallory, and Kathy, who were the only parents in the group, the rest sat quietly and waited…for at least twenty minutes before Ellie pleaded, "Mr. Cooper, could you find someone who can tell us what's happening?"

Nodding, Bennett found an intern and returned to the group. "This is what we know at present—my daughter is almost ready to give birth. It seems that even though this is her first child, she won't have a prolonged delivery. We just have to sit and calmly wait."

The information of the imminent birth of the child, who was going to not only have grandparents but assorted aunts and uncles did the opposite of keeping everyone calm. They chatted and planned how to help Taryn and Jesse once the baby arrived. Beverly brought coffee for all and felt helpless. She wanted to do more to help her daughter. Just then the doctor returned.

"Mr. and Mrs. Cooper?" Standing and waiting for the gowned young man to approach, the rest held their breaths. "Would you please follow me? Mrs. Walsh asked if you would like to join her in the delivery room." Holding hands, joy in every step, they rushed after the doctor.

While the family was busy, Linda, Ellie, Kathy, Melissa, Arthur, and Lorraine chatted among themselves. Lorraine hadn't realized that she was really part of Arthur's extended family until she sat sharing this intimate experience. She had married Arthur before the founding of 4G Investments and had over the years met everyone except Melissa Horn, but never until now had she felt accepted or seen just how important Taryn was to her husband. She had fallen in love with the quiet man because of his sensitivity that was so evident at that moment. With this new insight, Lorraine decided it was time to actively join her husband's second family. A baby was the perfect opportunity, and she was looking forward to it. These were special people drawn together because of a shared love. And that was something she valued.

"The sounds of a wailing baby preceded Jesse as he walked out to announce the arrival of his daughter, Jessica Diane Walsh, who instantly quieted when handed to her godfather. "Godfather of this little one will be a privilege," Arthur said as the baby took hold of his finger. As he gently rocked her in his arms, he turned to Lorraine. "Here, you hold the little one." Handing Jessica Diane Walsh to his wife, Arthur was reminded of the birth of their twins. That was twenty-two years ago, but the memory was as vivid as the sight of his wife holding little Jessica in her arms.

"Taryn is resting," Beverly Cooper announced, rejoining the group. "She said she'd be delighted to see you once she's settled."

As the bundled baby was gently passed from one to the other, she took the attention as her due and soon fell fast asleep.

Later, when Jesse and Taryn had little Jessica to themselves, Taryn asked, "Are you disappointed in not having a son? A boy named Jessup the third?"

Incredulous that she'd even ask, Jesse replied with his heart in his voice, "You must be kidding. I'm so grateful our child is healthy and your delivery went so smoothly. Anyway, I'll still teach her to throw a baseball like an athlete."

"Fine, and I'll take her to ballet." Lost in thought, she added, "I'm glad we gave the baby your mom's name, Diane. Now she will have your mother as a namesake in addition to the continuation of your family's heritage." Kissing his wife and then the fair down-covered head of his daughter, Jesse teared up. Taking a finger and gently lifting a tear, Taryn brought it to her lips, and kissing it, she thanked fate that her growing family was safe. Feeling well loved and exhausted by the arrival of her daughter, Taryn fell into a deep sleep for the first time in months.

The End

ACKNOWLEDGEMENTS

Each novel is an adventure during which I am blessed to have the support of a variety of skilled friends and associates.

FYI - An Unintended Consequence was brought to life through the guidance of Sharon Johnson, instructor and cheerleader to her many students. With her love of a good mystery and in-depth knowledge of the skill required to build a tale to excite readers, she inspired this writer to create a world inhabited with characters and actions that bring the good, bad and misguided to life.

My descriptions of smart women dealing with the crisis of fake news, also benefited from the expertise of Elinor Ruskin, Mary Karpin and Linda Paternoster, who are themselves, strong, intelligent, self-directed individuals. Additionally, they helped to spur me past incidents of writer's block. If they could bottle this particular skill they'd make a fortune.

A special thanks to Eric Liboy and Jeff Cohen, for their financial overview that helped to make 4G Investments a viable firm. And to Brian Gitt for his expertise in construction management.

My thanks also to the first readers who freely shared their comments and corrections. They are Joy Smith, Angela Knauss and Phyllis Arnold. I value their patience and friendship.

Without the final professional skills of editor, Kathy Rygg, author of a series of books for children, this novel would have been less dramatic, not a cohesive drama written to entice readers.

ABOUT THE AUTHOR

Patricia E. Gitt is the author of novels featuring women, mystery, crime and success.

As a former executive in public relations she worked with many outstanding women in finance, healthcare, fashion and pharmaceutical industries. She says, "I wanted to read novels featuring their strength, qualities that made them successful, and how they balanced dynamic careers with their private lives."

Patricia earned her B.S. from the University of Vermont, and her MBA from Fordham. During her career as an executive in public relations, she served as Chapter President of American Women in Radio and Television, and was listed in editions of "Who's Who of American Women", "Who's Who in Finance and Industry", and "Who's Who in Professional and Executive Women."

Her previous novels include *CEO* – a driven life examined, *ASAP* – A settling of scores and *TBD* – A game changer. Please visit www.pegpublishing.com for additional information.

Proof

Made in the USA
Middletown, DE
27 June 2017